I0817658

Something of the Springtime

A NOVEL BY

JOHN KING SPIEZIO

PASSAGE
PUBLISHING

Published by Passage Publishing

Cover design by Wide Dog

Printed in the United States of America

For information, contact support@passage.press

ISBN: 978-1-959403-28-9

Passage Publishing
www.passage.press

To my wife, for her Painter's Honeymoon

Something of the Springtime

Ne deah eall soþ asæd, ne eall sar ætwiten

Part I

IN WHICH PORTENTS GATHER

1

The cornerstone of a good life is a good humor. Believing this firmly, I had, over the past half a year, grown not only used to but fond of the constant inconstancy of weather in the English heavens. Besides serving as a ceaseless source of small talk, the rain, the dry, the rain again, the moodiness of this sky imbued the people who lived under it with a certain philosophical quality. One could never quite rest easy; one had always to be prepared for sudden, violent change. I found this temperament fascinating, and, at the risk of reading too much into a frivolous footnote on the national character, had attempted to adopt it as well as I might. Indeed, as I stepped out of Victoria Station, I was so pleased with myself at having so thoroughly taken on the gentlemanly habit of always carrying an umbrella at this time of year that I forewent a cab, for once not for want of money but of pleasure, and decided to return to the Club on foot.

I would have to send a telegram. And I had rather been looking forward to Collingwood's lecture. But as I approached

Buckingham Palace, as the rain excused itself with so little fuss as it had entered, as the setting sun brought out the warm pink hue that waits always but hides so often behind the cold face of the stones, I could not consider myself disappointed to have missed the train. I closed my umbrella, shook out the eager droplets (a benediction to the cobblestones), and proceeded onto the Mall.

I did like walking, especially alone. One could drum up imaginary conversations so easily to the rhythm of footsteps. This was the sorting which evens things out: not one-sided monologues of for or against, but a dance of two ideas finding each other in the middle. And now, there was plenty to ponder. The previous day, I had been summoned to the office of Gudbrand Vigfusson at Christ Church College. Though this man was, ostensibly, my immediate superior, I had met him only twice before: once when he asked me to tea shortly after my arrival at Oxford, and once more when he had attended a lecture of mine on the uses of the genitive case in Old Norse (which were somewhat counterintuitive for those who had been, like most of my students, trained primarily in Latin and Greek), and had loitered several minutes outside of the little room in the Examination Schools where I taught, waiting for me to collect my things and exit, so that he could shake me by the hand and congratulate me on the thoroughness of my understanding.

When I found his note in my pigeonhole asking to see him, I feared it had something to do with my having somewhat lost my temper at a certain shiftless student the previous day and threatening to use him as a prop to demonstrate the latter half of the tale of Wayland the Smith if he could not be bothered to memorize the vowel alternation patterns of the seven classes of strong Germanic verbs. This anxiety lasted through the first several minutes of our meeting. Gudbrand was a stony-faced man, and it was impossible to make out any sort of a mood, be it sanguine or cholic, through the dense brush of his thick Icelandic accent. I had to assume the worst.

But after our formal pleasantries of perfunctory comments on the weather, our students, the declining quality of food in the dining hall, Gudbrand supplanted my foreboding with mild surprise by asking me to keep a secret for him in the surest confidence. I agreed readily. He then told me that, during a visit to discuss a chronic fatigue which had set upon him recently, his physician had discovered an inoperably advanced tumor. He would be dead within a year.

He had refrained so far from telling any of his colleagues or students, as he did not want to drag them through an indefinitely long period of grief. However, for the sake of ensuring the continued existence of the position of Chair of Scandinavian Studies, which he himself had founded, he considered it necessary to begin making arrangements for his successor. He had been rather pleased by my work up to this point, and believed I could rise to the occasion.

I did not know how to respond to his thoroughly unforeseen offer, either when he first proposed it, or now, a day later, as I walked along the northern end of St. James's Park. Already, though, my perception had changed. I had very much enjoyed my time so far in England, but now I had to consider it as a place not just to see in passing but in which to build a life. I could no longer look with the eye of a tourist who wanders softly from room to room, gallery to gallery, nods here and there at a painting or architectural feature and says, "Yes, yes, it's all very charming." Instead, I was Figaro with a measuring tape, trying frantically to assess whether his bed was fit for purpose. I became fixated on the most minor details; I started taking in mind the finest aspects of rooms and faces and dress. Lengthy conversations began to transcribe themselves in permanent ink upon my memory.

Perhaps it was due to this sudden absorption in the world, and my constantly frustrated attempts to assign it a grade, that I had missed my train despite coming to London a day early to catch it. Perhaps, as the sequel would show, it was fate. Whatever the case, such earthly concerns were the whole content of my thought as I approached the columned entrance of the Oxford and Cambridge Club. However, before explaining my sudden reappearance to the man behind the check-in desk, I decided to retire these questions for the moment and ease into an unexpected second evening of luxury.

Yes: I would be keeping my rooms for another night; the Club was pleased to accommodate. Indeed, the very chambers I had left only three hours previously were not yet cleaned. I could return directly thither with nothing more than a signature and date in the little guestbook. Here, at the end of February, I had gotten almost entirely used to the new year, and had to scratch out and correct "1887" only once.

I tossed my suitcase beside the bed, gracing the canopy in scarlet silk, and, instead of undressing, returned immediately downstairs to make my repast. I took a chair in the dining room, ensconced in a ring of portraits of the various Kings George, and told the waiter I would be having whatever the cook should recommend. After a relaxed meal of mutton and Médoc, followed apace by some Roquefort and sherry, I looked forward to pairing the gentle burn of my light Virginian tobacco with the smell of wet stone that lingered yet on the buildings outside. I thanked the waiter for his efforts, collected my coat, and proceeded into the open air.

It was Friday evening; several parties passed before me. Here, a man in a silk hat whispered something to a small group huddled close together. There, a governess herded excited children with pockets full of sweets and a dear surprise for Father. A young woman in a high bonnet, on whose lips the words "Oh God, oh God" repeated themselves softly and automatically, like ripples on a silent pond, transfixed me as she passed on the other side of the street and disappeared onto St. James's Square. My gaze lingered there a while, then lost itself for what may have been a minute or what may have been a quarter of an hour. However long the interval, the fire in my pipe had burned out the next time I saw it.

I was snapped back to attention by a sudden flurry of laughter that erupted not far off my left. A group of something between half a dozen and a dozen men, well-dressed and merry, now drawn together, now stumbling out into the gutter or onto a doorstep, was proceeding as well as it could manage toward the Club. Though it was already quite dark, I immediately recognized the distinctly white, long-drawn moustaches and short, neat, triangular beard of Thomas Trimblay.

I had met Thomas only once before, and then only briefly, but he had already told at least a score of my more familiar colleagues (as I knew from so many reports) that he was intensely fond of me as one of those rare, capital fellows who is precisely as clever as he should be. I was more surprised than I should have been, then, when his wry smile followed the meeting of our eyes.

"James!" He clapped me on the back, then turned to those behind and beside him. "This is just the fellow I'd been telling you about! The American. Come now," he hunched us both over with the arm around my shoulder and lowered his voice to a stage whisper. "James, you can't begin to imagine how pleased I am to have seen you. There's the most wonderful party on tonight with the most distinguished guests and hosts and I couldn't possibly rock up with only these," he whipped his head there and back, "these boors!" He looked me in the eye, half-smirked, and winked. "I won't take 'no' for an answer."

We were both laughing softly now. "You haven't asked me anything."

"I don't have to," he winked again. "Come. We'll just stop here for a port."

I followed Thomas back inside to the Club bar, where we were joined by his fellows. We did have a port (Thomas insisted on ruby); he introduced me to the others as he quaffed.

"These are my Londoners," Thomas said with a sweeping gesture along the circle of the group.

"A pleasure to meet you all," I said with a tip of my glass to all those about me.

"We've just been seeing the oddest sort of woman," Thomas continued quietly.

"And which sort is that?" I asked.

"She's a seer," offered the man directly to Thomas' right, close enough to hear our private conversation.

"A seer, yes," Thomas picked up. "That's what they insist."

"And what is she really?"

"Someone who happened to hear of Tibet before they did," Thomas smiled. "But please, don't get me started."

I didn't. Instead, I made small talk with the other men in the crowd. I was studying Vikings? And what did I think of them? Did I know about certain references to the position of the constellations in the most ancient layer of the Vedic texts? I did not; as he and he told me more than I could be expected to remember, I saw Thomas slip away then return a few minutes later.

A second drink followed the first. While I sipped, Thomas whispered to me that he had gone and asked the barman to call us a cab. Some moments later, an attendant stood behind Thomas, coughed to get his attention, and began, "Sir..."

Thomas coughed in turn, much more loudly, and addressed the rest of the group. "Excuse me, gentleman, my colleague and I shall have to step outside." He downed his drink, indicated I should do the same, and proceeded through the doorway.

Though I would have been happy to pay for the cab, and could indeed make good on such an offer following my earlier forbearance, I cannot say I was insulted when Thomas, almost curtly (and certainly with little ceremony), insisted that he do so himself. Again and again I found it difficult to greet any word or action from Thomas with anything other than the sense of genuine comradery one gets from being on the inside of a joke that is at no one's expense in particular.

Thomas spent the ride, up St. James's, along Piccadilly, then onto Berkeley Street and Square, telling me at great length, though, in hindsight, in no great detail, of the exquisite quality of our soon-to-be host, who was possessed of the singular gift for condescending to the commons without the member of either class having become conscious that any condescension had occurred. I tucked these turns of his in the folds of a smile and gave little in the way of response beyond the understanding nods and here-and-there "Is that so?"s which Thomas was quite clearly happy to accept as the peak of refined interlocution.

In the meanwhile, I let my head rest against the cushion behind it and glanced at the buildings along side. I could not, with the port, declare myself sober, yet it would be hasty to call myself drunk at this point in the evening. All the same, behind the heady gaslights which lined our path at odd intervals, the façades shed their wonted rigidity and appeared, if not yet to dance outright, at least beginning to sway in time to the music.

We stopped with a jolt; Thomas leapt to the street. As I followed, I found my eyes fixed on the front of the building before me. I cannot boast of having been a guest at many Mayfair townhouses, be it before or after that night, and must admit thereby that the immediate effect elicited in me by the Barberry home may have been but a cousin, elder though no more distinguished, of that naïve first love of a farm girl who has never known a better face than the pock-marked cheek of a chubby vicar's son. That said, I maintain in good faith my simplicity was not the whole cause, as the stirrings took hold of me so forcefully, so suddenly, before I had moved my next foot from the carriage.

It would be beyond rude and quite frankly dishonest to describe the near houses as ugly or even as lacking in charm. Yet theirs was the charm of particularity, of just a little too much or too little. They were historical artifacts: an auntie's old dresses found up in the attic, by unfolding which one might trace popular aesthetics from the Regency down to our very own day. In the Barberry house, though, I noted the work of an architect guided by taste, not by style. I would later be told it had been built early in the reign of William IV; to me, then and now, it is timeless.

The masonry was of solid white stone; the entryway was flanked on either side by two arched windows. These windows were each bookended by Doric quarter-columns and continued, a third taking the place of the door, for three levels, before reaching a pitched roof of gray slate, out of which came four smaller, square windows framed in a copper of patinated green.

I must have tarried there in thought nearly so long as I have here on the page, for I heard Thomas say gently, at medium volume, "It's perfect, isn't it?" I looked down to see him gazing at me with the warm pride of a father at his child's First Communion. Not embarrassed but courteously now aware of the need to move forward, I finished my extended descent then followed Thomas up a short series of steps towards a bright light behind the already-open door. The porter greeted us kindly; the butler traced the razor's edge between efficiency and officiousness as he had our hats and our coats removed.

Now inside, I was once again struck by a lightness of touch in design. "Simple" does not describe the decor of the foyer. No: what I noticed were hallmarks of care. Beauty did not arise in this space as the mere sum of adjacently placed, glittering ornaments to be counted together like coins on a balance sheet. The eye that had ordered these objects knew harmony; the senses were not overwhelmed. Rather, the kinship between the amber tint of fire-topped candles and the reflection of scarlet carpeting in the crystal chandelier which held them aloft, the correspondence between a mahogany staircase hugging the wall and the small side table greeting us near the entrance, a vase of fresh flowers whose colors echoed those of the wallpaper behind them (*paly or and gules*), all of these things and, as I guess, many more which Thomas' urgent hand prevented me from noticing then as circumstances do now, invited the senses to sport themselves in a play of what might derisively be called visual tricks if they had not so evidently been arranged with that innocent, giddy zeal of a daughter hiding Easter eggs in what she takes to be a very clever location.

The sound of high-spirited conversation came from both the top of the aforementioned staircase and the hallway extending immediately before us. Thomas and I were shown down the latter and into a large drawing room with windows on the north and east walls through which one spied, even at this advanced hour, an enticing suggestion of gardens outside. I had hardly the chance to investigate further before I was shuffled into a near corner, charged with a glass of champagne, and enjoined to drink its health to the Queen.

Thomas broke the short silence, fallen over our circle (though no other part of the house) for as long as it takes to take one sip of wine, with, "Careful now, lads, our old James here is still in rebellion!"

"Oh?" said a voice from a scrunched-up face, whose thick, twitching eyebrows of meleed vanguard gray and loyal black suggested that the surprise was not merely sincere but perhaps even mixed with genuine apprehension. "Are you an Irishman?"

"It's more advanced than that, but let James speak for himself!"

"I'm an American," I found the words. "James Dalthey." I extended my hand and shook those of the strangers around me.

"An American?" sputtered a man with a gold-plated monocle, then asked Thomas, "And how'd you drag him in?"

"Entirely in spite of myself."

"I'm a scholar," I explained, "a visiting lecturer at Brasenose with Thomas."

"Oh?" picked up the man whose eyebrow, once quivering, now seemed to have found some rest. "You're a classicist then?"

"No..."

"No!" Thomas butted in. "James is a searcher! See: the Classicists consider themselves to have found something. But James is very skeptical. He's not convinced that anyone has ever found anything at all! Isn't that so?"

"No!" I insisted.

"No? What do you study then?" the Monocle asked further.

"I'm somewhere between linguistics and literature. I lecture on the Germanic languages generally but my real arena is Norse and Old English."

"Old English, then? You know, we had some of that at Winchester," the Brows told me.

"Old English, yes, and I'm terribly fond of it."

"A queer sort of thing, isn't it?"

"How so?"

"Well," the Brows drank deeply, "it is the sort of thing one would be able to like, and simply like. But the world has gotten so political. Everything now is a posture or emblem, in this part of the globe at the least. I'm not sure how things stand in America. Does this make any sense to you?"

"Yes, I have noticed that tendency somewhat, though much more abroad than at home, for the moment."

"And does it bother you at all? Do you feel that your field is being..." he finished his champagne and accepted a new, full glass, "sown with bad seeds?"

"Not so much that I lose sleep over it."

"Is that because you're aligned yourself?" the Monocle joined.

"No, on the contrary, I'm afraid I'm an absolute philistine."

"In what sense? I'm not sure I believe you."

"In the sense that, well, as our friend said," I gestured to the Brows, "I like art and simply like it."

The Brows nodded, appreciating the recognition. "There's a wisdom in that."

"I should like to think so as well, though..." This was all that I managed of the sentiment before I felt Thomas tap his hand on my waist then turn me towards the center of the room. A man stood there alone. "Excuse us," Thomas said with a look back to the Brows and the Monocle. "I think James should meet our host."

I was puzzled a second. I would not take that silent man as the host, frankly, of any party, nor as the master of the decorous home I had spent the last quarter-hour admiring so fixedly. He seemed stately and perfectly removed, unassuming; if I struggle to imagine using such words to describe his character at present, having known him firsthand, perhaps it is due to my own clouded judgment or stains on my conscience. For the moment, I was eager to uncover his mind.

"Yes, a pleasure," I said, locking eyes around the circle through the first three syllables. Over the course of the fourth, Thomas began walking me several feet to the right.

Through a glass of champagne (the one sign he belonged at a party), our host appeared looking at nothing in particular, but happily contained in a private thought of his own. That being said, he was not distracted or aloof: he turned readily towards us while some four or five steps remained in between and gave no impression of being anything other than grateful for the company.

"Thomas." I have spent great time considering how to punctuate this first word that I heard out of Arthur. It was not an exclamation, no, but neither was it said as a flat statement of fact. It was clear from the tone that Arthur was happy to see him, but he did not speak with surprise or relief. He spoke as if he had sensed Thomas waiting in the wings of the party from the moment the curtain had risen and was turning now to the guests beside him in the opera box to say, "Here, there's the man I was telling you about."

"Arthur," Thomas matched his tone. "I'm sure you don't mind, but I've taken it upon myself to invite this friend of mine tonight as I knew you would take to him so quickly as I did."

Arthur turned to me now. He was tall, his build slighter but not slight. His hair was a rich chestnut color and, close cropped, had the unmistakable appearance of having been shorn very recently. There might have been something sad about his countenance, somehow fleshy and bony all at once, but if there was, it lasted only for the instant between his eyes leaving Thomas' and meeting mine.

"Of course." If he had not been smiling before he was now. "Any friend of Thomas is a friend of mine."

I realize now that I haven't the foggiest idea how exactly Thomas and Arthur did come to be friends; it has never occurred to me to ask. While there are those about whom an observation such as the following would be made as a mark of shallow character, of superficiality, I hope to make it clear that, when I speak it in reference to Thomas, it is not only not an insult, or even a friendly criticism, but a distillation of what I would come to value so highly in his personality. That is to say: through a subtle alchemy whose precise mechanism remains a prized mystery perhaps even to its own master, Thomas was the sort of man that, upon seeing him speak with any other, one could not possibly guess how long and how intimate the friendship between the two had existed and had, therefore, to assume that it had been growing, fostered, cherished, even, for at least as long as the younger had been alive.

"Here," Arthur saw my drink empty before I had and plucked me a fresh one. "Arthur Barberry." He looked me in the eye again and shook my hand.

"James Dalthey."

"A pleasure, James." He raised his glass and looked back at Thomas. "And a drink to those who go between." We clinked with a hushed but lively "here here."

"Now what brought you together?" continued Arthur, speaking to both of us.

"Well you know the sorts of dinners they have at Merton when they think no one is looking..." Thomas started.

"Yes I know them very well, Thomas, but I'd never known a man you thought worth knowing on the morning after."

"Well, James..."

"Yes, James?"

"Yes, thank you." If Thomas had been speaking on my behalf up to this point I had been content enough with laughter and wine not to feel impeded on. "Thomas and I met at one of these dinners."

"And what did he find so interesting about you?"

"He..."

"Yes?"

"I...well, it isn't my place to say."

"But I can tell from your accent at least that you aren't a subject."

"No, not as far as I heard from my grandfather."

"And, if you'll excuse me, you do seem too old for a student."

"Yes, I'm a visiting lecturer."

"Ah! And young enough for that to be impressive!" If this was a slight it was said with a smile.

"Well my field is rather young itself, so most of us are green: all fresh, eager saplings, not too many old oaks blocking our sun."

"Brilliant, brilliant..." Arthur, who had been matching my gaze steadily throughout our conversation so far now looked towards an empty stretch of wall, then continued, "Yes, those old oaks are getting in the way in just about every forest aren't they?" He turned back and smiled. "But the fire comes as sure as the seasons!" As he laughed he gave me a look that so casually and comfortably expressed the assumption that I had not only understood the meaning of his words but had agreed wholeheartedly with their sentiment that I felt I really had understood and agreed, and laughed along with him.

"Not that I should be saying these things in a crowd," Arthur scanned the room as he sipped his champagne, "even in what they tell me is my own home." I realized I was at a total loss to say whether this was Arthur's first or twentieth glass of the evening. "But I forget myself. Excuse me, James, tell me, what are you studying then? One of these new maths they're drawing up at Cambridge?"

The suggestion was so ridiculous to Thomas, who must have divined (I know not how) that I had not computed so much as a single sum in over half a decade, that he nearly spat out his drink. He managed to catch this outburst in its path and convincingly recast it as a cough, then begged our pardon and turned off to the side.

"No, not quite," I began now. "I'm studying Germanic literature, Norse and Old English and that sort of thing."

"Really?" If the look on Arthur's face previously had been one of wry bemusement, it now expressed genuine interest, even excitement. "Isn't that remarkable? Would you believe it, I've just finished reading through that lovely translation Morris did of Gunnlaugur Serpent-Tongue for the first time since I was in school. Have you had a look at it?"

"I'm not sure I've even heard of it."

"Gunnlaugur Serpent-Tongue? I'm told it's a masterpiece by those who know better about these sorts of things."

The lines fell into place. "Ormstungu, yes of course! That must be the first saga they had us read. Yes, it is brilliant, though I can't say I'm familiar with Mr. Morris' translation."

"I'm certain there will be a copy somewhere at Oxford. I would have you read it over just to get your opinion as someone who knows the original."

"I'll be sure to track it down. In fact, I really should, as I'm meant to be translating a saga myself and ought to see how it's been done well before."

"And which saga is that?"

"Kormáks."

"Cormac's? Well," he sipped lazily, "I've no bloody idea what that is. And not, I take it, because the title is lost in translation."

"Yes, the title will be much the same in any language, but it is less well known."

"Then I'm sure it will sell. We're not the only ones interested in these things, and our numbers keep growing."

"So they tell me. In fact, that's more or less what brought me across the Atlantic. I'd heard the old stories were enjoying something of a renaissance in England, though the taste hasn't taken the American palate yet."

"A renaissance?" He smirked. "Sure, very much so."

"And it's not just in literature, from what I gather, but in the other arts as well. In fact, this very evening, before I had the pleasure of being invited into your home, I had meant to take the night train to Oxenholme to hear a painter named Collingwood give a lecture on his budding interest in the subject."

"Collingwood!" Thomas (by now recovered from his cough) blurted out. "Ruskin's lapdog!"

"I won't disagree with you," Arthur said, turning to Thomas, "but I should let you know that I am biased. I knew the fellow when he was still giving New College a crack. At the very first formal hall I attended he spilled the entirety of a glass of port on a certain prized waistcoat of mine which I had received from my father during his smells-and-bells fanaticism as a remembrance of my Confirmation. Of course it was irreplaceable, and of course I've never forgiven him, but he did strive so earnestly to make it up to me that I have never exacted any further revenge than to nod along in solemn accord with those around me who will refer to him casually as, say, 'Ruskin's lapdog.' "

"And how did he do that?" I asked.

Arthur finished a sip and savored the taste on his tongue for several seconds before realizing I had spoken to him. "Do what?"

"Strive so earnestly to make it up to you?"

"Oh, Collingwood? It really was rather thoughtful. He put together a book of sketches: caricatures of our tutors, Spooner as Odysseus absentmindedly plunging a red-hot cheese knife into his own eye. Little things like that. I remember one in particular he had done of the nunnery up at Godstow with the ghost of Rosamund Clifford downing a pint of scrumpy and lamenting how young men never keep past their third exertion."

"You're joking."

"I wish I were! In fact, I'm fairly certain I still have the little book bound up somewhere in the library."

"Can I see it?"

"See it? Of course, you can have it! Shall we have a look now?"

"Now? I wouldn't take you away from your own party."

"You'd be doing me a favor. This is Emma's affair." He downed several sips then placed his glass on a tray passing by. "Thomas, will you be joining us?"

"Me? No, I'm afraid I'm enjoying myself too completely," he answered. "And now that you mention her, I should go pay my respects to the life of the party. But please do keep me in your prayers." With this, Thomas excused himself and turned in the vague direction of the door we had entered through those many minutes earlier.

"Shall we?" Saying no more, Arthur turned and expected me to follow. I did; we exited by a second door along the same wall but well to the east of that by which we had entered earlier in the evening. The entryway remained open behind us, but immediately the sounds of the party became hushed. The hall along which we walked was wide, perhaps eight feet across, and well-lit by a series of candles on brass arms. Though the floor was bare, walnut, and creaked slightly, the walls were papered with a floral design much more rich, intricate, and, so far as I could judge, expensive than the simple stripes I had seen in the foyer, and crowned and based with a tasteful white molding. I had the sense of being in the servants' quarters.

We came to a staircase. The steps, like the floor before them, were bare walnut; like the floor before them, they creaked. It was dark, but I could make out the glint of a handle facing us from the top by the flittering reflection of far-off candlelight. Arthur had not spoken to me all of this time, nor even turned in my direction. He placed his hand on a rail of lacquered cherrywood, and I did the same as I traced his ascent.

At the top of the staircase, I was completely in the dark. By sense of hearing, I knew that Arthur had opened the door before him. By the same sense, I knew he had stepped onto carpet, as the clack of his shoes became a mossy muffle. I proceeded slowly in the direction of these sounds. For the final feet, I no longer needed to proceed with caution and by guesswork, as bright light suffused my full field of vision. As I looked at what must be the library, I would have liked to let my gaze linger a while on the portrait it suddenly beheld on the opposite wall of a woman with golden-blonde hair in a richly textured, green silk gown leaning a faded harp against her waist and standing before an overgrown hedgerow that covered, but revealed just slightly at the top, a clear blue sky. However, I found that it turned automatically, driven, perhaps, by a material curiosity greater than my artistic propensity, to see Arthur standing beside a pair of buttons, one on top of the other, escutcheoned on the wall by a small golden oval made to look like the rim of an overflowing basket of flowers.

"Electric light." Arthur met my eyes. "What will they think of next?" I laughed silently, finding no further response. Arthur turned and began walking towards a large bookshelf which formed the wall far to the right of where we had come in. From this distance, I could see that much of it was filled by series: identically bound volumes with identically lettered titles, differing only in the Roman numeral which followed the "Vol." an inch or an inch and a half or two inches above the bottom of their spines. These, however, occupied mostly the upper, more inaccessible rungs which could only be reached by a rolling ladder of matching cedar. The works on the levels that lie within arm's reach were more at odds with each other and, to judge by their somewhat weathered appearance, indeed there for the pleasure of their owner rather than for the impression they might make on a guest.

The other walls of the room were painted with a simple, light, perhaps plum purple. The ceiling was layered in white and richly, though not gaudily ornamented with wooden outgrowths of unfolding acanthus leaf here, jutting rosebud there. The floor was indeed carpeted, as I had surmised earlier, though not with a thick rug but with a thin piece of Persian work which fitted the space almost to the depth of its corners. The field of the carpet was jet, but a bouquet burst from its center and covered most everything but a foot of border with lilies and hyacinths, narcissus, begonia, drooping lavender and creeping ivy. In the center of this carpet was a small table of dark-finished wood. A book lay open face-up upon it. The slight smell of must upon all of the furniture, the harshness of the light about me, the completeness of the silence that shut out the party as soon as I closed the door, made me feel I had snuck into a wealthy man's crypt. As I traced the bleak beams to a slight chandelier above the central table, Arthur called me to his attention.

"I'm not sure what surprises me more," he said, "that I've managed to hold onto this or that somebody wants to see it."

I began walking with a quickened pace as Arthur gamboled to meet me to the right of the table in the center.

"Some of these really are quite clever, now that I think about it," he continued. "Quite clever." He handed me the book. It was small, bound in beaten brown leather, consisting of perhaps a hundred pages well-stained now with thumbprints. Lo and behold, there was Spooner, there was Rosamund Clifford, there was who must have been a companion of the young bachelors, whose name I should never know but whose cardinal vice I could divine, as George Plantagenet sitting with a contented grin at the bottom of the butt of Malmsey meant to have drowned him.

"Very charming!" I said, and meant it.

"Yes, in its own way of course." As I turned through the pages, Arthur had walked towards the row of windows and now lifted slightly the curtain that covered one with the back of his hand to peek behind. I cannot think what he expected or imagined or hoped not to see. He finished this cursory examination and turned to face me again with his hands clasped behind his back. “I’m going to have to ask you eventually, you know.” I did not. He must have picked up the confusion on my immobile face, for he continued: “Are you a Wagnerite?”

A short laugh escaped my lips. “No!” I said. I should like to make clear that I was not laughing (as some men would indeed) at the suggestion that I could be a Wagnerite. However, Arthur had prefaced the question with such seriousness, almost furtiveness of tone that I was thoroughly taken aback by the innocuous nature of the inquiry that followed. “Excuse me, no. I saw a performance of his *Tristan* in New York a few years ago but cannot say I know more about him other than what I’ve read from the critics.”

“Really? That’s it? So many of us are, you know. It’s how I fell into all this originally.”

“All what?”

“The mythology and such. I suppose I had always known it, even as a child, Siegfried, Tristan, Percival. But for me, as for so many others, Wagner is who really...” he had taken his hands from behind his back and now suspended them palm-up in front of his chest. They sank and rose repeatedly, as if their master were weighing something of dear importance. Nevertheless, the words they found fitting did not ring as spontaneous to me, but as having been organized well in advance, be it in imagined conversation or real. Whether my presence here was the long-awaited opportunity for the manifestation of a cherished dream, or merely another repetition of a routine, I could tell that Arthur was in the beginning stages of initiating me into his personal mysteries. “...who brought them to life,” he concluded.

"Is that so?" I said. "I hadn't realized that these stories meant so much to you. You mentioned the saga so casually, I had assumed it was just another one of several passing interests."

"Oh no," Arthur assured me. "Though it may have started in that way," Arthur began to trace a circle around the room with myself and the table as its center, "but the more I read of the material, the more I found something special in it." Arthur paused before the painting in the corner, turned to consider it for a moment, then continued his stalking. "They're very honest," he said, "the rough works. And there's an...emotional intensity that comes from their simple tact." Arthur stopped now a bit past the door through which we had come in, and faced me once more. "Do you know what I mean?"

"I do," and I did.

"You see," he continued, "I believe that this is what is really missing in our age: a certain frankness and authenticity of feeling. There are too many formulas, too many assumed opinions, too many things that we do by rote. But these older stories, and Wagner's magic that captures them, remind us of a...a more direct mode of experience."

"There's something to that."

"I think of this often, as I'm sure you can tell. Now, wouldn't you say?..."

I cannot say whether I would, for before Arthur had time to finish his question, the small door to the left of the bookshelves threw itself open with something between a smack and a crash. There we saw Thomas standing with his hand firmly on the door handle. A white scarf was flung around his neck which, if it had been there before, had gone unnoticed.

"Pardon me, gentlemen," he said. "I do hope I'm not interrupting anything."

"Oh no," Arthur looked at me smirking, and then back to Thomas. "This is a conversation for another evening."

"Good, brilliant, grand. Well, Arthur, your wife has sent me to fetch you as I simply insist on hearing that story about the Archbishop of Canterbury and she simply insists that no one, by right or by might, may recount it but your noble self. Would you be willing to crawl back down into our cave?"

"Of course." I did not sense annoyance or exhaustion in his voice, but mere acquiescence. "James, I expect you will join us?" I intended to, and said as much, placed the small book of Collingwood's sketches on the table beside me, and began walking with Arthur towards Thomas. After four or five steps, however, the bells from the Farm Street Church began to ring midnight and gave both of us pause. All of a sudden, I felt totally drained.

"No. I beg your pardon gentlemen." I turned to Arthur and extended my hand. "Thank you very much." Arthur returned the shake. "For everything. Excuse me Thomas," I turned now to him, "but I really must get some rest. I've forgotten even to send notice that I won't be at the Lakes tomorrow."

"Of course," Thomas said.

"Of course," echoed Arthur. "I'll have Albert get your things and call you a cab."

"Thank you."

Arthur brushed past Thomas and began walking with heavy footsteps down the hallway. I followed in his wake, joined by Thomas. Continuing down the hallway, we were thronged on either side by a series of open doors. Behind each was a room, well-lit, and full of its own family of colors: one yellow, one red, one pink or rich blue. Each was full of people talking loudly and laughing. I noted several memorable faces of both men and women, and even locked eyes with several passing pairs. However, my pace remained steady until I reached the head of the stairs I had seen at the start of the evening. Thomas and I began our descent.

"Being inducted, were you?" He said from behind me.

"Yes. How did you know?"

"He's like that with everyone. Or at least with everyone he takes seriously enough to feel the need to be taken seriously by."

We reached the bottom of the stairs where the butler, whom I now took to be Albert, was waiting with my jacket and hat.

"It's a compliment, really," Thomas continued. "You'll see what I mean. But for now," Albert helped me into my coat and handed me my hat. He thanked me as I slipped a shilling into the palm of his hand. "For now, I believe you have a cab waiting for you."

"Yes," I said. "Thank you so much for bringing me."

"Of course," he continued. "I wouldn't have done so if I didn't know you would make an impression."

I shook his hand, turned, and began walking towards the outside.

"I shall call on you soon," he yelled at my back.

"But not soon enough!" I turned only my head, waved, and stepped into the night.

My cab was indeed already waiting, as was a footman who helped me get in. Though I could barely keep my eyes open, as I retraced the path of my earlier trip with Thomas, I realized for the first time how accurate his descriptions of Arthur had been. Not once, over the entire course of the evening, had I become conscious of the fact that I was speaking with a member of the nobility, even a minor one.

I had liked Arthur. Or, at least, if I had not yet had time to form my own full opinion of the man, I understood why Thomas liked him. However, I could not shake the disquieting sense that Arthur considered himself to have intimated something to me without noticing that I had failed to grasp it. He thought of us both as being in on the same secret, though I could only begin to guess what he believed himself to have been getting at. Perhaps this was presumptuousness on his part, who saw any other person worth talking to as a version of himself, endowed with the same set of private associations; perhaps it was poor manners on mine, who should have spoken more and more openly rather than allowing myself to be understood as understanding. Perhaps it was late in the evening, I was not thinking lucidly, and I had invented these impressions out of half-digested sherry. Perhaps now, from the dim vantage of years, I am simply misremembering and coloring in the corners of a long-faded night with pencils sharpened much later and with deliberate intent.

Whatever the case may be, shortly I was back at the Club. Drawn by the gravity of my own fatigue, like the boulder of Sisyphus giving itself over to the other side, I exited the cab, entered the Club, made my way to my rooms and, without undressing more than my shoes, fell into a deep, dreamless sleep.

2

The bells of Saint Mary the Virgin struck noon. Precisely, or nearly, a day before, I had received a card from Thomas Trimblay asking if I would be pleased, weather permitting, to meet him by the church's garden for a walk to the Isis Tavern and an early Sunday roast dinner thereat. I had managed, over the past week, to recover from our last outing and graciously accepted his offer. There wasn't a cloud in the sky. Though the hunger I had saved from the previous night kept me mostly eager and alert for Thomas' arrival, shortly after the resounding of the bells had dissipated I found myself gazing distractedly at one of the empty niches which gird the Radcliffe Camera for what must have been at least three quarters of a minute.

As ever, he caught me off guard.

"Hullo, man!" I felt his hand on my shoulder. I smiled, and turned to see Thomas doing the same. He put his other hand in my right for a firm handshake. We began walking down St. Mary's Passage. An almond tree had recently been planted in the western corner of the church, right next to the arched entrance which opens upon the north side of High Street. I noticed as we waited there for a break in the oncoming carriages that the first buds were now coming in.

"I have to tell you," Thomas said as we came up on the other side of High Street and began walking down Oriel, "I've just caught up over tea with a most interesting man whom I had not seen in the longest time. We read our Greats together when the Queen was as young as we pretend she is now. Then, much like you, he thought he had exhausted Homer. But instead of due north, he headed east. Of course now the government requires his dutiful service in translating our God and our Law into good Classical Sanskrit. And he's more than happy to live in Bombay for ten years at a time eating mangoes and humming his *ragas*."

"Is that so?" I was content, at the moment, to fall into what was beginning to be the pattern of our conversations.

"Yes," Thomas continued, "Jonathan Fox. I'll have to introduce you soon. He's staying at All Souls." He paused as we finished crossing Oriel Square and stepped before the Canterbury Gate of Christ Church. He puffed eagerly at his pipe, and I noticed for the first time the odd smell of the smoke that came from its bowl. He must have noticed me staring, for he removed the pipe from his mouth, raised it slightly in the air, looked me straight in the eye, and said, "He brought me this."

"I didn't know they grew tobacco in India."

"They don't! Here, try it."

I accepted the pipe and drew lightly from its tapered end. The smoke did not come on harsh, but I found myself coughing slightly as I handed it back to Thomas.

"You'll get used to it," he said.

We turned onto Merton Lane, then down the narrow stretch of the Grove behind that college's chapel towards the kissing gates that lead onto Christ Church Meadow. Having passed through these behind me and dusted himself lightly on their other side, Thomas looked at my face again.

"Not that, I blame you," he said.

"For what?"

"For...for turning to the Pole Star," he winked. "Life is only so long and variety its spice. And I must say I have thoroughly enjoyed what I've read of the stuff. But for me, the good life begins and ends on the Mediterranean."

"Well, I was never much of a classicist myself."

"No?" he replied with genuine surprise. "I thought that you all started out as philologers."

"No." The pipe was back in my hand. I had gotten used to it by now. My gait, which was already relaxed, now slowed to a stop at the dusty northwest corner of the fenced-off Meadow proper, where cattle graze within, along the Broad Walk which stretches from Saint Aldate's Street all the way to the Cherwell. As I collected my thoughts, I turned towards the Meadow, beheld a particularly large pair of horns, then began walking with Thomas down the suitably named Poplar Walk: an avenue of trees which forms the Meadow's western flank.

"No," I repeated. "Of course I read some at school. But when I was sent off to Harvard I thought I would be a philosopher. I'm almost embarrassed to admit it."

"Oh? If that's so, you're the first philosopher I've ever met who would be embarrassed of his vocation. Most every one

I've ever met is just dying to dangle everything he has out in front of you."

"Yes, and that's precisely why I fell out with the stuff."

"How's that?"

"Because it seems to me," I found I was suddenly very excited, "it seems to me that it is almost an open secret that these questions the philosophers deal with do not have proper answers. Is the universe limited or infinite, is man's will bound or free? It's not as if the right answer hasn't been hit on yet, or that half of the philosophers in the world are either too thick or too stubborn to admit that the other half is right. The questions do not lend themselves to definite or final or incontrovertible solutions in the form of falsifiable truths."

We stepped aside momentarily to let a governess pass with a pram, then continued our walk along the edge of the meadow.

"And yet," I began again.

"And yet!"

"And yet!" I smiled softly. "And yet one still believes one thing or another. And not only does one believe it, but one will devote one's entire life to proving it to you. At times, indeed often, by means of force. And it is here that I find the truly interesting question: why is it, when one cannot be sure of any abstract idea, that one nevertheless finds oneself believing in one or another? And what are the fruits of these ideas?"

We had now nearly reached the southwest corner of the Meadow, some yards short of where it meets up with the Isis. Thomas stood aside and gestured me through a second pair of kissing gates which would lead us by a narrow alley up to

St. Aldate's Street and onto Folly Bridge. I thanked him and continued.

"Have I made myself clear at all? These are things I have thought about in great depth before, and written about articulately. Yet all of a sudden I feel as if I were talking nonsense."

"Oh no, I understand you perfectly." Thomas puffed the pipe thoughtfully. "You had the good sense to recognize all of this philosophizing as chasing after the wind. So instead you've become interested in what sort of person finds himself believing what sort of thing, in seeing how he arrived at this position and, well, how all that, shall we say, works out for him."

"Yes," I exhaled. "That's it exactly." Halfway across the bridge we both stopped, simultaneously transfixed by the driving technique of a farmer who passed with a modest cart of produce. He whipped his horse over the small peak in the center of the bridge with such regularity, so matter-of-factly, as a matter of course, almost automatically, that both he and the horse seemed totally bored through the flagellation and lost in their separate reminiscences of sunnier days and much younger lovers.

After they passed, Thomas and I continued.

"Of course," he said. "I understand you perfectly. I've often had similar concerns myself. But those came at a younger age and kept me safe from getting involved with philosophy in the first place." We reached the end of the bridge, turned left, and crossed over that smaller span which passes behind Grandpont House and onto the southern towpath of the Isis.

"What's interesting to me," Thomas resumed, "is that, presumably, you now think you find these answers in the sagas."

"I do. Or I hope so. Or, it's in some parts in all literature. Or, it's not that I find answers *per se*, but I see them come to life and explored."

"Yes, as you alluded to earlier." Several boats passed us on the river, eight men and a howling coxswain to each, preparing for the rapidly approaching Torpids. Thomas took a moment to strike a new match and relight the pipe before he continued speaking. "So you're a psychologist."

"Yes, I suppose I am."

"And your books are your patients."

"No, the books are my schedule. The characters are my patients."

"Have you developed a diagnosis?"

"I do see some recurring tendencies, instincts that crop up across different places and times."

"Such as?"

"Such as," we stopped by the swimming pool and watched the boys jumping a moment. The pipe passed back and forth.

"Such as," we resumed, "a tendency in the patient to confuse himself with the outside."

"I don't follow."

"I mean to say that characters are often confused with who they are in themselves and who they are in the collective mind, the *Anima Mundi*. Let's look at your Homer. There, it's the obsession of his characters with *kleos*, with how they will be celebrated after death. For the heroes of the epic tradition live in a world that itself contains the epic tradition. This is not the sense in which our world contains it: to us, it is a fossil, or a sarcophagus brought over from Egypt. I do not mean to place myself amongst those who assess the value of classical literature with the eye of an antique dealer, to break it for parts and pawn what one can off to the proper sciences of history. No. I mean only to say that we cannot *join* the epic tradition, nor *merge* with it. As much as we may, and do indeed, enjoy these great works of poetry, we cannot become their subject. The hero can, and in a way, must.

"For the hero has a bitter awareness of this potential, which is vexed thereby into a duty. His cardinal drive seems to be achieving this *kleos* and becoming the subject of Epic History, to the point that his concern for how he *appears* completely overrides any concern for how he *is*. Do you see what I'm driving at here? The hero does not have a personal sense of happiness or fulfillment or purpose or meaning, or what have you. Rather, to be happy, 'blessed,' to him is to be seen as blessed in the eyes of others. So he performs the deeds and behaves in the way that will make his audience see him as blessed, even if doing so makes him miserable in the here and now.

"One may be inclined to assume that Homer is caught up in the same race as his Achaeans. Very well: then what are we to make of Odysseus' trip to Hades? Why does Achilles say there that his entire life had been a waste, that he had rather have been an unknown slave than a glorious hero? At that point, Homer must appear to be putting himself on trial, and indeed finding himself guilty. And so the epic tradition becomes, by its own assessment, something sinister, or worse, even paltry and childish."

"And we're both too sentimental to settle for that!"

"Why yes!" I laughed. "Why yes we are! Though for a while it did lead me to the conclusion that one should make art as our Lord commanded us to pray: hidden up in our rooms. Now I assume that Homer must have had motives much more profound. So what is Homer's view? It seems he sets up his own characters for failure. He sees their motives as flawed, perhaps wholly misguided, yet seemingly grants them the very recognition they craved. He must have a reason for doing so. What, then, is Homer's opinion of the motives of his own characters? What does he make of these men and their actions?"

"Yes, yes, but neither of us can ask the gentleman since he's stopped returning our calls."

"Neither of us can say. But we can say that, one way or the other, he must have thought it was *important*. Out of everything he could have said or recited, he chose the stories that he did, and he portrays the characters in the way that he does, because he's trying to get something across. And not only does he believe as much, but his audience does. Otherwise, they wouldn't bother listening to him. And the princes of the cities and palaces he plays in must think it's important as well. That's why they have it written down, when paper is not easily come by. And not only did they find it important, the generation after them found it important, and every generation even down to our age. And in this time, which many fairly disdain as obsessed with the practical and the rigidly material, still it is considered important. Yes: so important that they will pay you, a man who would otherwise be by many miles the most competent and efficient coal mine manager or railway controller or government bureaucrat or mid-level financier in all of England's Upper South, nearly *almost* as much as they would pay a coal mine manager to read these texts and wax poetical on them mostly to yourself but perhaps to a small group of friends who also do nothing but the same in between glasses of port and strolls down the pub. And because of this, this, glaring *anomaly*, I have to think there is something indeed in it, and something of great importance!"

"Aye." Thomas stopped for a second to puff on his pipe and look at the river. I appreciated the pause, feeling slightly embarrassed at having become so animated. Under normal circumstances I did indeed consider myself, as I had said to the Brows and Monocle, a perfect Philistine who liked art and simply liked it. I believe the sharp change was in part the influence of the odd tobacco, but not entirely: these questions were suddenly much more pressing as they were, ultimately, Gudbrand's unanswered offer. I was silently weighing the import placed on literature as the import placed on my vocation, my life's work. What would normally pass as the subject of idle chatter between friends had become a subtle crucible.

"But you see," Thomas continued, "I would do it even if they didn't pay me." He started walking again. "Nor do I do it because I consider it 'important.' I'm not even sure what that would mean. No. I do it because I like it. And I imagine these princes you are so baffled by, from Albert to Peisistratus, acted from very similar impulses."

He slowed, held the pipe close to his bent-over face, and began to frown at it. He produced a matchbox from his pocket, drew fire, drew smoke from the pipe with several sucks on its lips, and continued walking. He handed the pipe to me.

"Now Homer himself," he resumed, "may be an entirely different matter. He was not a prince. In fact, many say he was a slave. Perhaps his poetry was merely a career, a craft like any other. What relish he may have taken in it is beyond us to say."

At this point, we had reached the Isis Tavern. Fog had settled in, and I began to feel rain on my hat and my fingertips. Thomas looked up at the sky, then down at the pipe in his hands. He knocked it against the bottom of his up-turned foot and shook the ashes onto the ground. He wiped the dirt off the pipe with the back of his hand, replaced it on his inner jacket pocket, and looked me in the eye. A smile curled half of his face.

"Come on."

He opened the gate and we entered.

THE TAVERN was neither full nor empty. It hosted enough guests to keep a buzz of good cheer in the air, but Thomas and I did not have to wait for an opening before seating ourselves at a small wooden table in the far right corner. Though the rain had only just started, and the day had been fine before, a fire was already lit in the hearth now beside us. It was stone, black on the inner rim with soot, with a thin mantelpiece on top. There had been placed several pieces of comic porcelain: a schoolboy tugging a milkmaid's braid, a well-feasted Falstaff falling off of his roan. On the walls about the place were a pair of oars, a deer's head, several species of dried wild flowers bundled together with twine.

Two beef roasts; two pints of ale. Thomas and I could make only small talk now, as we had both suddenly discovered that we were far more starving than we would normally be at this time of day, even after a walk. So: had my students stopped using the strong declension when they should use the weak? Had they finally twigged the difference between a predicate and an attributive adjective, then? And had any of his managed to work an ethical dative into their prose compositions yet?

"Yes, but in the most daft way imaginable. *Mihi sum Caesari*. Can you imagine? I can't even begin to think what they're teaching those boys at Winchester these days. Oh!" He took another sip from his pint glass. "That reminds me!" He cut off a piece of his Yorkshire pudding and doused it with relish in his gravy as he absentmindedly left me to stew in anticipation.

"Reminds you of what?"

"Your Wykehamist. Arthur Barberry. He'll be there tonight."

"Where, exactly?"

"At the dinner!" Thomas read the confused look on my face. "Blimey, that's good on you. You had me so thoroughly entertained on our little walk over here that I completely forgot to mention." He let me simmer again through another round of sips and doused chewings. "That fellow I mentioned earlier, Jonathan Fox." He saw me stare at him somewhat searchingly. "Our tobacconist," he winked. "They're putting him up at High Table this evening at Christ Church. And, well, apparently he and Arthur have had some sort of correspondence, some political intrigues I respect myself too much to know much more about, and he'll be joining us as well."

Thomas had finished his pudding and was now cutting his carrots into small bits. He took these one at a time on his fork, pierced a bit of beef behind the bit of carrot, then ate the two together at a gulp. I had just had the last bite of my meal and spoke now between sips of ale. "How lovely for the lot of you."

"You'll be joining us, of course."

"Me?"

"Yes. Oh, bugger." Thomas swallowed the last of his ale then replaced the glass on the table with a thump. "Yes, I forgot that as well. Of course, you're invited. I mentioned you to Jonathan, described you as...as a...the sort of fellow who...well, never mind, I described you in a rather pithy way, and very complimentary to your excellent character, and he insisted he simply had to meet you. That old Sillett remembered that every other Sunday is when he meets his mistress at the Harcourt Arms and had to give up the seat he had accepted earlier, leaving it open for you."

I had begun to accept the offer when Thomas interrupted.

"I don't care what else you have planned, James."

"I haven't got anything planned."

"Of course. Well." Thomas stood up, took the coat from the back of his chair, put it around his shoulders, and checked the watch on his waistcoat. "Half two already. I was meant to be at the Prince of Wales in Iffley an hour ago. Dismal place..."

I stood up as well, prepared myself to leave, and followed Thomas outside. The rain had stopped now, but the sky remained overhung with dense gray clouds. A chill wind was blowing from across the river.

"Well," Thomas turned. "Thank you as ever for your company. I'll be heading over the lock." He gestured towards the small stone bridge to our right. "I'll meet you by Old Tom at six tonight." He brought the pipe back out from his pocket. "Feel free to be late."

"Only as much as necessary."

We parted ways. As I walked back towards the center of town, I meditated on Thomas' ability to engage in any register of conversation with the same amount of zeal and concerted interest. Later, on an only tangentially related note, he would tell me that there was no logical reason that one should ever not be enjoying oneself. At that moment though, alone on the towpath, I believe I could have formulated this motto myself on his behalf.

With our every encounter I had come to admire this quality in Thomas more and more. There were many men I had known, especially in England, who used humor as a defense against the earnest. There was something rude, or flippant, or even pathetic in their demeanor. Thomas, on the other hand, shot his quips not like arrows to pierce the bleeding heart of sincerity. Rather, he spoke them to put one at one's leisure. They were little ladders he sent down, inviting you to join him at his height of perfect ease.

I busied myself with these thoughts as I passed by Old Tom (where I would be meeting my own Old Tom later), crested the minor hill onto Cornmarket Street, past the Tudor bawdy house, turning right onto Ship Street, briefly down Turl Street (why had I taken this long way?), along Brasenose Lane, over the walls of whose northern side I could hear fellows in the Exeter gardens at bowls, and finally back onto Radcliffe Square where I had begun my day.

I turned towards Saint Mary's, took only a few paces, and entered through the open gates of Brasenose College. I saluted the porter, Andrew, of slightly less than average height and slightly receded, short black hair, who, though normally wont to return my gesture with a chuffed grin, seemed not to notice me today as he was busily engaged in giving unheeded advice to a downcast, slightly green student standing beside him with a scholar's gown and disheveled blonde hair.

I passed along the northern rim of the Old Quad, then mounted the stairs in the far corner and proceeded to my unlocked rooms on the second floor. Over a pot of black tea, I spent the rest of the afternoon looking over a series of exercises my students had submitted the Friday before. To my dismay, most of them had not yet twigged the difference between an attributive and a predicate adjective and had made a number of errors in the expectedly ensuing confusion between the strong and weak declensions of adjectives. All the same, I found I enjoyed the frustration. I thought of my father, patient, adjusting me time and again as I fumbled a bowline or fell from a horse.

Shocked to alertness by the bells of Saint Mary's playing half-way through their tune to show that this hour was now halfway passed, realizing that so much time had glided away unnoticed, I returned to Gudbrand's proposal in my mind. It had been curing long enough now that I could begin to consider it in earnest and not just in muddled outbursts to colleagues. A man in a more noble spirit may say that I had an epiphany that my work was "meaningful," but, at that moment, I was thinking only of Thomas' earlier turn of phrase: I had discovered that I "liked it." I replaced my pen in its well, tidied the papers on my desk, and began dressing in my formal clothes, deliberately but with no sense of urgency.

The clouds had cleared from the sky and the wind had died down. It was a pleasant evening, and still very bright as I caught sight of Thomas outside of the massive gate of Christ Church. He was gazing in the other direction and puffing gently on his pipe when I greeted him.

"Ah, James," he said without a start. "I had hoped you would be a little later. They've gone into the Senior Common Room already, and waiting here to show you the way was my only excuse for taking a last moment to myself."

"I told you I would be no later than necessary. If you had warned me your necessities were such I could have invented any number of delays."

"No, no," he sputtered. "No matter."

Thomas continued puffing on his pipe, but turned around and waved me to follow him. After passing through the gate, we went up a short series of steps on the right to the raised walkway which runs along the entire outside of the main quad, then up a longer flight of steps to the Senior Common Room located above the dining hall where we would later be eating.

Upon being shown in, I recognized one or two fellows from Brasenose who I believed to be classicists, as well as the chaplain of the more recently founded Keble College. I had met this man on a number of occasions before, as a general, intellectual, perhaps aesthetic if not religious *per se*, interest in the so-called "Oxford Movement" of Anglo-Catholicism had brought me to a number of the Sunday Evensong services over which he presided.

I remembered at that moment that, while we spoke briefly in the doorway of his chapel after the previous Sunday's worship, he had offered to host me for tea and a more extended theological discussion after the following week's Eucharist if I should elect to attend. I had completely forgotten to send the, *stricto sensu* unnecessary, but, for the sake both of general good manners and for the particular fondness I had begun to develop towards the man, requisite word that I would not be attending. He and I locked eyes shortly after I entered the room, and, as I felt quite keen to excuse myself to him, I was happy to see Thomas leading me in his direction.

"Jonathan!" Thomas said to the man beside the chaplain. "This is the man I was telling you about."

Jonathan struck me with his being at the same time tall and of muscular build, yet completely unimposing. The immediate impression one got upon seeing him was of gentleness. There was a calm in his appearance: soft but not spongy, relaxed but not tired, an ease of pace that was never sluggish. Indeed, I very soon came to recognize in him a quickness of wit and ready intelligence that were exceptional even in these sorts of circles we moved in which were composed of individuals who prided themselves on such qualities.

His hair, mostly gray, had receded to that accidental tonsure which so many men adopt in their venerable age. He wore it comfortably, as he did a pair of bifocal spectacles with a yellow metal frame. He spoke with a voice that came off as quiet, yet always was perfectly audible. "Ah, yes. James, is it?"

"Yes," I met his extended hand. "James Dalthey. And Dominic," I turned to the chaplain (a thin man with a round face, close eyes, and neat blond hair). "I beg your pardon for having missed you earlier today."

"What's that? Oh the tea!" He seemed genuinely to have forgotten. "Never mind. In fact, it's rather a good job you didn't come. An old friend of my father's dropped by who felt perfectly justified in occupying the entirety of my afternoon. But, 'the evils of the day...' Would you have some sherry?"

"Yes, thank you."

Dominic gestured to a servant who brought two full glasses which Thomas and I received with gratitude.

"Now Thomas was telling me," Jonathan continued after a brief clinking, "that you're studying ancient Germanic languages. You must be working with Vigfusson, then."

"Yes!" I responded with pleased surprise. "I didn't think you'd have heard of him." It occurred to me that, in the near future, other total strangers may be dropping my own name in a similar fashion.

"Well, those of us trying to bring in a little..." he smiled at Thomas, "color to the study of literature have to stick together."

"Of course," I said. "And Vigfusson has done so much in his time here. In fact, he established the visiting position which I am currently filling. Unfortunately he has not been as active as I hear he had been in previous years. And I, for my own part, whether it's under the influence of the local climate or merely the greater resources available here on the subject, have found myself turning much more to Old English than to Norse, though I had originally secured the role due to expertise in the latter."

"Really? The climate or resources aside, do you have any inclination for why this is, other than personal taste?"

"I can't say for certain. For one thing, I've been commissioned by the Press to translate a saga, which is quickly driving me to see Norse as work and English as pleasure."

"A blessing," his smile wore the words' understanding. "Which saga?"

"*Kormáks.*"

He laughed like I'd mentioned a friend. "Yes, I believe I know the one. Something about cursed lovers and a missed wedding, isn't it?"

"Precisely," I laughed back, impressed, then became slightly quizzical. "Do you read much Norse literature?"

"Oh no, only as much as I read everything. But I remember it stuck with me because I felt something of the *Shakuntala* in it."

"I can't say I'm familiar."

"That is a shame. Remind me to send you a copy. Goethe has a funny line about it, about the heroine's name containing the entire world. But," he finished his sherry, grinned at another, and continued, "as I said, it's a blessing. If we never have anything we *must* do, a duty, we can never have the joy of flouting it for something else."

"Well, I should be clear that Old English isn't merely 'something else.' There is a particular intellectual, or even personal connection I feel as well. You see, something that strikes me is that the Anglo-Saxons converted to Christianity much earlier and, if I may speak frankly, more fully than their Scandinavian cousins. And living now, in a society so thoroughly Christian, a world so thoroughly Christian, I am fascinated to see...to see how this came about, and was seen by the people who were living through this change."

"Bless you," Dominic said smirking, "for suggesting we live in a Christian society. I suppose America always catches its colds a little while after they have run through the old continent."

"Yes, yes," Jonathan tutted. "Excuse our friend, but this relates very closely to what the two of us had been discussing before you joined us."

"Oh?" Thomas, who'd seemed not to be listening, joined as he started another glass. "What's that then?"

"We were reopening old wounds," Jonathan explained wryly. "I'm sure you know nothing about it, James, but it caused something of a national scandal in our day. In fact, it's what got me into studying Sanskrit in the first place."

"Oh this..." Thomas let out softly.

"Yes, this," Jonathan volleyed. "You see, James, when Thomas and I were, well, still a bit younger than you are now, there was quite a stir over the election of the second-ever Boden Professor of Sanskrit."

"Oh?" I said.

"Yes. I won't bore you with the details. But, in the papers and in the minds of the people, this little academic row came to represent the general uncertainty over how the native Indian religion ought to be treated by its conquerors. Some argued for an appreciation of the Hindu texts on their own terms as great works of poetry or thought-provoking philosophy. They were accused by the other camp of being, sort of...taken in by the entire thing, to have gone intellectually native, become crypto-pagans almost. These others, furthermore, believed that one need only know Sanskrit well enough to dismiss it. And while this latter camp won the battle..."

"They seem to have lost the war," Dominic came in where Jonathan had flagged.

"Yes, well, that is your point of view," Jonathan now resumed. "Though I would be curious to hear yours as well, James. The heathens you deal with, their stories, their art, their ideas, or what we can suppose of such, have enjoyed much more public favor recently than those of my own subjects. Does our friend have a point? Has the world gone pagan overnight?"

I very much appreciated the thoughtful question, but had no idea where to begin answering it. I was spared the embarrassment of floundering through a perfunctory answer by the tinkle of a small bell coming from behind my back. I turned, as did Thomas, to see an attendant who informed us that dinner would begin shortly and asked if we would be pleased to proceed to Hall.

"Never mind," Jonathan assured me. "We'll sort this out later."

We followed the attendant out of the room in single file, down stairs, around turns, in through the grand set of doors that lead into the Dining Hall. Around us on either side were two columns of tables populated by students in their gowns who had stood at attention to welcome our entry. We continued to the far end of the room, and stood behind the chair of our assigned seats as Grace was read aloud in Latin. I looked over and noticed Thomas muttering the words along under his breath, then remembered having heard that he was banned from leading the Grace at Brasenose while still an undergraduate after an unfortunate incident wherein he had recited the prayer with such Mediterranean gusto (rolling the "r" at the start of "rex aeternae gloriae" for, if the impression I had heard was anything near correct, at least a full thirty seconds) that the solemnity of the event had been totally ruined and the dinner guests overtaken by fits of raucous laughter.

The prayer ended, we said "amen," then seated ourselves. Immediately we were served with dishes full of a thick stew and tucked in severally. As I found it reprising the beef chunks and carrots from lunch, I felt an instinctual, domestic comfort in the consistency of English cuisine.

"Do you think he'll be let in?" Dominic said, nodding at the empty chair to his right.

"Who?" I asked.

"Arthur Barberry," replied Jonathan. Only at that moment did I realize I had not seen him so far. "Have you had the pleasure?"

"Only once, and that briefly. Though he seemed to have much more to say when I left."

"Oh he always has plenty to say," Dominic continued, prodding wet carrot, "when he finally decides to arrive. Not that I mind in a general sort of way. One gets used to a lack of punctuality when living amongst intellectuals. But with Arthur," he collected his thoughts with a spoonful of stew, "with Arthur it isn't natural, it isn't his character. A scholar misses Grace because his head just wanders off in the clouds or the mountains of Anatolia. Arthur does these things deliberately to flaunt how little he cares for ceremony, indeed, for his own station. To show how he's just like you and me. And yet, it is only his station that lets him get away with things like this!"

"Oh come now, Dominic," Thomas put in.

"No, I'm sure I'm quite right. You know just as well as I do that, if I had missed drinks and showed up to High Table a quarter of an hour late, I would not only be turned away at the door but made to know in no uncertain terms that I should never be invited again. Arthur, on the other hand," I noticed Dominic was halfway through the glass of wine which had waited before each of us at table, "will not only be let in, but the president will make a point of pulling him aside at Second Desserts to let him know how very clever and liberal and progressive he found the entire thing. The entire show. For that's what it is: show."

Dominic darted his eyes among the three of us, then resumed eating his stew with a hand that was shaking slightly. We remained quiet and I, for one, found myself lost momentarily in the inarticulate din of conversation and laughter and clattering of silver on plate from the other end of High Table and the rest of the hall generally.

"Yes, well," Thomas hacked at the ice with a cough as he picked up his spoon. "That remains to be seen." We finished our stew in what was the first uncomfortable silence I had experienced in Thomas' presence thus far.

The dishes were cleared away; our wine glasses were refilled. I looked at Thomas and saw he was prepared to begin speaking again. He cleared his throat but did not make it past "Well," before we raised our eyes in turn to meet the sound of heavy footsteps. Arthur had arrived and, apparently, been let in. He walked directly to what he correctly assessed as his seat beside Dominic, pulled out the chair, lifted the napkin daintily from the empty, ornamental place setting, sat down, placed the napkin in his lap, looked around our small cluster of faces with the peevish look of a schoolboy who has successfully framed another for the theft of certain lost biscuits and said simply, "Pardon me, gentlemen."

"Pardoned, sir," Thomas tilted his glass, "and well met!"

"I trust you've been keeping yourselves thoroughly entertained in my absence." We locked eyes. "Ah, James! With you here I reiterate my previous sentence in earnest."

"I'm happy," I said, "to be one thing that could make you speak honestly."

"Not that I want to insult the rest of you," Arthur picked up, "but fresh blood brings new life to rehearsed conversation."

"Yes," Jonathan agreed. "It has been a pleasure getting to know you, James. In fact, if I'm not mistaken, we're still eagerly awaiting your thoughts on a certain topic."

"Oh really?" asked Arthur. He turned to hand the bare plates to a servant, looked this man square in the eye and, as if he had saved him from drowning, whispered, "Thank you." Without pause, he shot his gaze at his empty wine glass, clinked a heavy, ruby-laden ring against its side, then winked back at the servant. "What's that?" he turned back to face us.

"Well," picked up Jonathan, "what, with James and I specializing in...in more exotic forms of pre-Christian literature, both of which are coming into fashion in their own way in our home culture, and with Dominic's repeated concern over the state of the national religion, well, we were simply...assessing the claim one hears from certain quarters that old Europe is falling back into...into old, barbarous ways."

"Yes," Arthur, as quietly and carefully as before, thanked the servant who filled his wine glass before taking a further sip. "Yes, it's inevitable."

Dinner plates were now being set before us: a leg of duck on a bed of mashed potatoes and red cabbage. I was content, still lacking the presence of mind to arrange my thoughts so articulately as the considerate people with whom I was dining deserved, to let Arthur speak in my place for the moment.

"Inevitable?" Dominic asked, looking back and forth between Arthur's face and the bit of duck he was cutting and which, after speaking, he snatched into his mouth with unbroken eye contact.

"Yes," replied Arthur, as yet unaware of the food in front of him, swirling his glass of wine. "Inevitable."

"And why is that?" Dominic prodded.

"Because," Arthur continued, having, with imperceptible speed, escorted a bit of duck into his mouth and now chewing, "of the inherent contradictions in Christianity." He paused to let us digest his idea and sip once more from his glass. "Europe was bound to wake up eventually from, what did Kant call it?, its 'dogmatic slumber.' "

"Oh?" Dominic feigned surprise. "And what are these 'inherent contradictions?' "

"Simply, Father," Arthur winked at me, "that Christianity hates life. It was all well and good in the early days, with Perpetua and Felicitas throwing themselves at the lions. Because that's what Christ really wanted. He wanted his disciples to care nothing for life, to spit it out with aristocratic contempt. To love heaven so much that one comes to hate the earth. But," another forkful and sip, "one has to live! And so the religion would either die with its suicidal martyrs, or betray its original character and, shall we say," he lifted his glass to the three of us in turn, " 'find a way.' "

"I've heard things like this very often before," Dominic said, who had now finished his duck and was lightly dabbing his lip with his napkin. "And as much as I, well...as much as I would be willing to entertain the idea, I've yet to hear a good suggestion of an alternative. I mean to say, that is, if, if one is not going to aim for heaven, well, what exactly is one going to aim for at all?"

"I couldn't have framed it better myself!" I saw chewed bits of food in Arthur's wide grin. "In the absence of heaven we aim at the earth! Don't you see? Once we get past the idea of some other place, some other time, we can face the world as it is and finally get what we want out of it, make it what it ought to be."

Our plates were cleared once again.

"I see," Dominic said. "And I imagine you have a jolly good sense of what the world should be instead?"

"Yes!" Arthur roared, so loudly that I allowed myself to assume, as I had formerly only supposed, that he had been already quite drunk before joining us. "Yes I do. I foresee a life of...of spiritual aristocracy. Instead of breeding slaves and browbeating them into submission, we will rear wolves, and lions, titans of the will!" He finished his glass. "This, you know," he pointed to us all singly, "is the true project of eugenics: to free man from what he has been and prepare him for godhood."

"Not that I'm trying to insult you," Dominic affected concern for the cake now before him, "yourself or your station, but it seems to me that the very idea of 'aristocracy' is itself '*dys*genic,' to coin a phrase. For, as the men I know you read suggest, it is the struggle for survival against nature that drives to that much lauded vigor of the fittest. And what is aristocracy but the selective removal of not only certain individuals, but indeed an entire class of individuals from 'selection pressures'? The little princes of Spain never sweat for their dinner. They're never hot in the summer nor cold in the winter. And I don't mean to say this out of moral indignation, as if 'how dare they enjoy so much while the rest of us struggle?' I'm simply pointing out that," he took a moment to pass the port to the left, "that to talk about 'aristocracy' and 'eugenics' in the way that you do is not only misguided, but, on your very own terms, absurd!"

"Very good!" Arthur clapped him on the back and looked to the rest of us with beaming pride. "That's precisely why we mean to do away with them! To overturn men's exorbitant privileges and put them to work!" An onlooker, one of the classicists I had recognized earlier, stared at him confusedly before Arthur met his gaze, leaned aggressively in his direction and asked, "Wouldn't you say?" The man turned back to his cake.

For several minutes we ate, for the second time, in an uncomfortable silence. Arthur moved his eyes from one face to another awaiting a response. After building up nerve from his lingering cake, Jonathan put down his knife and said, "Yes, at any rate, you're getting at something I have often thought on my own. Whether in its absolute, divine core or in its human execution there are," he cleared his throat, though less artfully than Thomas, and began to speak now truly quietly, not just with his wonted gentleness, "problems with Christianity, which have led it to the position it is in now. And, should one like to save it," he looked with compassion at Dominic, "one must be frank about these things." He sipped his port cautiously. "For now, that's all I have to say on the matter."

Quiet again.

"Tawny," said Thomas. "That's all *I* have to say on the matter."

We finished our slices of cake like mice. From the center of High Table, we heard the pounding of a gavel. The president of the college had stood; we all followed suit. He uttered a few words in slurred Latin, which we followed with another "Amen," then proceeded once again in single file behind him out of the hall.

We traced our earlier steps of the evening in reverse, and made our way back to the Senior Common Room for Second Desserts. As I entered the room I saw that the far end, which had been bare but of some portraits of dons in full academic dress during the earlier part of the evening, was now filled with two long tables. Each was layered by a thin white cloth with a simple lace design around its outside border. Upon these cloths on silver trays were several clumps of grapes and a variety of cheeses, both hard and soft.

We were nearly the last to come in. Already, several people had clustered around the food. Though I doubt he very much depended on the assurance of others, in this or in any situation, the fact that he would not be the first to cut the cheese made Thomas very comfortable in begging leave of our little group and making way to serve himself. I begged pardon in turn and followed him. When I reached Thomas he was already nibbling a bit of Mimolette. He handed me a dish with some of the same and said, "Here." After a minute or so he spoke further.

"Of course, he's not entirely wrong."

"Who?" I asked.

"Arthur," Thomas wiped his mouth.

"No, of course not entirely."

"The problem is," he chewed vigorously, "the way he goes about these things. Dominic knows him perfectly. He's trying more to prove something about himself than about the world. So when he happens to be correct, or even insightful, he just so *happens* to be. Pure coincidence."

Thomas accepted a glass of port. "Finally," he smiled at me contentedly. "Nor," now resuming his original point, "do I believe, if you really pinned him down and asked him, he would be able to distinguish between the things he is right about and the absolute rubbish."

"Speak them all and let God sort them out."

"Yes!" Thomas chuckled. "A fair tactic. But surely you see, as I do, that he really will be a good man once he stops being so embarrassed about the greatness of his birth?"

"I'm not sure I see it yet, but I imagine I'll witness the sequel whether I choose to or not."

As Thomas reflected, we spied Arthur walking towards us.

"Hello again, gentleman. The president has just been talking my ear off. I suppose he considers himself very progressive. All I know is, thank God for this cheese plate, for I doubt I could have stomached much more of his conversation without an excuse to excuse myself."

Arthur took up a dish of brie and tucked into it softly. I noticed his cheek was quite pale. If I had seen him now for the first time in my life, I would have said he seemed ashamed.

"I do think I said rather too much myself tonight," he resumed.

"Oh?" asked Thomas. "Is that so?"

"Yes...Not that I'm too concerned about of fending the sensibilities of an old priest. But, frankly, I'm not sure even *I* believe it. That is: I don't think I really meant even half of what I said this evening."

Thomas had moved onto grapes. "Well, nothing wrong with a gentleman's Third!"

"I suppose not," Arthur replied absentmindedly. He focused on finishing brie. "But enough of that. Tell me, gentlemen. Here we are at the end of Hilary, isn't it? A very exciting time."

"Yes," Thomas told him. "I'm nearly done whipping my students into shape for their Moderations. I've got one who should do just brilliantly if he can put aside his genius for a moment."

"A common quandary," Arthur smiled. "And you, James?"

"Me? No, I'm not busy at all," I said almost truly. "I spend the better part of my days meditating on how much I shall enjoy the holidays."

"I'm glad to hear it. And how will you be spending them?"

"I will be working in a sense, I suppose. I've got a grant from College to do some archaeological work. You see, I'm developing a theory about the location of the storied Battle of Brunanburh, and have placed it in the north end of Yorkshire near a town called Boroughbridge."

"Really?" Arthur asked with gentle and genuine interest. "I believe that's our old friend Æthelstan."

"Presumably, yes. But though it's celebrated as the moment England was born as a nation out of petty, squabbling tribes, firm details are hardly extant."

"And now the American digs for the roots." He licked his fingers. "Well, what's the evidence for your theory?"

"Between the few of us, not very much at all. But my guess is as good as any, and I wanted an excuse to visit the area."

"That's quite a coincidence. You know, I've just purchased a home in the area."

"You don't say?"

"Yes, though I've no bloody idea what I'll do with the thing. My work keeps me in London. It was Emma's idea, really. We're still in the process of getting some things moved in, but we did intend to spend the coming month or so there. If you don't mind a lack of appearances, then, why don't you visit us for a weekend?"

"I'd be delighted, thank you for the offer."

"Of course. It's the least I could do. And that reminds me," he glanced at his wristwatch, "I really must be back in London tomorrow morning, and will have to leave now if I intend to catch the last train." He put down his mostly empty dish. "If you will pardon me, gentlemen. It has been a pleasure, as always."

"Of course," Thomas said for us both. "And don't imagine we'll tarry here long after you."

Arthur thanked us, shook our hands, then went around the room bidding similar farewells to a handful of other guests. Thomas finished his grapes, put down his dish and turned to me.

"Well. I meant what I said." He wiped his moustaches lightly with a handkerchief. "I can't keep my wife waiting all night. You wouldn't happen to be looking to share a carriage to Summertown?"

"No, thank you, my rooms are in College."

"Of course."

"But I am getting tired myself. I'll see you off before heading in as well."

"Of course."

We found Dominic and Jonathan, who were now speaking with the president and the second of the classicists I had recognized earlier. We thanked them in turn for their company. I promised to make good on the former's offer of tea soon, and to meet the latter for at least one pub lunch before I went up north and he, via London, back to India.

The night had grown chilly. The clouds had dissipated completely, and overhead I could see the distinct, jagged teeth of Cassiopeia. Thomas and I returned to the St. Aldate's Street gate, where a porter quickly flagged down a cab. I helped Thomas in, thanked him again for the invitation, and started my walk back to College.

As I approached Carfax Tower, I realized that the time was within but a few minutes of precisely ten o'clock. I had often passed by this place shortly before or after the tolling of its quarter-hourly peal. Whenever I did so, I thought about the miniature soldiers, in mock half-Roman, half-medieval dress, who stood suspended some dozen feet in the air on the tower's eastern face directly below the clock. They were bookends to a pair of small bells, that on the left being even smaller than that on the right. I always wondered if these two sentinels, who did bear hammers as if to strike, were purely ornamental, or if they were indeed the source of the two short clangs which came from their area at every fifteen minutes. Gazing up from below, I believed myself to have seen a slender steel rail under the feet of each attendant, along which he might be guided back and forth, as well as two chains attached to their backs, which might yank them to hit. Despite the soundness of this hypothesis, and the evidence to back it up, I was not content with conjecture. I needed to catch them in the act, yet always managed to be just too early or just too late.

Now, at this odd hour, despite the wine and confused, half-remembered bits of conversation floating therein, my mind had the presence to stop. I stood at the juncture of High Street in perfect stillness with my eyes fixed firmly there above. Shortly after, much as I had expected, the two little men, first the left and then the right, moved slightly forward then snapped back to crack out the peal of the bells.

Finally seeing it done, I cannot say I felt satisfied. I was perhaps pleased for a moment, but quickly became conscious of having been rather silly to have spent so many minutes, on this frigid evening, and mental energy, over the past several months, on something absolutely trivial. I continued staring at the men for several minutes after they had become still, hoping the mystery might draw back its veil. For the first time in several years, I felt the urge for a cigarette.

I'd kept Gudbrand's secret for over a week. Despite a few stirrings (that earlier, fatherly feeling), I had not come closer to choosing a path. But now crept a sense that the final decision was already made in advance, indeed, on my behalf. It is possible I was merely indulging in cheap mysticism; there is certainly something romantic to the idea of fate. Yet it is also an opiate to that *vertigo* which comes when facing absolute freedom, and the most ready tonic for remorse.

Eventually, I came back to myself, laughed slightly, lowered my eyes, and proceeded to the right. I entered College through the High Street Gate and walked along New Quad. On a Sunday night, it was silent. The only sound came from the chapel, whence I heard someone playing, with the minimal number of stops, something between Buxtehude and Bach up in the organ loft. No lights in the library. None in the Old Cloisters. Hall had been empty for hours. I reached my staircase, nudged open my door, discovered I was exhausted, and prepared myself for bed.

Part II

IN WHICH WE HEAR THUNDER

1

Rest needs preparation. Though I had intended to do so much earlier, I began packing my bags only two days before leaving for the North. This made it Saturday, the tenth of March. The previous evening, I had attended a dinner with Thomas, his fellow tutors, and their second year students to celebrate the end of their exams. I must have drunk more than I usually did with Thomas, even more than I had noted the effect of at the time, for I woke up slightly before dawn feeling extremely dehydrated. I stumbled out of the bedroom into my reception area, and helped myself there to the entirety of two large, glass bottles of water that waited on a squat wooden table in the center of the space.

Each done at a gulp, I did not suffer from the headache or nausea which are the custom of such mornings after. My only symptom was a vague sense, comforted if *mal* at ease, that I had been through Hell in the distant but not wholly forgotten past. All the same, I felt no inclination to return to sleep.

A pair of modest windows lined the room's eastern wall. They looked out onto Old Quad, over the opposite wall of Brasenose, and, jutting up from the middle of Radcliffe square, the eponymous Camera. A late frost had set in; looking at the grass below, I saw that it was covered in a sheet of cracked crystal ice.

The light began to come in. Purple, then orange, then concord of pink crept into my line of sight and poured color out onto the stones. As the disk of the sun became visible beyond the south side of the Camera, I realized this was the first time I had seen it rise since the seasick, sleepless evenings of my voyage across the Atlantic.

I lingered watching Phoebus mount his chariot up the sky until he was level with the bulbed cap of the Camera. As whenever I caught sight of dawn, I wished I had taken my modest though considerable artistic talent more seriously in youth and kept painting at least as a *violon d'Ingres*. I could lose myself in those colors forever.

But the world waits for no one. The seasons, the sun, the moon, the tides, turn and turn and turn with little regard for their beauty or our appreciation thereof. The colors bled out to an even blue. The nascent warmth melted the frost at the tips of the grass into seeps of dropping dew. The stones became yellow and brown and dun. I took a suitcase from the dresser and began to collect my things.

In the absence of anything else needing doing, I allowed the process to drag itself out over several hours. I walked slowly between the closet, the chest of drawers, back to the suitcase on the desk. I lingered, deliberating over pairs of socks, trousers, notebooks, pens. When a maid from the kitchen came to offer me tea, I accepted after fumbling myself decent enough to answer her knock at the door.

I stood by the window again while I sipped from the cup of white china. The students who were returning home for the following six weeks had begun carting out their chests. Teams of servants bumped and excused and stumbled around each other with arms full of bursting valises. The sight of vigorous activity made me realize I was hungry. The tea had come with some biscuits, but I wanted a bite more substantial. I put on a cape, took my hat, and walked out of College.

Some two hundred yards to the east down High Street, there is a pair, directly facing each other from opposite sides of the road, of coffee shops. That on the north, named the Queen's Lane Coffee House for the pleasant little alley at whose delta it sits, advertises itself, established in 1654, as the oldest coffeehouse in Europe. That on the south, with the rather continental title of Grand Café, boasts, by means of a large sign in its window, to be the site of the first coffeehouse in England (circa 1650). This set of rival, competing claims, in such close proximity, is bound to give any thinking man pause. But, with a minimum of inquiry and archival research, the truth is easily discovered.

The Queen's Lane Coffee House has been continuously open and operational as a coffee house since the aforementioned date of 1654. This makes it truly, and by a rather considerable margin, the oldest coffeehouse in Europe which one may still frequent. The Grand Café, meanwhile, occupies a building which, according to a casual remark in the diaries of Samuel Pepys, hosted the first coffee house in England, indeed around the year 1650. However, through the intervening ages, it had since become a toyshop, a bookbinders, a warehouse for the nearby University College, and even, if rumors are to be believed, certain things which, for the sake of avoiding libel, I will not put into print.

Therefore, while the Café's claim to be the site of the first coffeehouse in England is technically true, it is only in a strict, legalistic, I dare say surreptitious, sense. The sign in its window seemed to me, after I had done this deep digging, like a pound of flesh which one should have refrained from demanding rather than fashioning into a medal. The bad taste which came into my mouth whenever I saw it, coupled with the unnecessary, gaudy interior design of the place, marble and crystal and gilt column capitals, an accidental *pastiche* of a third hand description of Paris, prevented me ever from choosing this location when deliberating between the two. Perhaps the excellent quality of its scones and cucumber sandwiches would have left me eating my words. I am content to remain ignorant.

And so, as several times before, I refrained from crossing High Street and entered the Queen's Lane Coffee House. I was on friendly terms with the owner and his wife, the latter of whom, Mildred by name, greeted me this morning, sat me by the fireplace, and immediately served me with a fresh pot of coffee and a miniature jug of cream. She was short of stature, I daresay even tiny. Her build, meanwhile, was plump without being fat. She wore a brown dress with rows of white dots, and a clean if well-used apron over her front. A red kerchief was wrapped about her chestnut hair which was pulled up in a series of loose buns. She spoke with rather received pronunciation, but there was an airiness in some of her front vowels which reminded me, as she had mentioned once in conversation, that she had spent a part of her childhood in a remote section of Cardiganshire.

"Cold one, isn't it?" she asked with more interest and cheer than a strictly ritual conversation required. I was, if not the first, currently her only customer, and she was happy to grant me her undivided attention.

"Yes," as I warmed to the coffee. "I see springtime comes late here in England."

"Oh, that's Old Blighty. Everything in fits and starts. But then when spring is here you will know it!" She poured me another cup, needing not ask if I needed more coffee. "Will you be eating with us as well, sir?"

"As if I had ever refused..."

"And what will it be, then? If I may, sir, I would suggest the devilled kidneys."

"It will be devilled kidneys, then."

"Very good, sir."

With term at its end, I felt I had earned this restful fatigue as the prize of good effort. I loitered about my coffee and kidneys as I had earlier about my packing. The warmth of the fire, as well as that of my own digestion, must have made me forgetful of the weather, as I found myself suddenly determined to take a constitutional about the University Parks for what would be the first time since the previous November. I would, however, first stop at my rooms to pick up a walking stick. Having paid, replaced my cape, picked up my hat, and left an extra twopence on the table, I said farewell to Mildred and walked out of the shop.

As I passed the gate of Brasenose, my pace was slowed to a stop by the porter, who informed me that I had been sent a telegram. I thanked him, slipped him a farthing, and continued to my rooms with the message in hand. I did not bother removing my coat, but took a letter opener from my desk and slid it along the lip of the envelope from Western Union. The note read as follows:

Mother suddenly ill STOP Dead STOP No time come home STOP Letter tell soon STOP

Your,
Elizabeth

I sank into the couch by the central table. I was stunned before sad. Even once I had time to make sense of the information in my hand, my emotions were jumbled up with rage that my sister had not put aside her old Puritan thriftiness even long enough to pay for a telegram which would explain the situation properly. Had the third sentence been meant as an imperative? "No time, come home!"? Was I expected to wait the two weeks needed for her letter to cross the ocean in order to get clarification?

For a moment, my mother stood before me. Then, she sat down on the spare wooden chair pulled out from my writing desk. Her face was sullen, disappointed, perhaps, but unsurprised. It was the same look she had worn when I had seen her for the last time, five years earlier, when I told her I would be leaving Massachusetts to accept a teaching position at New York University. She had a notable gift for never quite paying one her full attention: then, she had been embroidering a floral pattern with a small hoop in her lap, now her lips were silently muttering a prayer.

At that time I was ashamed. She understood without words how embarrassed I felt, that I feared myself dilettante, that I had taken the role for a want of direction. She was the sole who did not congratulate; she was the soul that I could not convince. She: living proof I convinced not myself. I should have invited myself home for Christmas.

And then, she was gone. I shook as if from sleep. If I thought there too nearly I'd drive myself mad. Instead, quite mechanic, I gave into the plan of things, collected the walking stick I had come for, left my rooms, and returned onto Radcliffe Square. To the northeast corner, up Catte Street, past the Kings Arms and onto Parks Road, one foot following the other, all very regular. The blue gates of Trinity. The little cabin past Wadham as if built for a dwarf. That Natural History where Huxley trounced Wilberforce. Its hidden Pitt Rivers, flooded with death masks and cursed shrunken heads. And then, there, outbreaking, the cracked lines of Keble, churning on yellow and red.

Well, that was it, or at least a something. I would finally take Dominic up on his offer for tea in his chaplaincy rooms. Could he say a word? Well shouldn't I ask?

I told the porters I was a visiting lecturer at Brasenose. Could they show me in the direction of the Chaplain's office?

Around the corner; up a flight. Stumble, regain, step. Knock.

"Hello, James, what a pleasant surprise!"

Yes, I would take a seat. Hat off. Cape off. Here, tea and biscuits.

"To what do I owe the pleasure? I don't believe I've seen you since that ghastly night with Arthur Barberry."

I could focus on the tea. "Yes. Please excuse my having been so aloof. You know how things get towards the end of term."

"Yes, of course, but, James, are you feeling quite well?"

I looked down and noticed I had spilt a bit of tea on my upper thigh. "No, Dominic. I should apologize as well for barging in here like this, but I've just received a telegram from my sister telling me, in so many words, that my mother has taken suddenly ill and died."

He was confused for a moment. He put his cup of tea down on the table before us, then rested his chin in his hand, his elbow on his knee. He stood up. He turned and walked towards a window looking out over the quadrangle behind his desk directly in front of me. After staring thereout for some seconds, he pivoted gently and remained standing with his right fist on the desk.

"I'm so sorry, James." He stalled. "Please accept my condolences." He started and stopped. "Did you have any idea?"

"No. I'm...as you can tell, frankly I'm in shock." He covered his eyes with his hand. I couldn't disturb the still face of the tea, and placed it unsipped on the table. "This is all that I've heard." I groped about my jacket pocket after the telegram paper as Dominic headed towards me.

"Here."

He took the message from my hand and surveyed its contents. He furrowed his brow. He kept his eyes fixed on the page as he felt his way back to his seat and lowered himself gently back into it.

"When did you receive this?"

"Immediately before I came to see you."

"I see." He looked at his tea with something like disbelief. "Was she a religious woman? I know you are..."

"Yes," I replied. "Very much so."

"I see. I can offer a prayer for her at tomorrow's Eucharist, if you like."

"Please."

"Of course." We had no more to say as he finished his tea. "And please do join me afterwards. I can have a small dinner prepared."

"I will do, thank you very much. If you'll excuse me." I stood up and collected the articles I couldn't remember having strewn about the room. "Thank you very much."

"Of course." Dominic saw me to the door.

Slowly I was coming back to myself. Again outdoors, I breathed deeply the slight nip in the air and found it bracing. I left Keble and continued to the University Parks, where I allowed myself to be distracted watching local schoolboys at cricket. The circles, between the cypresses and oaks. How could I have been there so long?

But the sun had set; the sky was getting dark. So out of the Parks up the Banbury Road to North Parade. Left onto that little avenue, then into the Rose and Crown pub, past the first room where, by my side, a group of tardy students at the piano sing snippets of the *H.M.S. Pinafore*. Greeting the barman behind a row of taps in his harbor behind the clatter. A steak and ale pie. Pint of bitter. Eating alone and in silence. Then, cape back on, hat reclaimed, "God keep you too!" and back on to the street.

2

I must have made it home, for in the morning, I was in bed. I cannot say if I slept. I cannot say if I dreamt. Over the course of those hours, ideas and intimations, thought and memory, bled in, through each other, a fantasy quadrille. The curtains were completely drawn, and I may well have remained unaware day was starting if not for the regular knock at the door. I shot bolt upright; the ghosts fled my field of vision. I was still dressed from the previous evening, and proceeded directly to answer the call.

"Tea, sir?"

"Of course, please, come in."

"Thank you, sir."

This was the same girl who had brought my tea the previous morning, indeed every morning for the past several months. Yet, through a combination of lack of sleep and still undigested grief, I felt as if these habitual things I saw now were somehow strange, suspicious in their familiarity, vaguely alien, seen from a great distance through the cracked lens of an antique spyglass.

And so, as I stood beside my desk and watched the girl bend at her waist, place the full tray on the round reception room table, remove therefrom the dish and cup, then lift the kettle to serve my first portion, I had the unshakeable impression of watching a deeply reverend and thoroughly perfected ritual belonging to an endlessly perplexing but fascinating culture. I suppose England is a foreign place, but it had always seemed so close to my own native country, and especially that little corner of it I had inhabited since birth, that I saw it less as a stranger and more as a rather elder brother who only comes home for the holidays. Names of towns and streets, a shared literary tradition, bonds of blood and history, but even smaller things, certain mannerisms in the people, concerns, fears, things left unsaid in half-finished sentences, had allowed me, so far, to feel at home even when abroad.

Of course, the greatest commonality was our shared language. But perhaps language is a trap. Perhaps it is like a child's pacifier. It soothes us as the gears turn and our mouths open and close and our heads nod assent. We know the meaning of any given word, and comprehend the syntax of the sentence containing it. Therefore, we are content to assume we have understood everything perfectly well and been understood in turn. All the while, glances of the eye, a sudden shift in tone, the private history of a certain term or turn of phrase to the person employing it, are completely unnoticed or, indeed, entirely undiscoverable.

At this moment, I am back in my third-year rooms at Harvard. It is mid-December. Aleister Freely, who, though two years elder, had immediately taken a liking to me when I was a freshman, has now begun graduate studies down at New Haven but is back in Cambridge to see family. Paying me a visit, he speaks of the long summer he has just spent visiting, at last, the country whose culture and language he had spent so many years immersing himself in from the cold corner of a library in frozen Massachusetts.

He removes an envelope from his jacket pocket, held closed by a thin red string wrapped around two circular seals, one on either side of the lip. He opens it, begins removing its contents, and invites me to come look. On the table he places a series of photographs, one after the other. Most are monochrome, but a few have been colorized.

Here is Aleister, barefoot, in silk robes with a chrysanthemum design bursting over each breast, a sword at his side. Here is a sloping avenue along a hill lined with cherry blossoms. Small pieces of paper hang from the branches, covered in fast, jagged writing, like traces left in sand by birds taking flight. Here is a girl in a lily-white *kimono*, kneeling on a mat before an iron kettle on a raised platform.

"*Chadō*," Aleister tells me. "They consider it an art of refinement. We don't have anything quite like it."

I pick up the photograph. I am transfixed by the look of effortless yet perfect concentration on the girl's face. She is sublime. She is God guiding the wheel of the universe.

"What is your name?"

"Excuse me, sir?" The girl looked at me with such sudden shock that I knew I must have blurted out the question.

"Excuse me, I didn't mean to startle you. Only I just realized that you and I have seen each other most every day for nearly half a year and that I had never bothered to discover your name."

"I see, sir. Catherine, sir."

"Thank you. Catherine. And I am James."

"Of course, Mr. Dalthey, sir."

She had finished pouring the tea and now stood upright faced towards me. She was thinner and taller, with red hair in thick curls under a white knit bonnet. Her dress was of cotton, green, long-sleeved, aproned. I took her to be about nineteen years old. I noticed the tea had always come with two settings, and gestured towards the empty cup.

"Would you have some as well?"

She stifled a laugh. "I couldn't, sir."

"I insist."

"Really, sir, I must keep working."

"I see." I fished through my pocket as I walked her to the door. All I could find was a crown. "Thank you, Catherine." I handed her the coin. "I'm to be out of town for the next several weeks and hope that, in my absence, you will please yourself even half so well as you have always pleased me."

"Sir, I couldn't..."

I put my hand up to stop her.

"Yes, sir. Thank you, sir. Thank you very very much, sir."

I closed the door behind her and stood in the hallway a while listening to her descending footsteps, then returned to the tea set in the reception room. I was not sure if Dominic's sect was Catholic enough that I would be expected to have fasted before receiving the Eucharist. All the same, I did not feel like eating even if I were permitted, and left the biscuits on the dish untouched. I did, however, pick up a small card from beside the kettle which Catherine must have been entrusted to give me though forgetting to mention it. I opened the note and read the following in a neat, flowing hand:

Dear James,

I heard from Dominic of the loss of your mother. Please accept my sincerest condolences. Helen and I will be leaving first thing this morning to visit our son in Florence. I have included a slip in this envelope with our address in that city. Please do not hesitate to contact me there if you are in need of a sympathetic ear.

Your friend,
Thomas Trimblay

I turned over the words several times; they read like a prayer. I retrieved the slip from the envelope with Thomas' address and copied the information down in a small book I kept of such information, then tucked the note back into the envelope and placed that in the drawer of my desk for safe keeping.

It was customary, as I knew, amongst many ancient peoples, for one in mourning to look one's absolute worst. One wanted to appear so beside oneself with grief that one had lost the ability even to maintain basic hygiene. A memory of this tradition hidden somewhere in the blood may, I hoped, have excused my disheveled appearance and erratic behavior over the previous day to Dominic, to the barman at the Rose and Crown, to Catherine. Now, though, I had the sense of being come back down to earth. I felt obliged to shape myself up, and looked forward to a little ritual cleansing. I shaved, changed clothes, and finished a second cup of tea.

This morning was quite as chilly as the previous one; I decided to wear a black overcoat over my jacket instead of the simple cape I had gone with yesterday. Even with that, I had begun to shiver slightly by the time that I reached Keble Chapel.

By the brickwork of its exterior (alternating broad red with thin yellow, and checkerboards of both about the windows), by its architectural style (Gothic revival), the building blends in with the rest of its college. It is, however, significantly taller, and the series of stained-glass windows and peaked, wrought-iron crosses which dot its upper level betray its sacramental character.

I entered, still some quarter of an hour before the start of the service, to see that the place was quite so empty as was to be expected after the end of term. In fact, I counted only two bowed heads, one of which belonged to a fellow I had been introduced to before and the other to a man who appeared to be a groundskeeper. I seated myself somewhere towards the center of a central pew. I considered reciting some of the prayers I remembered from my childhood, but instead began to gaze up at the mosaics adorning the interior walls.

Above the altar, Christ enthroned. Around his outstretched right hand, seven stars. Cradled in his left, an open book bearing the Alpha and the Omega. Before his feet, seven candles. From his mouth, a sword. Coming to worship from either side, saints and martyrs. Cecilia with her organ. Peter with his keys. The Magdalene with her case of ointment.

To my left, the life of Moses: the prophet horned with light bearing down the Commandments; the brazen serpent hung from the tree, here a cross; water gushing out from stricken rock. To my right, the life of Joseph: the dream of sun and moon worshipping his star; a bag of gold for sale into slavery; lording over repentant brothers.

The colors of the mosaics reminded me of a set of the Marseille *tarot* I had seen at an antique store in New York shortly before embarking for England.

I feared that turning my head completely around might be somehow irreverent, as I really ought to be meditating on the divine rather than ogling the scenery. I refrained, therefore, from looking back at what I knew, from brief, previous glimpses, to be a depiction of the Last Judgment. I lowered my head, and found that the words of the Our Father came flowing as easily as the waters of a spring, frozen fast by winter, now finally set free by the early April breeze.

The service began shortly thereafter. I fought hard to focus, not quite in outright delirium as on the previous day but still in something of a haze. My attention managed to regain its posture when, as part of a series of petitions, Dominic asked those in attendance to offer a prayer for the soul of Prudence Dalthey, recently deceased. This left me sufficiently self-aware to approach the altar and receive communion from Dominic's hand after he chanted the spare *Agnus Dei*.

By the time I was standing just outside the chapel, waiting for Dominic to change back into plainclothes in the vestry, I was fully recovered. When he came out, greeted me, and shook my hand, I even managed a smile. I thanked him for his remembrance, then followed him to his rooms.

THE FURNITURE around which we had sat the previous day was moved slightly to the side. In place of the short, broad table was a taut, taller one. In place of the couches were a pair of upright wooden chairs with thin red cushions as seats. As

Dominic and I entered, an attendant helped me out of my coat (Dominic had not worn one on the short walk) and showed us to our respective places.

"The cook really is very good here," Dominic said, reassuring, not boasting. "I will have to have you back some day under more cheerful auspices."

"Of course," though I struggled to picture a time past the present.

"Do you drink beer, James?"

"Yes, and especially on an empty stomach."

"Are you very hungry? I can have them bring a bit of bread or something."

"Oh no, I don't have much of an appetite. It was a little joke for myself, I suppose."

"What's that?"

"It sounds so silly now that I hear myself say it, but I spent several minutes this morning deliberating over whether or not I would be expected to have fasted before receiving the Eucharist."

Dominic laughed like a Sunday-school teacher. "I see. I hadn't even thought of that." Two pints of ale were placed before us. "Thank you, Robert," he graced the attendant.

"I did wait, just in case. Though I didn't feel like eating anyway."

"I see. Well, I'm certain that the Lord appreciates your conscientiousness. The specifics like this are often trivial, but He likes to see your mind is in the right place. Well," Dominic hoisted his glass, "to Prudence."

"To Prudence," I returned the toast, regaining more spirit. We savored the ale a while, then were presented with white dishes under silver lids. Robert removed the covers and placed them on a small cart he had wheeled out in front of himself. He informed us we would be eating baked chicken breast, with carrots, parsnips, and a light vegetable gravy, then enjoined us to enjoy ourselves before excusing himself and pushing the cart back out of the room.

We began eating. "Of course," Dominic covered his mouth as he chewed, "men of my cut of cloth get asked constantly why we aren't simply Catholics. And of course, Newman himself converted. But, at the risk of seeming frivolous, I must say I think that your little dubitation is one of the cardinal reasons." He sipped at his ale like a bird at a fountain. "To myself, at least."

"What do you mean?"

"I suppose that, when they were starting out, the Protestants wanted to cut through all of the nonsense. When they looked at the rituals of the Church, they saw nothing but pageantry. The services were," he pecked at a large bit of chicken, "were like these fossils they keep digging up in Dorset. Of course, everything was in Latin, so no one had any idea what was being said or why. In general, things were being done purely out of habit; there was no authentic religious feeling, any sense of awe or love or joy."

"I see," I had nothing to add but did wish he'd continue. "Go on."

"With that in mind, I understand the need to get...to get as far away from Rome as possible. But after a while," Dominic put down his fork and pirouetted his hand. "After a while, this terror, this hatred, this abhorrence of any sort of ceremony, it became a habit unto itself and drove past anything within the bounds of reason. I mean," he checked to see we were alone, "have you been to a Quaker service? 'Meeting of friends'? And of course, we had the Puritans, who had just no idea *what* they were doing." He caught himself. "I hope you're not offended by that."

I laughed at the very suggestion. "Offended? No, of course not. If I were so fond of the Puritans I would still be one. Not that they're really around anymore."

"No, but their descendants are, I suppose...what?, Congregationalist?"

"Yes. And even outside of the church, that pride has seeped into our culture."

"I have no doubt."

"I often wonder," though articulating the thought on the spot, "how I would have taken to Christianity if...from a different angle. If I had been brought up in your sort of tradition, or even just somewhere other than New England. I imagine I could have really believed it. But it's only very recently I've started peeking my nose into other forms of the faith. I fell out with what, at the time, I assumed must be its only species."

"Understandable," Dominic herded his last bites. "And why was that?"

"The typical reasons. I went to school and decided it was all illogical hogwash." He said by a snort he had been there as well. "But, if I may remember myself as a little more romantic than I actually was, I saw something sinister in it as well. It was a cold religion, and desperate. One whose adherents wanted to die as quickly as possible to get this life over with."

"I should like to say that is merely the Puritanism. And also what we try to push back against." We nursed the last drips of the ale. "In bringing back the ceremony, I know to our detractors it seems silly if not outright sacrilegious, but we are trying to cultivate a sense of life itself as something beautiful. Something to be loved and cherished. A gift in itself, not just a cross to bear."

We had stretched out our pints for as long as we could. "And that brings me back to the point I should have liked to make earlier," Dominic knotted the bow, sensing the end. "As much as the ceremony moves us or edifies us, we don't do it at the threat of hellfire like the Catholics. God cares about beauty, as it helps us see Him. He doesn't care if...if the wafer touches the back of your teeth or whatever superstition."

"Yes, I see what you mean." The sun had passed its peak and now, sloping towards the west, was shining brightly into Dominic's room; we basked in its silence awhile.

"Well," as a cloud sent a sudden *frisson*, "I should like to thank you again." I stood up and scanned the room for my coat.

"It was the least I could do."

"Now, if you'll excuse me, I've barely slept and need to rest before my journey."

"Yes, Thomas mentioned. I'm sure you'll have a lovely time."

"Surely. And in Trinity," Richard, summoned by a bell, had returned to help me back into my coat, "I shall have to attend another service."

"And dine with me under better circumstances!"

"Of course, yes, good day!"

I descended the steps and was pleased to discover the day had become much warmer over the course of my meal. My intellect was refreshed and, seeing as it was not even two o'clock by the time I had entered my rooms, I decided to pluck a copy of *Kormáks Saga* off the shelf and read it seated in my deep easy chair.

I ought, I supposed, to be writing out the translation of the text as I went, as I had already for the first several pages. All the same, I found I could not pick up a pen; I wanted nothing but to be sunk in the words. I was at a good place for getting lost: everything up to that point had been background, scene-setting. Now, the eponymous hero was finally to meet his great love.

He was sat in the meadhall while she was outside with a friend. All it took was the sight of her foot on the threshold, and Kormák began to sing:

At the door of my soul she is standing

Hearing his poetry, knowing herself seen, Steingerd turns her gaze inside. The lovers meet eyes for the first time. While Kormák is struck by her beauty, already he senses, if vaguely, what is to come:

But the star that is shining upon me,
What spell shall it work by its witchcraft?
That moon of her brow shall be mighty,
With mischief to her and to me.

I paused at the end of this verse, unsure what sort of spirit had given Kormák these words. She was a muse beyond that of poetry; he was here prophetic. Was this vision a blessing or a curse? Would he have done differently, could he, if he had met his fate blind?

I lingered in wonder, the book in one hand and my chin in the other. There were no thoughts as such in my mind, only sensations and intimations. Uneasy and searching for perhaps half an hour, I fell in that very position to sleep.

3

The train was waiting when I stepped out onto the platform. As a boy helped me on board with my luggage, I was pleased to hear that I was to be the only passenger in my carriage. Though the brief remembrance at the service, my lightly engaging conversation with Dominic afterwards, along with plenty of sleep, had helped my *psyche* immensely, nevertheless, I was very much looking forward to a few weeks of solitude.

Perhaps the mind has a hidden sort of memory of future events. Perhaps I had a presentiment of how I would be feeling now those few weeks ago when, booking a ticket, I had chosen to forego riding one of the new luxury trains which were becoming so popular. At the time, not quite sure of why I had felt this urge so strongly (the difference in price was a matter of shillings, which my grant from College would cover in either case), I had settled on a vague preference for this direct though slightly chillier journey to a more comfortable one which would have forced me to tarry a while in Euston station waiting for a connection in London. At the risk of superstition, I consider it possible that I, or some part of my self, had known in advance that I would be the only passenger to York that morning who still preferred the older trains, and that I made my choice for the sake of traveling alone.

The whistle blew and the train left on time. I checked my watch and saw that it was precisely three minutes past nine o'clock. I would be in York by supper. For the first few hours, through the first few of the eight stations between here and there, I allowed myself to be entertained in idleness. At Kettering, though, as the train went once again east before north towards Peterborough, I began to feel that I ought to make some use of this in-between time.

I opened my suitcase to retrieve my copy of *Kormák*. The acquaintance involved with the University Press who had asked me to do the translation had repeatedly expressed a lack of urgency, but did ask that I prepare it "whenever I had the time." Here lay the time spread out and waiting before me, but the book was nowhere to be found. After a few confused minutes of searching, then several desperate ones, I realized that the volume must have slipped out of my hand when I had fallen asleep reading it the previous afternoon and secluded itself somewhere underneath my chair.

I did have with me some blank pages of a notebook, some pens. For the first time since my teenage years, I spent the day in drawing. I had, at first, been brought to the practice by a private tutor as part of a suite, along with penmanship and the violin, of activities in which my father considered it necessary for a gentleman to have at least some ability. Though he died when I was twelve, at which point I had already been sent to Exeter, I carried on with this art out of my own interest long after setting down the rosin and accepting I would never have a lovely hand.

I liked drawing, loved it, really, as I felt that it wove me into my surroundings. One cannot draw what one does not see, or at least, if one tries, then one will do poorly. To draw something even so simple as a chair, one must give one's attention to it completely. Every detail, every curve, every crack, every light change in color, and, in them, the spirit that breathes in through image, must be searched out, known, and carefully recreated. One cannot draw as one lives: by habit, putting objects to use and then shoving them back in the corner.

Though I had neglected the activity for so long since, it had been more than an adolescent fancy. Indeed, until my seventeenth year, I had seriously considered taking up an apprenticeship or going to an art college. But at that age, I turned from images to words and began to consider myself a philosopher. My mother, though mildly distrustful of the term and anyone who used it to refer to himself, was happy that at least, under this banner, I would be following in the family footsteps to Cambridge, rather than dying of consumption in a drafty Parisian boardinghouse.

The old muscles and instincts were coated in rust, my little tricks and techniques with a thin layer of cobweb and dust. I made several aborted attempts to capture how gently a certain river flowed beside us for a stretch of the long way to Newark, or how a certain shrub perfectly accented a certain hillock. By Retford, though, I had gained my footing and produced a striking likeness of two trees, a dale, and even a small herd of kine. Shortly after Selby, only fifteen miles out of York, the sun began to set. Instead of trying to recreate the colors I now beheld with nothing but scratched black ink on paper, I decided to spend the final hour or so of my journey in simple, silent admiration.

We pulled into York station only slightly late. It was now half past seven, and the sky was becoming more and more dark. As it was for only one night, I briefly considered, though not usually one for spontaneous extravagance, shelling out fourteen shillings for a room at the immediately adjacent Royal Station Hotel. However, I felt agitated, anxious to be back in the open air, wanted to make good use of my legs now that I could stretch them so fully, and decided I would see something of the city on foot before finding lodging.

I walked up the Station Road along, under, past the cold city wall, past Barker Tower, over the Ouse. It struck me that I should have to research the etymology of that name, for, as I crossed over the river and watched it churning sluggishly in the thickening blackness like downhill molasses, it seemed so perfectly to ooze that I was unwilling to attribute this homophony to mere phonological chance.

Passing stout Lendal Tower, by the gates of the Museum Gardens, I regretted that I should not have time to immerse myself here for a while before catching the early stagecoach meant to bring me the final score miles to Boroughbridge. Indeed, I briefly weighed the option of sending an apology rather than my person to the small inn there whose only room I had reserved for the coming three weeks. Straining, I reined in my eyes, fixed them on the looming figure of the Minster, walked further in its direction, then caved to a sudden impulse towards Blake Street.

At Saint Helen's Church, on Saint Helen's Square, this became Davygate (and indeed all "Streets," "Gates"). Turning thence onto Stonegate, I broke into the thick of the shops.

As I ricocheted between the lingering pedestrians and the narrow, jagged walls, smelling bacon and beef and puff pastry, I realized how hungry I was. Would I stop at the Punch Bowl? No: I'd heard blood-chilling tales of a catastrophic fall in the quality of its gammon since its fame in Whig history had spoiled it with a steady income of itinerant patrons. But there, not far off from Petergate, I spied a sign, darkly colored but freshly painted, for the Thirsty Hermit, presenting a man with a long white beard in a flowing black, cowled robe with a walking stick in one hand and a shining pint of lager in the other.

I entered, ducking my head below the low doorway, and beheld a broad room. A staircase was immediately before me, and the bar lay towards the left in the back. In between were a dozen or so tables, three of which were occupied by single men in decent clothing eating sausages or livers or pie. At the bar, a man, presumably the publican, of medium height, ruddy-round nosed, bald but with scattered bristles, exceptionally friendly (perhaps deliberately so to make up for the initially off-putting impression caused by the black patch over his right eye), informed me that his house could not only feed me but give me overnight shelter a minute's walk from where I would be meeting the Royal Mail coach in the morning.

I accepted his offer, he accepted my coins, and I returned to the staircase I had seen earlier to leave my suitcase in the lodging rooms atop before starting dinner. As I put away my things, I noticed a lump in my coat's inner pocket. I removed the object and discovered it was a short history of the Oxford Movement that Dominic had given to me several weeks prior. I had worn the coat so infrequently since then (perhaps only twice) that I had completely forgotten that I had put it there. I decided to skim its contents over supper.

After thoroughly enjoying the suet pudding which my host recommended as his wife's specialty, I realized that it was nearly ten o'clock and time to prepare for bed. I put down the book and sipped the last of my bitter. I had just begun to stand up when I heard a voice slightly to my right.

"What are you reading?"

I looked over and saw a small man with snow white skin about high, plump cheeks and hair of copper red in a black suit and necktie.

"Excuse me?"

"What were you reading there?" He nodded towards the book open face down on the table. He had a thick cockney accent, of the sort I had previously believed only to exist within the confines of mean-spirited caricatures.

"A book of theology. Well, theological history." I seated myself once more.

"Theology," he stood up and began walking towards me.

"Don't be bothering the customers again!" the barman yelled at his back. I gestured to indicate that everything was quite alright.

"Theology, theology," the young man continued. "Do you know what I read?" He pulled out a chair beside me. "Do you mind?" he asked, having already seated himself.

"Of course not," I assured him. "What do you read?"

"The Bible." He winked at me and gulped down half a pint of beer he had carried over with him. "Have you ever had a yard of ale?"

"Now that you mention it, I don't think I have."

My companion turned around to the publican. “Billy, could we have two yards of ale?” then quietly to me, “Billy takes care of us.”

“Aye,” Billy shouted back, “but you’ll be in bed by midnight or you’ll be on the street.”

“I’m Daniel,” the man now introduced himself while Billy brought our ale in long, bulbed glasses. “Do you know what that means?” He took one of the yards and handed it to me before helping himself to the other. “Cheers,” he nodded thanks to the barman.

“No,” I said, finding nothing in Latin or Saxon.

“It means,” back to me, “‘God is my judge.’ What do you think of that?”

“I believe it’s a very wise sentiment.”

“I think on it a lot. Here, drink it faster, like this.” Daniel demonstrated how to gulp down the beer while turning it slowly with one hand by the bulb at its end. To my surprise, emulating his technique, I was able to finish what must have been at least a pint on my first go.

“You see,” Daniel continued, “I haven’t always been as cleaned up as I am now. My father left my mother when I was young. And I was never much good at helping her like I should’ve. So she was better off without the burden, and I wound up sleeping rough in London nearly two years.”

I set once again at the yard, growing in courage. “I’m very sorry to hear that.”

“Aye, it’s good ain’t it?” Daniel was nearly halfway through, outpacing me effortlessly. “It’s bad out there,” he switched to his solemner tone, “but not in the way people think it is.” He laughed as if remembering something private. “It’s almost a party, really. The drinking, smoking, chasing birds all night, and catching them more than you'd reckon." He laid a heavy hand on my shoulder. "It's the cold, though. And the embarrassment. You stop feeling like a human being."

"I can imagine." The ale paved the way for this sudden soul-bearing. "Like you've turned back into an animal."

"Aye," he stared into the distance a bit, "it is like that." We both looked away, in our own reflections. "But that's why I say 'God is my judge.' Cause He judged me, and sent me an angel."

"How's that?"

"My wife," he gestured up and back with his thumb, "upstairs. She's asleep already, bless her. She doesn't take to drinking much."

"Oh? Was she on the streets with you?"

"No, she wouldn't last a day! But she saw me one time near off Seven Dials, and said she knew I needed help. She brought me to her church. They cleaned me up, gave me a place to stay, some work." He took my hand and stared at me directly in the eye. "She saved my life."

"She did." I was rapt in his gaze.

"Now, why she fell in love with me," he laughed deeply, happy to be his own joke, "and why she stays with me, I can't begin to tell you."

"Dumb luck."

"Aye, dumb luck."

I saw him eyeing my glass and hurried to finish. "And what brought you two up to York?"

"That? Well..." He took his time choosing the words. "You know how people find you once you're back up on your feet. My father, though I hadn't seen him nigh on ten years, turns out he had been living around here. I don't know how he heard, but he heard I was in some money, and decided he was owed a part of it."

"Gosh, I'm sure you must have been shocked."

"Of course, but you know? I would have given it to him too."

"Did you?"

"Well..." he turned back to Billy and raised two fingers. "Like I said, I would have, but the old man went and died on me as soon as I got back to him."

I could hardly come up with a way to respond, and appreciated having a fresh yard to center me. "I'm sorry, I don't even know what to say."

"That's alright, I wouldn't either. But come on, drink up!" He tilted my glass back towards me. "So Mary and I, we came up for the funeral. I was kind of angry at first, you know? Him leaving me and my mum behind, us struggling so much while he was out drinking away the money that should have bought us bread. But do you know what? I got down, kneeled in front of that casket, and I forgave him." He looked straight through my face. "That's all you can do in the end. Forgive them."

I cannot remember ever having been so repeatedly at a loss for words in so short a span of time. I thought of my mother, of her own funeral I had missed. I wanted to express the feelings I had so slowly been coming to terms with, but any phrases I could think of to frame them felt inappropriate, insincere. Daniel must have read the feeling in my eyes, for he did me the favor of changing the subject entirely.

"And what about yourself? I take it you're not local."

"No," I let out, again speaking readily, "in fact, I'm just passing through. I'll be leaving first thing tomorrow morning."

"Ah, a shame, that. But it's good you saw York. Didn't you love the Minster?"

"I'm afraid I haven't got a good look at it."

"You're joking."

"I'm not, unfortunately. My train got in only an hour or two ago, and I came straight here."

"Oh, come on. You've got to see the Minster!" He turned around. "Billy, my friend..." back to me searchingly.

"James."

"My friend James and I are going for a walk to the Minster."

"Nay, you're not going nowhere but sleep," Billy had seen this before.

"Ah, come on, it's right down the street. And he's leaving in the morning."

"Alright. I'll wait up to let you back in. But you'll not be drinking more!"

"Of course not!" Daniel turned back and winked at me. "For the road." We raced through our yards, which had still been half full. As he handed the glass back to Billy, Daniel assured him we would not be more than fifteen minutes.

It really was a very short walk; I blinked and we stood before the entrance. By night, the colossal structure was even more impressive than during the day. The subtle gaslight fires of the streetlamps around us nestled into the surface of the stone and spread a pulsing amber hue around its entire overwhelming mass. The church seemed to be a single glowing ember at the heart of the ancient city.

Daniel pointed to the carvings around the central door. "Look," he instructed. "That's creation." I saw a hand reaching down from heaven. From its palm a widening gyre spiraled clockwise. Rays of light shot out like a wide-spread fan from the fingertips, in the center of which was a perfect sphere. The waters below this commotion were stirred.

Then, another pair of hands. Man and woman standing between them, back to back. Perfect, pure, eyes to the stars.

Following along the arch, above them, a tree. The snake coiled round it. Woman enticing the man with the fruit.

"This is how people learned the stories," Daniel told me. "Before they could read. They would look at these and they would understand."

We began walking back.

"Here," Daniel nodded at the building's southern side. I followed him towards it. He instructed me to lay my hands on the stones.

"Men built this. Can you imagine living like that? The constant, crushing labor, but every second of it a prayer? Can you imagine building the house of God?"

I couldn't, and expressed so through silence.

"We built this. And the spirit is still in us. Can you feel it?"

I could. "Yes."

A longer silence. The tolling of midnight. I pulled back my hands and turned to my partner. We walked onto Stonegate and approached the Thirsty Hermit. He stopped me outside of the entrance. "Things are going to change for you soon. You're going to start noticing things, numbers, coincidences. And you'll remember me." He put his hand on my arm, and then opened the door.

4

I was ready when the coach arrived. For the first time in weeks, perhaps over a month, I had fallen asleep with intention, then woken up fully rested and by my own impulse. These were the final minutes of the seventh hour, but I was dressed, packed, and even had time spare to enjoy a plate of kippers and eggs and tea before settling up with a fresh-faced Billy.

There was a slight nip in the morning air, as was to be expected from how far north I now found myself. However, the sun shone so hot and bright, though still at so low an angle, that I felt suspended somehow in both fire and ice, and all together comfortable in the middle. Even if the weather had been less agreeable, I had only to wait there on High Petergate, beneath the statue of Minerva (painted in what I'm told is the true classical style) for a handful of moments before my ride approached.

We traveled east along Petergate, Kings Square, Colliergate, south over the bridge, and finally west far off past the station where I had alighted before. We traced the Ouse upstream at more or less of a distance until it became the Ure, at which point we were nearly arrived. Over the first hour of the afternoon, we made the final few miles along the York Road into the town. I hopped off on the stones of the Old Market Square, then walked over the Tutt to my lodgings on Fishergate.

These were to be above a small pub named the Crown. I had engaged the rooms from that day, Tuesday, March the thirteenth, through the night of Monday, April the second. This provided me with a full three weeks in Boroughbridge. However, it was not until the very moment that the publican's wife, Constance (on the latter end of middle age with hair now fading from yellow to white and slight lines about her full if somewhat angular face) asked, while showing me to my rooms, how I intended to spend my time, that I realized I had no idea whatsoever besides the most general inclinations.

I had received my grant from college under the pretense of scouting the town's environs to see if they could possibly fit as the location of an obscure battle that had been fought nearly a thousand years prior. The idea of such an inquiry read well on the page, but was ultimately unnecessary and bound to be fruitless. Without so much as seeing the place on a map, I knew that the battle could have taken place there, for it could have taken place anywhere. And now, being arrived, I had neither any sense of what exactly I was seeking, nor the confidence I would be able to recognize it if I should stumble on it by chance.

It was far from the sea, but not too far. It was flat, but not too flat. The Vikings had been there, the Celts had been there, the Angles and Saxons and Scots had been there. I suppose it would be odd for the poet to speak of the Northmen heading directly thence back to Dublin, but I was by no means the first scholar to suggest a location on this side of the Pennines.

And so, for two weeks, I explored the supposed site of ancient Brigantum, mistook smatterings of pebbles for dashed floor mosaics, overheard lines of Propertius in the gentle riverrun. I visited twice and a third time the series of menhirs on the outskirts of town, near where the Great North Road now stretches on to Edinburgh, and wondered what sinister spirit had inspired the locals to refer to these shafts of stone as the Devil's Arrows.

By late morning on Monday the twenty-sixth, with a week left to prepare it, I finished a thorough draft of my report on the expedition. For the reasons mentioned in brief above (though here construed with great prolixity), I declared it beyond the shadow of a doubt that the Battle of Brunanburh may very well have taken place here in Boroughbridge. Perhaps the memory of that bloody quarrel, rooted deep in the minds of the people, was the origin of the sinister name of the nearby megalithic site. Local legend stated the Tempter had thrown those stone javelins intending to hit nearby Aldborough, but that they had fallen short and landed firmly planted where they remain today. Surely it is within reason to imagine that these "Devil's Arrows" were the very devilish Northmen, who were stopped in their tracks before they could reach the next town and do further damage? All that was needed was a simple mistaken reversal on the part of the poet, from Boroughbridge to Bridgeborough (which did indeed sound much more like the name of most English towns, and was a slip of the tongue I had heard both myself and natives of the area make on several occasions), and a casual misspelling (so endemic to the *Anglo-Saxon Chronicle*) on the part of the scribe to account for the "Brunanburh" form found in the manuscript. What was beyond the denial of any reasonable man was that more research was needed in the area. As I put down my pen, finished a final rasher of bacon, and swam in the calm face of my coffee, I almost believed I had convinced myself.

Though I was pleased with my work, and somewhat surprised to have produced anything at all, I was now unsure of how to proceed. I had exhausted my interest in Boroughbridge. I could break poor Constance' heart (who had grown rather fond of the sole guest she had served since the previous summer), end my stay a week early, and return to Oxford. Or perhaps I would take the time now to see more of York, as I had been so desirous of earlier. The wretched woman must have sniffed out my treachery, for, as I was in the midst of resolving firmly on the latter of these two options, she came up from behind and broke my concentration by shoving two letters in my face.

"The post, Mr. Dalthey," she spoke as if saying something slyly suggestive. "It seems someone is very popular."

"Yes, Constance, yes. Though I come all the way here to the far edge of Christendom to spend a moment alone with you, they still manage to track me down!"

"Oh, cheeky!" She giggled like a schoolgirl and returned to the bar.

Both letters had been successfully forwarded from Brasenose (I would have to thank Andrew for his diligence). I knew the sender of the first by the tight, aloof handwriting alone and did not bother to scan the return address. I opened the envelope, then removed and unfolded the slightly browned paper to read the following:

> Dear James,
>
> By now you have received my telegram. It is unfortunate you had to wait for this more detailed explanation, though it was sent to you at the very same time. Mother began coughing last Thursday, the eighth. By the time the doctor arrived that evening, nothing more could be done. We will be holding her funeral at the church here in Worcester where, as you know, mother attended services every Sunday until the end of her life. By the time this letter reaches you, she will be interred; I pray you not to regret your inability to attend.
>
> Your,
> Elizabeth
>
> PS - I am now handling affairs of estate and will alert you promptly should anything prove needful.

I had forgotten to expect this letter over the past two weeks, for it was largely superfluous. I could have (and had, in one or two moments of quietness) composed its entire contents with very near accuracy on my own. Now that it was come, I elected to let it slide into the deeper recesses of my mind and carried on to the second of the pair.

The hand was large and clumsy, like a child deliberately underperforming at sport to make his spectating parents so painfully aware that he was only participating in the activity at their repeated insistence. Somewhat embarrassed on its behalf, I read:

> James,
>
> Thomas (bless him) sent me a note about the beastly affair with your mother. Do keep your chin up.
>
> I know you will be knocking about the moors now, but trust the porters at Brasenose can manage to forward a letter. I myself have been kept back in London by a series of unforeseen events which command the entirety of my attention. Believe me: my baser nature would love nothing better than to be enjoying the sort of leisure you do now. But a great man must follow destiny while he has the chance. She doesn't knock twice.
>
> Fortunately, I write to you at last prepared to depart. I will be in Yorkshire shortly after this letter reaches you, and would like to reiterate my invitation to host you for a weekend. Would you care to pop around on Friday the thirtieth? Send a telegram to Mayfair with your address in Bridgeborough, and we'll have a phaeton collect you around ten.
>
> Best,
> Arthur

I had just as thoroughly forgotten Arthur's offer of a visit as I had forgotten my sister's promise to write. I was, however, delighted by the prospect. I was ready now for, desirous, even, of familiar company. Furthermore, having seen how remarkably Arthur kept his home in the narrow constraints of the town, I was curious to see how his taste might have manifested itself on the grander scale of the stark open country.

And so, a short walk to the post office to send Arthur my address, then a final triduum of breaching then falling from Dominic's history, of slipping Constance little sketches of her shape, so generously recreated by my pen, bent between the beer taps and dishes of pork crackling, of asking a farmer about town if he had ever seen anything queer by the menhirs, no, thank you sir, not in that sense, but anything, say supernatural?, until Arthur's phaeton arrived much more punctually than I could have expected and began bearing me northeast to Corbenic.

IT WAS a long ride for a phaeton, and lasted until nearly three o'clock in the afternoon. However, the weather was so mild, just verging on hot, that I embraced the jaunty, open air journey. Being close to the driver (a thin man, with no hair on his head but a set of thick, white mutton chops) made him feel like more of a fellow than a servant; perhaps under the effect of the sun, I engaged him in friendly conversation some halfway through our trip.

"Beautiful day, isn't it?" I offered cheerily.

"Aye," he said, with a pipe in one hand and the reins in the other, "bit too much though."

"How can that be?"

"There's been no rain here all season. The farmers will be starting to worry."

"Well, the season is early yet. It's April brings the rain."

"Aye," he puffed on the pipe and stared straight ahead. "We can hope, sir. We can hope."

He pointed out flowers and plants and animals: merlin circling overhead, golden plover dashing among the heather, whinchat hiding in the bracken.

We approached a densely wooded area. A gate of simple wrought iron with arrow-topped pickets guarded the way which curved slightly behind the trees. Though there was a porter's lodge beside it, of heavy, rough stone with a peaked copper roof, the driver got down and opened the gate himself. Having driven us onto the other side, he descended once more to close the gate behind us, and began along the path through the forest.

We passed what felt at least another mile of oak and ash and birch and rowan, long left then right then left then right again. Shortly after we rounded the final corner, Corbenic came into view. I cannot say what exactly my expectation had been (something between a medieval castle and the palatial yet always modestly named country homes I had become acquainted with from postcards), but my first sight of the house left me in confused disbelief. It was seated in a brief clearing, of carved limestone blocks of ripe yellow hue. There were two stories of four windows each under a pitched awning of gray slate, then a roof of odd tiles. The sides, bearing two windows more close together than those on the front, completed a neat, rectangular base. From this vantage point, the entire edifice seemed to be an outgrowth of the large hill behind it, whose peak was well beyond sight. There was an expanse of lawn on either end for about fifty yards, beyond which thick forest resumed.

The phaeton drew directly before the arched wooden door. The driver said nothing, but resumed smoking his pipe, cleaning his nails, and seeming generally patient for me to realize I was expected to alight on my own. I took my suitcase from beside me and did so. Before I reached the door it had opened.

"Mr. Dalthey," a woman of advanced age in faded muslin and spectacles greeted me. "We're so happy to have you. Though I must apologize, things really aren't ready."

"No, no," I assured her. "I am honored to be your guest under any roof."

"How kind. Arthur did say you were kind. Here, your room is upstairs."

The space I had entered was close unto pitch black. It was lighted on either side by twain candles held before brass plates, but their meager light did not allow me to perceive anything other than the scantest of details. The floor was of wood, badly warped, that creaked loudly. The steps of a staircase, immediately before me on the right, were of the same material and character, while the risers reflected with fresh-painted white. I followed the woman up; at the top of the landing, she opened a door on the right. I was pleasantly surprised to find it suffused with light from the window at its far end. There was, to the left of the doorway, a mahogany vanity with a large mirror surrounded by an arch of curling floral designs and a pink wash basin full of water with a rounded lip. To the right of the window was a bed, sized to fit one man comfortably but no more, with black posts and white sheets.

"This will be your room, sir." The woman stepped gently inside. "Please sir." She took the suitcase from my hand and placed it gingerly, with almost anxious care, on the woven quilt which sat atop a cedar chest at the foot of the bed.

"I'll let you make yourself comfortable, Mr. Dalthey. Then Mrs. Barberry will meet you in the parlor."

"Thank you."

There was nothing on earth now to make me comfortable. I did not feel unwelcome; the greeting I had received had been, if spare, thoroughly kind. All the same, I regretted my coming there. I felt as if I had stepped into a wayside country church, curious to inspect its interior, only to be interrupting a funeral with no attendant other than the priest. Had I imposed myself? Had Arthur invited me only as an empty gesture, which our cultural differences had prevented me from recognizing as such? Would it be ruder now to leave?

I stepped cautiously to the window, steeped in these thoughts for a long time, until a single, gentle knock (more a tap) came at the door. I opened it to see the same old woman.

"Are you quite ready, Mr. Dalthey?"

"Yes."

Perhaps she had noticed how dark the house seemed to my eyes, for she now bore a slender, tapered candle upon a burnt copper holder. The light led me back down the creaking steps then, through an open passage without a door nuzzled on the wall opposite the staircase, into a spacious drawing room.

This space too was flooded with light. On the wall to my left upon entering were two windows; a third was on the wall ahead of me. All three were treated with curtains of delicate white lace hanging from fluted rods of polished cherry. The space between them, and around the rest of the room, was papered with robin's-egg blue and a repeated print of bursting white lilies in columns, floor to ceiling. Above and below were twin frames of white molding. In the center was a rosewood table of medium height whose long, slender stem and broad base, along with the white cloth covering its circular top, had the appearance of an overflowing fountain and completed my overall impression of stepping into a secluded garden. Below it was a round rug, burgundy, which spread to fill most of the floor. On it, close by each other on the further side of the table, sat a pair of identical fauteuil chairs of rich walnut, upholstered to echo the rug, in the fashion of Louis XV. The ceiling, which continued the white of the molding, seemed impossibly high.

Nestled into the corner to the right of the single window across from me sat an upright pianoforte of tawny beechwood with a matching stool. After the woman I had taken to be the maid excused herself to prepare our tea, I began walking towards the instrument. As I crossed the floor, a plain golden oak, I discovered that it was in much finer condition in this room than in the hall and did not groan beneath my weight.

I found, on and about the piano, sheet music for a charming mix of classical and romantic pieces. On the scrollwork stand attached to its upper panel was the second of the first set of Nocturnes composed by Chopin for Madame Marie Pleyel. On its top was an old edition, well-used if not well-loved, of Bach's *Well Tempered Hammerklavier*. Beside that was a copy, less worn but perhaps more cherished, of Liszt's first *Année de pèlerinage*. The keys were exposed, and in clean condition. I tested them with a few bars, poorly remembered and fumblingly executed, of the "Melody" in C major with which Schumann opens his *Album for the Young*, and judged them to be very much in tune.

"Mr. Dalthey?" Emma walked on air. I turned to see her coming towards me at the pace of snow melting down a hillside in the noonday sun. "I didn't mean to startle you."

"Only for a moment."

She stopped beside the table while I went to meet her. She wore a simple dress of eggshell crape; the only adornment was a light stole of tulle hovering about her waist like mist on the mountaintop. Her hair, uncovered, the color of straw, had been woven into a single braid and wrapped about the crown of her head like a victory laurel. She waited with her hands folded beneath her breast in silk, four-button gloves, the same color as her dress.

She was tall for a woman; we stood almost eye to eye. When I reached her, she put her left in my right. I bowed slightly.

"A pleasure," she said.

"Charmed." I met her eyes and saw they were gray.

"Would you have a seat?"

"Yes." I helped her into one chair, then sat in the other.

"Grace should be with us shortly. She does take rather long with these things, but only because she likes them to be perfect."

"A respectable habit."

"Yes, I've always thought so. Though I know how some people get when they must wait for their tea."

"In a room like this, I could wait till the end of the world."

"Yes, it is coming together now, isn't it?"

In a moment of silence, I found myself studying her profile. I knew Emma to have lived something close to my thirty-three years; while her face did seem middle-aged in its own way, this was not in the traditional sense of being halfway between youth and senility. Rather, it gave the impression of belonging both to a débutante and a dowager at the same time. There was a rosiness in her cheeks, which were full but would not be called plump, an eager readiness to laugh on her lips, full even when stretched, as so often, by a smile, and an alertness in her quick, steady gaze which were more usually the qualities of a young girl who had not yet fallen out of love with the world. There was, meanwhile, an overall impression of quietness about her, of the content, somewhat removed wisdom that comes, if ever, at an advanced age.

"Thank you so much for visiting, especially under these strange circumstances," she continued.

"And thank you for taking me into your home."

Grace, as I now took the maid's name to be, entered with a china tea set (white with dark blue finishes) on a silver tray, offered me milk and sugar (I would have neither, Emma the former but not the latter), then excused herself to begin dinner in the kitchen.

"It's so different from being in the city," Emma resumed as if we hadn't stopped. "Here, we couldn't put up the sort of staff Arthur likes to have even if I let him. And though I had very much sought out the solitude, I must say it has taken some adjustment to being just the two of us."

"Yes, I'm certain it gets lonely." The tea was hot and richly steeped. "Speaking of which, when will Mr. Barberry be joining us?"

"Excuse me?"

"Is Arthur getting dressed, or...?"

Emma laughed gently, placed her cup on its saucer, and set this pair on the table. "I knew he would forget to tell you."

"Tell me what?"

"Arthur isn't coming."

"Excuse me?"

"Arthur is in London, completely wrapped up in his political games."

"He mentioned he had been delayed, but was leaving nearly a week ago."

"Yes, he made such and similar promises to me as well. But he's completely absorbed." She steadied her hands on her tea. "He's met an Irishman, a critic, a scraggly bearded fellow who lives with his mother, and is convinced he's found his second self. They're up every night, he says, drinking coffee past midnight, finishing each other's sentences, setting the world right. And writing. He believes they're writing a manifesto. And Arthur insists it simply has to be done before a demonstration they've planned on Bloomsbury Square next weekend."

"Incredible."

"I apologize for his not having told you. I ought to have done so myself."

I now understood the quiet in the house, and the vague sense I had earlier that I should not have come.

"Of course," Emma let out, "I found it perfectly strange that a husband would ask another man to spend a weekend alone with his wife. But Arthur refused to have you think he entertained such hang-ups."

"I hope my presence here doesn't make you uncomfortable."

"Oh no, not at all," though she didn't seem sure. "As I said, I was beginning to get lonely."

"How have you been keeping yourself busy?"

"I walk. Sometimes alone, sometimes with Grace, sometimes even with Martin, the driver. It's a queer thing to do, I suppose, but there's no one around here to notice me." She finished tea quickly and was now pouring a second cup. "And the country is absolutely beautiful. I think the locals may be onto something when they call it 'God's own.' "

"I'm surprised you can manage to walk at all through these woods."

"The woods? Yes, the little hectares around Corbenic are rather dense. But in the back, there's a path which leads out around the hill into the open, sweeping valley around the Swale on the other side. The effect of moving so suddenly into the light is breathtaking."

"I can picture it clearly." I drew a jagged sketch in my mind.

"That's what we can do tomorrow. It's a few hours on foot down to Thornton Bridge. If we're too tired for the uphill journey, I can send for Martin to collect us." She nodded playfully at the piano behind us. "Unless you had better practice your Schumann."

"No," I blushed. "A walk would be perfect."

Playing with the tea leaves, I realized my apprehension had evaporated. Indeed, I could not remember the last time I had felt so at home with myself, even with Thomas. Grace entered shortly after I had replaced the cup in its saucer and invited us to the dining room. We arrived there turning left from the drawing room, then entering through a doorway on the right hidden underneath the staircase.

The walls of this room were scarlet, while the molding and ceiling continued the theme of white from the drawing room. White, too, was the cloth laid out on the dining table of medium length which occupied most of the space. Around it were six chairs, one at either head and two along each flank. These were Chippendale style, acacia, with a slightly *rococo* quatrefoil carved as the back. Their cushions were thin, alternating lines of yellow and gold.

It was just five o'clock. The room received plenty of light from two windows (without treatments) on the wall to our left and a third behind the far head of the table. However, a pair of white candles in simple copper sticks had been lit and placed towards the center. Emma invited me to seat myself by the window, and took for herself the place nearer to the door. Immediately thereupon, Grace returned from the kitchen (located, as I surmised, behind the drawing room on the other side of the hallway from the dining room), and placed a full glass of red wine before each of us. We lifted the drinks and said "cheers." Grace had returned before we finished our sip and presented two plates of thick-cut beef in a rich brown gravy. She thanked us profusely for our patience, entreated us to enjoy, and excused herself to eat her portion in the kitchen. The silverware (polished, with a single rose towards the end of the ridged handle of the fork) was already before us. We armed ourselves with them, thanked Grace, and dug in.

"This is delicious!" I exclaimed. I will blame the fact that I had not eaten since my early breakfast for this unwonted outburst.

Emma laughed through her hand and her wine. "Yes, Grace is a miracle."

"Has she been with you long? You seem to know each other like sisters."

"Yes, since I was a child. My father brought her on as a nurse, but she proved so capable at everything and so eager to serve that we kept her on in a sort of general capacity straight through to adulthood."

"That's lovely. And your parents, then, are they in London as well?"

"Oh no. I was born in Stoke, if you've any idea where that is."

"So your father was in the pottery business?" I asked wryly.

"Yes!" Emma burst. "I'm always surprised when someone has heard of us."

"Well, before you flatter your ego, I should tell you it is only because my mother had in her possession a certain prized set of Wedgwood creamware, the history and unique value of which I heard repeated every Sunday over a roast supper from the time I was old enough to sit upright to the time I was old enough to dine alone." The beef made me ruminate. "I suppose it will go to Elizabeth."

"Who's that?"

"My sister. I apologize if I change the tone, but I should mention my mother has just recently passed."

"Gosh." Emma looked like she'd seen blood. "I'm so sorry."

"Thank you, I appreciate that. It was an intense shock at first. I was raving mad for a day and a half. I was especially upset not to be able to attend the funeral. But my time in Boroughbridge allowed me all of the solitude I needed to recover my self."

"That sounds perfect, really. Well, not perfect of course, but under the circumstances..."

"I understand."

Emma cut through her meat like she was bowing a violin. "When my father passed five years ago, I was an absolute shambles. I could have used a few weeks alone in the country. But," she jabbed a piece and swallowed, "Arthur and I had been planning the wedding for years and all of his relatives had already made arrangements. So of course we just had to push through."

"Gosh."

"I didn't mind terribly. It's what father would have wanted."

"A very practical man?"

"Oh, thoroughly," Emma laughed, "but in an idealistic sort of way. He insisted on my having the best education. He thought there was no reason a woman shouldn't be able to hold her own and support herself."

"A progressive."

"You could say that, though he would have recoiled at having the term applied to himself. No." She finished her food and dabbed her lip gently with a napkin. "He believed in me. And he disliked progressives because he thought they didn't believe in themselves."

"An important nuance."

"And one I think about often."

The sun had now set on our day and our meal. The light from the candles, whose necessity I now appreciated, cast a warm glow about the room. We bathed in a comfortable silence some minutes, while I looked out the window beside me and made out the shape of a small kitchen garden.

Grace returned at a moment so precisely perfect that I wondered if she didn't have some sort of magic mirror through which to watch us finish our wine.

"Will you be needing anything else?" she asked hopefully.

"No," Emma answered, with a hand on her arm. "It was perfect."

"Yes," I followed. "The gravy was delicious!"

"Thank you, Mr. Dalthey. It means so much, I'm still getting used to the kitchen here."

"I hope you don't mind," Emma said, now looking at me, "but I keep rather early hours."

"I wouldn't have you change them on my behalf."

"If Arthur were here, I suppose you would go back to the drawing room for a cigar. We do have some whiskey, if that's your drink."

"Oh no, that's quite alright. Thank you very much for the offer, but I suppose I should be rested for the walk tomorrow as well."

"As you like it."

Emma and I proceeded out of the dining room while Grace stayed to clean up. We creaked step by step up the stairs, and bid each other goodnight at the top of the landing. Having closed the bedroom door behind me, I paused a moment and stared blankly into the distance. For a moment, I was anxious for the following day to begin as soon as possible, in a mood akin to stage fright. Then there crept in something sinister, a sense that there was something untoward about this nervous excitement, about my feeling any strong emotion at all at the rather mild prospect of a stroll and some idle conversation. I shook off a *frisson*, and ignored this apprehension as well as I could as I undressed. The room was so perfectly pitch-black that, with my head against the pillow, I could not quite tell whether my eyes were open, nor can I say what was blindness or sleep.

5

I was awake, rested, washed, and dressed when Grace knocked at my door. Leading me down to breakfast, she explained that she and Mrs. Barberry had, as was their custom, begun the day several hours earlier. She hoped I would not mind eating my bacon and toast alone. Beneath the groan of the steps, I made out a slight hint of music coming from the way of the parlor. After following Grace into the dining room, I asked her to leave the door open behind her while she went to fetch my plate.

I could hear clearly now. It was a plaintive piece in a minor key, *adagio*. A second theme began in turn, pivoting to the relative major. A certain call and response pattern of thumping bass notes, then a tender treble trickle reinforced my suspicion that this was Beethoven.

Grace brought my plate. I thanked her, and once again asked her to keep the door open. As the second theme ended, and I dipped my toast in the runny yolk of an egg, the first theme returned and developed itself through a series of major and minor keys. The second theme resumed its course. While this development excited me with fewer sudden changes in key, I found myself deeply moved by its tone. That high, lilting melody line of its latter part, a young girl chasing butterflies, so light and cheery in the major, almost childlike, had become a tortured echo in the minor. I saw a man haunted by thoughts of his happiest days, now lost forever in unravelling time.

Without realizing my haste, I had finished in a hurry. I stood up from my empty plate and tea cup without waiting for Grace to clear them. I attempted to move silently through the hallway, but the oak floors must have been creaking even more loudly than usual. As soon as I looked into the drawing room, just as a friendly recapitulation had begun to resolve the piece, Emma stopped suddenly, stood up from the bench, and turned towards me.

"Good morning, Mr. Dalthey." She wore a white linen dress for the occasion, with lace about the neck and slight ruffles about the front and the long sleeves. Her hair was loose today, and spread out like a fan along her shoulder blades. She began walking towards a wide-brimmed straw hat and a gingham ribbon of red and white upon the central table. I had taken this set, at a short glance, to be a picnic basket before she placed the former item on her head and wrapped the latter around to keep it in place.

I gestured back towards the piano and stepped in its direction as she tied a bow below her chin. "Something for the *Unsterbliche Geliebte*?" I asked.

"Excuse me?" she looked at me quizzically.

"Was that Beethoven you were playing?"

"Beethoven? No, but I see why you thought that. Mozart, if you can believe it."

"You amaze me."

"He amazes us all."

Grace was at the door behind me. "Excuse me, sir. Will you be needing anything else?"

"No, thank you, Grace," Emma let in. "Unless you would like more to eat, Mr. Dalthey. Or a cane? It will be several hours down to Thornton Bridge."

"Oh no, that's quite alright," I assured them both.

"Please do make sure Martin remembers we may be sending for him later." Emma chimed.

"Yes, ma'am," Grace accepted.

We bid the woman farewell as she opened the front door and bid us the same. From there, we turned right, then right again around the side of the house. I beheld there a slender path, paved only by the beating of footsteps, leading from the pea gravel of the drive we now stood on, across the lawn, and into the woods. I followed Emma down.

The forest on either side of the path was thick with rich-smelling pine trees. Their needles and cones, sticky with resin, were littered about underfoot. The sun above filtered through the branches enough that we could see the way before us, but the sky itself remained totally obscured.

After about a quarter of an hour, the path began to curve to the west, and I remembered that we were skirting the base of a hill. This curve continued for about five miles. We were then, having traced half the circumference of a circle, diametrically opposed to the point where we had stood when the curve began. From here, the path took another sharp turn north.

Suddenly everything was clear. The trees stopped short in a straight line on either side. Below, the ground dropped drastically then gradually then drastically again before mellowing to a gentle decline around the meandering river Swale before rising back up to meet the mountain peaks on the opposite side. The path before us meandered as well, going neither left nor right as a rule, but along stone walls, through fields, past houses and mosses and rocky outcroppings.

The overwhelming color was green: the lighter shades of grasses and the darker ones of shrubs or odd trees. But what really bewitched the eye were the purple or scarlet or pink waves of heather which undulated in the wind across broad swaths of hillside like drops of wet paint God had let fall from his palette. The sky above was perfect blue. The sun stood at its center. What clouds there were, tufts of floating cotton, cast large black shadows which grazed at their leisure among the slopes.

Emma, who had been walking in front of me down the narrow woodland path, stopped at the point where the trees broke off and stared off into the valley. I reached her, and found myself similarly transfixed.

"It's perfect, isn't it?" she stated more than asked.

"Perfect."

These were the first words we had spoken since leaving the house. Now, however, as the path had become broader, we were able to stand two abreast and begin a conversation.

"Arthur told me you were a visiting professor," Emma started.

"Yes. Well, a lecturer, technically."

"I see. Would you care to explain what that means?"

"It means I'm not a fellow of any college. Though Brasenose give me rooms, and I'm affiliated with..." I spooled in the line. "It means I shall have to do something else next year."

"Do you have any idea what that may be?"

"Not in the least!" I laughed, realizing that I had not given serious consideration to Vigfusson's proposal in well over a fortnight. "Though I have had an offer."

"Oh? And what's that?"

"Frankly, I should like to tell you, as I have not yet had the opportunity to discuss it with anybody at all, despite having received it at the end of last month. But that is only because I have sworn to keep it in confidence."

"Your secret would be safe with me."

"Well, then, without going into the details, my supervisor, the Chair of Scandinavian Studies, has offered me his position."

"My. That must be awfully flattering."

"Yes, though I hadn't thought of it that way."

"Why not? Don't you want the job?"

"I suppose I do. It's prestigious and I enjoy the work. But it would mean staying in England possibly for the rest of my life."

"And you're not sure you can handle the weather."

A laugh stumbled out. "No, I find the weather charming. But it's a difficult decision to make, choosing a new home country."

"I understand you perfectly well. Of course, I love England very dearly. I could never live anywhere else. But I don't expect a Frenchman or a German to feel the same way as I do about moors or cliffs or hedgerows or constant rain. I imagine they have a similar sort of feeling to mine, but about their own specific things in their own specific countries."

"Certainly, and I do miss certain things about my home country. But I think America is different as well."

"How so?"

"Because we've only been there for half a dozen generations. And that doesn't just mean a lack of...of old buildings or ruins or what have you. The attitude of the people, their relationship to the land, to the soil, to each other, is totally different." We paused for a moment to watch a bee hop about a crop of violet devil's-bit, then continued walking. "I often think of it as a nation of runaway children. The people who went there, whether from England, or France, or Germany, left their nations behind, be it for idiosyncratic religious obsessions or the promise of wealth and power. They did it because they wanted to be alone, to stand on their own instead of as part of their people. And so, one cannot have or doesn't have the same ties or feelings as an American about America as an Englishman can about England or a German about Germany. And precisely because the country was founded by turning away from and giving up on those ties and feelings."

"I can see why Arthur liked you," Emma seemed amused. "He's very fond of that romantic sort of nationalism."

"I wouldn't consider myself a nationalist though, really. But..."

"But you think it may be time to come home?"

"I'm not sure it's still possible."

"It's always possible." Emma stopped and turned her head to a patch of oxeye daisies on a gentle slope up from the path on our left. "But the people you knew may have become strangers."

"That is what I fear. My ancestors left, let us say, two hundred years ago. And since then England has gone on without them. It's continued growing, changing, developing. It's forgotten them, too."

"Not entirely. Or not as much as you may think. A century is shorter than Americans suppose. You and I can still meet and talk and understand each other perfectly well."

"Perhaps." We walked in silence for a while. The path wove back and forth in such a way that its grade was only slightly downhill despite the steepness of the face that we walked on. On the right, we saw a man in a field surrounded by sheep in a torn tweed jacket and cap, a black knit sweater, and mud-caked boots. He waved, wished us a good afternoon; we returned the pleasantries before passing him by. "But what would you do?" I asked.

"When?"

"In my situation."

"In your situation? I've never had to think about it. But I'm certain I could be perfectly happy as an Oxford don: formal dinners thrice a week, all the arcane rituals, the pageantry, being paid to tell precocious young men that they've quite misunderstood everything."

"Yes, somehow I think you'd take to it."

"Immediately."

"The ideas, then. You called it 'romantic nationalism.' Surely it's something you've thought about."

"It is."

"And?"

"I find it strange. It seems that the thoughts and inclinations are more or less correct in themselves. But it seems odd to me that they should have to be spoken, that it would even occur to one to speak them in the first place. One loves one's country, one loves one's people. But that, to me, seems like a matter of course. And so, to make something so intellectual out of it, it's like trying to build a philosophy around pointing out that one has ten fingers and toes as if this simple fact were one of the best-guarded secrets of the universe. Does that make any sense?"

"It does. But it also leads to the question: why exactly *does* one feel the need to make a movement of these things then? And not just one odd bloke in the corner of nowhere, but so many people, so many who are celebrated and prominent?"

"You ask as if you know the answer," her teeth shone through a smile.

"I know one or two, but would like to hear yours first."

"I suppose, on the one hand, people feel these things, a given nation in particular or the concept in general, are somehow in trouble, under attack. And I suppose in a way they are, from certain quarters. But still, the overall effect is...hysterical isn't quite the word, but...forced, perhaps? Unnatural?" She adjusted her hat and collected her thoughts. "If a man were constantly going on about how much he loves his wife, to the point that he could not utter a single sentence no matter the topic of conversation without mentioning his thorough and pure-hearted devotion, I would get the impression that he was not only most certainly not in love with his wife, but that he may very well have murdered her and was now trying to throw people off of the scent."

Again a laugh slipped. "I would as well. It goes back to what you said earlier, that these things should almost be taken for granted. I can picture an odd sort of Cato, ending every speech with *ceterum censeo, digiti numerandi sunt*, or some such."

"He was getting senile; he may really have had to check."

"Yes, I suppose one ought not to hold that against him."

"Well, I've told you mine. Let's have your answer."

"Mine? I don't have much to add. I think you're quite right about these things. I will say, though, that I see this particular phenomenon as part of a larger one."

"As everything is."

"Of course."

"But let's hear about this one."

"Well," I stumbled briefly on a partly outcropped stone, then regained my posture, "to carry on your metaphor, a man like that insists so constantly that he loves his wife so dearly because he knows that he should. He tells you so often because he's trying to cover for himself, to convince you, but also to convince himself and allay his sense of shame. Is this reasonable to conclude?"

"Yes."

"Then I think we can apply that same psychological pattern to the sort of nationalist you described. He talks so much about his country because he desperately wants to convince not only you but himself that he does indeed love it."

"I believe you're onto something."

"And it isn't just a simple matter of a man trying to live up to his patriotic duty. You see, I believe that, at the end of one's life, or even just at the end of a day, one wants to be able to point at something and say 'There, that was it. That's what it was all for, what made the pain worth it.' One feels the need to redeem the world, to justify it somehow. And this justification can be anything, a person, an event, in this case an entire nation."

"So one wants to be in love."

"What do you mean?"

"What you're talking about is what I've heard about love. That sudden sense of clarity, of direction, of purpose and meaning. I've heard, not just from poets or novelists, but from friends and relatives, as I'm sure you have as well, that this is how it feels to fall in love."

"Yes, I suppose it is like that. But I'm reminded as well of the old iconoclastic impulse, the commandment to destroy all our idols, to stop worshipping the creation and worship the creator. Because one shouldn't be in love with a person, but with life itself. One should be in love with the world."

"You can't blame people for falling in love. It happens to everyone at some point."

"Of course, I'm just being extreme."

"And really, James, if we want to be consistent, what you're describing is the very pitch of idolatry. It's idolatry so perverse it can no longer recognize itself as such. All you've done is conflate the creation with the creator and labeled the world as God."

"*Deus sive natura?*" I said with a wink.

"Precisely."

"That's a heresy I'm willing to risk."

"As am I. But do let's keep each other honest."

"I'm being quite serious, though."

"As am I."

"I truly believe the soul has this thirst, this need to be enamored of existence. People sense that the love they should have is gone or faded or broken, and they fixate on this nationalism as a way to try and relight the fire."

"Gosh, I forgot that was how we got on this."

"But do you see what I'm getting at?"

"I do. And I agree."

"This is what has kept me from Christianity. It seems, in a way, to be an attempt to get away from that very spiritual need. One needs to love the world, does not, but instead of fixating on a nation like those others we mentioned before, the Christian scoffs at the world like sour grapes. We laugh about the Puritans, who took self-denial to such an extreme. But, in fairness, I think their harsh way of life is the most honest response to Christ's commands. 'Love not the world, neither the things that are in the world. If any man love the world, the love of the Father is not in him.' Indeed, I think this may very well be why they abandoned their people, their families, their homes and their blood and their history, to come to America as we said before. 'If any man come to me, and hate not his father, and mother, and wife, and children, and brethren, and sisters, yea, and his own life also, he cannot be my disciple.' "

"I can tell where you're headed here. But the Bible is a romance as well. Even if God orders us to hate the world, He loves it Himself: so much so that He 'gave His only son,' yes?"

"A poor choice of words on the part of the evangelist."

"On the part of God?"

"We won't settle this today. But we can return to turning over the earlier question of why one isn't, if one isn't, in love with the world."

"Perhaps we have broached the world's trust."

"What do you mean?"

"A joke, but there's something in it."

"Explain."

"Forgetting for now the argument over whether or not such love is even real, we should all agree that, if it does exist, while feeling or sensation may be a part, those passive experiences are not all that constitutes it. To be in love is also to behave a certain way, to make choices and sacrifices to keep the fire alive. We know what this means in human terms: marital fidelity, duties about the house, a shared pocketbook. But do we know what it means to be in love with the world? And not just to feel love but to live it? To be beholden to the world? To have a sense of honor and commitment towards the world? To owe the world something, but to owe it as a debt of gratitude? See, what you're suggesting as being 'in love with the world' is only one half of the equation. You see it merely as a certain joy or exuberance. Whereas I am suggesting that one has lost this joy or exuberance because one hasn't been acting like a very good lover."

"And what might these duties to the world be, then?"

"I'm not sure, but..." she laughed at herself, "gosh, I'm completely changing the subject and I'm sure you'll think I'm quite silly."

"No, please, go on."

"Yes, well whenever I think about these things..."

Thunder cracked overhead. I had been so absorbed in the conversation that I hadn't noticed the dark clouds roll in and lay a thick sheet over the heavens. Rain began to pour in heavy buckets. I had forgotten my umbrella.

"Oh, God," Emma cowered beneath the brim of her hat, then pointed to a speck of a building in the distance across a field on the main road. "There's a pub there. We can wait inside and send for Martin."

I leapt over the low stone wall between path and field, then gave Emma my hand to help her over. We ran through the clover and grass, squelching in the mud and howling in spite of ourselves. We were drenched when we entered. Emma walked forward and greeted the woman behind the bar before us.

"Sorry," she stated, late middle-aged, "we don't serve drowned rats."

We were too shocked with cold to catch her humor.

"Just a little joke," she softened for our miserable sake. "How can I help ye?"

"We were out on a walk and were caught in the rain," Emma put plainly.

"I can see that."

"Would we be able to wait here while I send for my driver?"

"Aye, it won't be me, but I know someone who'll go for him. Have a seat while you wait." The woman gestured to the broad, sprawling space on her right, where laughter resounded as rain beat the roof. We saw several tables, but almost all sieged by full plates and half-empty glasses. By luck, one remained with two seats near the fireplace.

"Thank you very much." Emma slipped her a gold sovereign which she had hidden somewhere, then we followed the woman to the table.

"Will ye be eating anything with us?" she asked when we'd seated ourselves.

"What do you have?" Emma asked innocently.

"The liver is good tonight. With onions."

"We'll be having that, then."

"And two pints of ale," I chimed in.

"Of course, sir."

"Ale?" Emma asked quizzically when we were alone.

"Yes, it's always the thing to have."

"I don't doubt you, but," Emma continued laughing as she took off her hat and rubbed her hands beside the fire, "I'm not sure I've had beer in my life."

"You'll like it."

She didn't. In fact, she called it "perfectly awful," but drank it all the same with her liver and onions. Having devoured my portion with relish, I nearly stopped shivering and regained my composure when I saw her giggle and point out a chunk stuck in my teeth. I was flushed, covered my mouth, set the piece loose, and swallowed.

Behind me, by the far stone wall of the pub, were two empty stools. As a man with a guitar seated himself on the one to the left and slightly behind the other, the room became suddenly silent. Then, a young woman, almost a girl, with raven black hair and a long oval of a face seated herself on the other. The guitar began strumming chords across all six open-tuned strings, and the girl began to sing.

The king has been a prisoner,
And a prisoner long in Spain

She fluttered about her "long" in such a way that I finally understood why a beautiful woman's voice is compared to the lark. She continued to give us what was the queerest ballad I have ever heard. It told the tale of a princess, Janet, young though no longer a maiden, who had become the lover of a commoner, Willie o' Winsbury, during her royal father's extended absence. Outraged at this treason, the king has Willie brought before him and intends to have him hanged. However, upon seeing the young man, the king is struck to the quick by his beauty and discovers pity.

"And it is no wonder," said the king
"That my daughter's love you did win.
If I were a woman as I am a man,
My bedfellow you would have been."

The strangest thing of all was the end. The king offers Willie his throne if he will make his daughter an honest woman. Willie agrees to be Janet's husband, but rejects the kingdom. And so the ballad ends:

He's mounted her on a milk-white steed
And himself on a dapple grey.
He has made her the lady of as much land
As she'll ride in a long summer's day.

The singer rose from the stool when she had finished, and bowed slightly towards the cheering and clapping and stamping and hollering before her, in which Emma and I played no small part. As the applause died down, I looked behind Emma and saw Martin hovering about our table.

"Excuse me, ma'am," he intoned to his mistress, "the carriage is here."

"Of course, thank you very much, Martin." She wiped down her hands, put some coins on the table, and collected her hat, then we followed Martin out of the pub and into the carriage.

THE RAIN beat on. Martin had thought to bring an umbrella, and Emma used it to shield herself while she hurried the short way from the carriage to the front door of Corbenic. By the time I caught up to her there, Grace was waiting behind the open door and shooing us in. She apologized profusely as if the storm had been her own doing, and let us know that a fire had been lit in the library.

I followed Emma up the stairs to a door opposite my quarters, which she opened and showed me into. It was completely dark outside now, and I could make out few details of the room despite the warm glow cast about it by the fire. On the wall behind the fireplace were shelves of books whose titles I could not begin to read. On the floor before the fire was a thin rug of thistle and floral patterns in tan and red and gray. Upon this were two armchairs of soft green velvet, one with its back and one with its face towards me. Emma sat in the far one with a cream-colored quilt on her lap, while I stood near by the hearth.

We remained in silence for a while. She gazed at the blaze while I tried to make out the shape of a constellation above the treetops outside the window.

We turned to each other, locked eyes, and laughed.

"I don't think we ever finished our conversation," I said as a matter of fact.

"I don't think we have to," she looked now away.

"But you had been in the middle of saying something."

"Had I? I don't even remember."

"Yes, though you did say it would make me think you quite silly."

"Then allow me to continue feigning amnesia rather than risk embarrassment."

"Only out of courtesy; I would very much like to hear your thoughts."

"On what subject, again?"

"I believe it was on our duties to the world."

"Yes, 'duties to the world.' What could I possibly know about something like that?"

"Perhaps nothing. You did warn me you were going to get off track."

"Then perhaps you can bring me back," she let out her smile.

"And how would I do that?"

"Tell me your own thoughts. That may get the old gears turning. The topic was, what, God? Love? Small things. Nationalism?"

"I've no idea what more I could say on that topic, but that I am beginning to think I am much more American than I had realized."

"How do you mean?"

"Well, when I left my home country, I left it in the rosy dawn of a golden age. Our technology, our commerce, our science and industry, were ennobling man, enriching his mind, lifting millions from poverty, banishing hunger and disease to the forgotten recesses of ancient history. Ignorance and want were cast out like shadows; wisdom and knowledge had become the stability of our times.

"But as soon as I reached Europe, I was told that ours was an age of decay. Not only was the progress I had heard of back home illusory or futile, it was in fact the symptom of a gross disease. Order was slipping. Things were coming apart. I even heard that God was dead. You cannot imagine how jarring all of this was to me at first."

"And what do you make of it, having settled in?"

"Still nothing definite. That's why I had hoped for your word."

"I don't know what to tell you; I'm just as unsure. Though I do believe I can relate to your sense of shock."

"Oh? Have you visited America?"

"No, never," she almost poo-pooed. "But I have been to Paris. And they are even more advanced in their despair than the English."

"Why is that?"

"I couldn't tell you." She shook her head slightly as she spoke. "Perhaps they've never recovered from the revolution. But whatever the reason, there's something hazy about the city, warped, delirious, but hysterical, not giddy. It's somewhat in the art, very much in the literature, though not quite yet the music. And it does seem to be getting, I daresay, worse, but certainly more and more in that direction. And that odd sort of sensibility, meanwhile, appears to be spreading out to the rest of the continent."

"So perhaps the *Légitimistes* are correct?"

"No, I can't say so. Or, I can't quite agree with them fully."

"Why not?"

"Because, well, because they're just as pessimistic as the people they criticize. They point out that these moderns have a morbid obsession with ugliness, and that's true. But instead of dismissing an off-color painting or an atonal étude as beneath their contempt, they tremble before it like a horseman of the apocalypse. They bandy on about beauty being absolute and transcendent and eternal, but in the same sentence weep and gnash their teeth and lament that beauty is over, that order is shattered, that heaven has fallen. So in their way, they agree with the atheists: God really is dead!

"Do you see what I'm saying? That, in a sense, it's sort of... sort of *crass* to be worried about beauty. Because if we really believe in it, and really take it seriously, as I do, shouldn't there be some inevitability about it? I realize this is obscure, but they talk about beauty like it's God in a sense. And we don't really have to worry about God, do we? We have to worry about ourselves, in our proximate ken. But if God, if this beauty is real, and is absolute in the way we'd like it to be, well then...well, it exists completely regardless of us. So to be worried that it's dying or going to die or is going away is ridiculous on its own terms. And if it seems to be dying, musn't that be a problem with our vision? Absolute things are eternal. If they're fading, then, then...that's in ourselves, not the stars. And if they aren't eternal, then we're deluding ourselves to get so fussy about them in the first place."

"Yes." The fire was burned down to embers.

"Yes, I think so too."

I wasn't tired; Emma gave no indication of being so herself. I turned and began to scan the modest but ample rows of books which had waited behind me throughout the conversation. My eye fixed on a slim, leather bound volume, flaked-yellow leafed, with the words *The King of the Golden River*. Below this I noticed, in far smaller print, the name of John Ruskin. I was unfamiliar with the title, though knowing so much from its author, and brought it out for a closer look.

"What's that?" Emma could smile again.

"Something by Ruskin. I've never heard of it."

"Oh, gosh," she laughed, then arose and started walking towards me. "It's a children's book, not any sort of criticism.

Father bought it for me when I was very young. Even though I had just started reading, I already thought it was sort of silly for me." She took it from my hands and flipped through the illustrations. "I wonder what I would make of it now?"

I took it back from her, then sank down against the wall to sit on the floor by the fireplace. Emma sat beside me, draped the quilt over our legs, and laid her head on my shoulder. We took turns, reading a few pages aloud in turns, passing the book back and forth. Knowing something of Ruskin, I could guess there was meant to be a political message behind the little fable of greedy older brothers who lose their wealth through negligence, and the youngest who regains it through kindness (and the help of a magic dwarf). But the slight clumsiness of the ideas only added to the childlike atmosphere, and helped us get carried away instead of being deeply pondered. We were warm; we were close. At some point, we must have fallen asleep.

When the light woke me, Emma was replacing the book on the shelf. I arose as well and walked to the window in the center of the wall opposite the doorway. I looked out, and saw that the entire spread of grass, the path through it, as well as the trees about the edge of the lawn, were all covered in a thin layer of snow. It was April the first.

"I suppose we will have breakfast."

I turned back to Emma. "Yes, breakfast. Then I'll be back in York for my train."

We ate our eggs and our toast very naturally, and spoke very plainly. Did I feel that my students were ready for their exams? Did I have any other plans for the term? And when would she be back in London? We carried ourselves so ordinarily that I was able to convince myself nothing extraordinary had passed between us. It had not been a dream, for nothing of particular note had happened. I had spent a pleasant weekend with a pleasant friend. I packed my things, thanked Emma and Grace for their company, mounted the phaeton beside Martin once more, and made way for home.

Part III

IN WHICH THE STORM BREAKS

1

One cannot arrive at the same Oxford twice. Spring had come suddenly; though reaching town well after sunset, I needed no more than half-moonlight to see this was not the old city I'd left. The trees had begun overflowing. The river was eddying, teeming. And even the air: as I walked from the station, I carried my coat, or else the heat verged on oppressive. The fragrance of flowers which burst from each bush and each branch was inescapable, unmistakable: the season was known at one hint of perfume, though she tried to sneak up and surprise me.

In the morning, the twittering song of the starlings rang through my rooms as I unpacked my suitcase and settled my things. Catherine, the servant girl, brought tea, and laughed as she filled my cup and heard stories about Daniel at the Thirsty Hermit, about Constance at the Crown mumbling bits of "Locksley Hall" just so not-quite *sotto voce* that it was clear she intended me to overhear. She drew my attention to a letter on the serving tray, which I opened after closing the door behind her. It read, taking up nearly an entire sheet of paper in its large, majestic, widely spaced hand, as follows:

> Dear James,
>
> I write hoping you enjoy much deserved rest. However, I also express urgency. Please send word and let me know when you can meet to discuss your future.
>
> Sincerely,
> Gudbrand Vigfusson

I took a pen and paper off of my desk, and jotted down a short note letting Gudbrand know I would come speak with him the following day at noon. Eager to enjoy the weather, I decided to deliver the message on foot. After leaving the slip with the porters at Christ Church, I remained unsatisfied with this short journey, and resolved to pay a long-overdue visit to Port Meadow.

And so, to the tune of the buskers on Cornmarket, past Saint Mary Magdalen, stuffed with weeds and cracked tombstones, past the high steps of the Ashmolean, where students share cigarettes and say words like "rococo," towards Worcester College, which reminds me of home. So down onto Walton, then down into Jericho, the *Sublime Porte* of the press, that Greek slab of a temple. Past the observatory, carved with the Eight Winds, then at last turning on the Well Road.

I linger as I go by a row of terraced houses on the south side of the street, and observe a series of lunette panels depicting the life of the prophet Elijah. Here he is, being fed by God's ravens, by His servant Sarephath, by His messenger bearing bread and wine. Here, he leaves the cave, casts his mantle onto Elisha as the latter plows his field, then confronts wicked Ahab in the vineyard of Naboth. Here, he splits the stream with the tip of his cloak, before being taken in the angels' chariot to heaven.

Behind me, where Southmoor and Longworth meet and flow down onto the main path, the true well, once a spring, now a fountain of capped Portland stone.

Over the canal, over the railway, over the Castle Mill Stream, finally, through a wooden gate, onto the broad expanse of the Meadow. Looking south, I see stretching above the treeline the Sheldonian, the Camera, Saint Mary the Virgin. Looking north, the blurred outline and wafting smoke of Wolvercote. Here, at the hub of the wheel, I stand above time.

The low-lying center of the Meadow has been completely flooded by the overbrimming Isis. Gulls, geese, ducks, swans, and herons sport about the waters. All around what remains dry graze herds of cattle and free-roaming horses. As I begin the dusty path across the Meadow towards Binsey, I see a young girl at my side run away from her distraught, chasing mother to offer an apple to a chestnut mare who eats eagerly from her hand. Behind me, a voice.

"Excuse me, young man."

I turned to see a small woman, bent low with age, with deep lines about her tanned face and around her closed eyes, wrapped in a black shawl and dressed in dark fustian. A wooden cane trembled in her hand.

"Yes, ma'am. How can I help you?"

"Do you know the way to Margaret of Antioch?"

I had been to that small church once before during one of the many reconnaissance journeys I had taken about the area shortly after I first came to Oxford. "I do."

"Would you be happy to guide an old woman thither?" She opened her eyes long enough for me to see them clouded over with cataracts.

"Of course, ma'am."

"Thank you, young man."

I took her by the arm and walked with her. Slowly but deliberately, we crossed the meadow, the bridge over the Isis, past the strawberry patch, the thatched roof of the Perch and the line of houses beside it, the feral cats, between fields of sheep feeding their new lambs. She spoke to me as we went.

"Do you know the tale of Saint Frideswide?"

"I can't say I do."

"Of course. I can tell you're not from here," she laughed.

"Please tell me."

"She was a princess long ago, one of the first of our people to find the Lord. She was very, very pious, and pledged her chastity to Christ. Now, a powerful but wicked king, King Agar, had heard many tales of her virtue and beauty. He wanted her for his wife. The princess would not break her vow to the Lord, and went into hiding in these woods when Agar brought a savage army to claim her. She prayed and prayed unto God, and He struck the wicked king blind to protect her.

"Now, the heart of Frideswide was so pure and so innocent that she took pity even on the wicked king. She prayed to Margaret of Antioch, the Holy Helper. She knew the princess' pain. She too had been wooed by a wicked man, and was tortured and killed for refusing him. She heard the prayers of Frideswide, and told her to strike the ground with her staff.

"A spring of water came up from the spot where she hit. The princess took some of the water and rubbed it on the eyes of Agar. His sight was made clear. He had a change of heart, and withdrew his great army. And Frideswide made her nunnery where we stand today."

There we were in the churchyard. The woman raised her right hand and pointed to a spot beyond the graves.

"The well is still there. Would you lead me?"

We wove through the peeling tree trunks and stood before a rectangular pit, about six feet long and a shoulder span wide, paved about and supported with stone. At her request, I descended the brick steps, under a Latin inscription whose letters were too worn to read, to a small pool of water below. I cupped my hands and took some of the water, thick with clumps of moss. I returned, and held my offering before the woman. She dipped her fingers into the water repeatedly and splashed it around her face, soaking in every drop with the cracked plane of her palm.

"Would you bring me into the church, young man? I should like to pray."

I led her back to the warped wooden door, under an archway of Norman pattern, and into the chamber of cold stone. I sat her in the closest pew, and myself across the aisle. Above were stout rows of bent timber ribs and censers of faded metal hanging from chains. Before, above a small altar, was the twisted crucifix.

After several minutes, the woman stood up and walked to a miniature chamber organ in the back corner of the church. I heard her foot stamp eagerly at the bellows beneath to fill its lungs with air. Then began the running strains of a baroque fugue. When she finished, she remained seated before the keys in silence. I went to her side and asked if she would need help returning home.

"No thank you, young man." She looked up at me. Her eyes were shining emeralds. "I shall find the way."

"Really, I would be more than happy to..."

"No, no." She placed her hand on mine. "I would like a moment alone."

"If you're absolutely certain..."

She smiled gently, then turned once more to the organ. As she began to play, I collected my coat and returned outside. The air hummed about me as I walked; I felt I could hear the rhythmic pumping of her foot, the clack of the creaking keys. The breeze carried her notes. They followed near at my heels all the way back to the Meadow.

2

Gudbrand's office was up a single flight of a broad stone stairway that led onto Tom Quad only slightly south of being directly across from the tower and gate. I knocked twice on the heavy wooden door as the bells were ringing twelve. As their sound faded out, his loud voice called me in.

Gudbrand sat pitched behind his large wooden desk. He had been writing: a pen and several sheets of paper were before him. On either side of these lay a stack of ragged manuscripts (the youngest being half a millennium old) arranged in order from thick folios on the bottom, quarto, octavo, and a handful of miniatures sprinkled about on top whose tightly packed script must have been illegible to any man but Gudbrand himself. The wall to my left was a shelf full of books, less ancient than those on the desk but equally worn from constant use. Goethe, Schiller, Cervantes, Racine, Dante, Tasso, Ariosto, Boccaccio, Pushkin, Mickiewicz, even the dialogues of Cicero and Plato, all in their respective original, stood alongside editions of Shakespeare and Marlowe and Spenser and Milton which, in their many centuries, had most likely never left the city of Oxford. If I had not known the man's modest character myself, which cared nothing to impress, I would struggle to believe the reports I received from countless colleagues, experts in German or Russian or French, who stated quite plainly that Gudbrand was fluent in them all. Nor was this gift of his a mere hobby or parlor trick: he had read everything I saw on there, often more times than the scholars who studied them professionally, and could quote them at length with nuance and feeling and most evident, profound understanding.

He gestured with his hand to a long, deep-cushioned sofa and asked me to sit. I did so, facing towards him. In between us was a round, wooden table, upon which sat a small marble bust of Homer, the only piece of art in the room. He gestured once more, now to a tea set on a tray on this table, asked me to help myself, then continued speaking as I did so.

"Your trip up to Boroughbridge?"

"Very good, sir."

"And you've written your report?"

"Yes, sir."

"Very good. You will present on it some time in the coming term."

"I would be honored to, sir."

Gudbrand nodded and stared at me intensely over folded hands which stood up at right angles from where his upper arms rested on the desk in front of him.

"James." He opened his mouth, began a syllable, then stopped and buried his face in his hands. It stayed there a long time. He arose, walked to the window at my right, and stared out of it with his back towards me.

"I need," he cleared an empty throat, "I need to know that my work will go on." He placed one hand on the window sill. "I know it is very difficult to leave one's homeland. I have not seen my own in many, many years." He removed the hand from the sill and put it to his eyes. "I will never again." He was quiet a while, and visibly shaking. In that moment, I realized for the first time that he was human. He half turned to the bookshelf with an outstretched arm and open hand. "But these things I have loved, the poetry, the stories, all of it so beautiful. I..." he walked to the desk and stood perpendicular to me, head bowed, with both fists planted firmly beside the manuscripts. "I need to know these things will outlive my memory."

We locked eyes a moment, but I could not match his gaze for long. I looked back out of the window where he had been standing a moment ago. More than of this offer alone, I was thinking of my entire academic career up until that very moment. I was ashamed of the sense that it had always been something of a whim. I had a knack for these languages, I enjoyed reading their literature, and things had more or less fallen into my lap. I felt childish, almost petulant, to compare myself with Gudbrand. I could feel the intensity of his care, his dedication, devotion, how deliberately all of his life had been executed. I was unworthy of bearing his title, and yet, perhaps I was ready to change.

He straightened his jacket, pulled out his chair, and resumed sitting, staring at me over his folded hands, as if he had never moved from the spot. "You must make a decision."

"Yes, sir."

"Before the start of term."

"I will, sir."

He coughed again. "And your translation of *Kormák*?"

I thought of the text on my desk, open but otherwise untouched since my return from Yorkshire. "It is coming along very well, sir."

"Undoubtedly." He continued staring at me. His eyes were blue and cold, having taken their shade from the glaciers back home. "That is all, James."

"Thank you, sir."

I stood up. He walked towards me and extended his hand for a firm shake. "Thank you, James. I trust you will make the right choice."

I HAD to talk to someone. Thomas was still in Florence; Dominic was off leading a pilgrimage to the Holy Island of Lindisfarne. At last I remembered my promise to Thomas' old classmate, Jonathan, broken in the flurry of business and pleasure at the end of Hilary term, to meet him for a pub lunch before heading to Boroughbridge. I pushed through the crowds along High Street to All Souls College. The porter there drew a long sigh of relief from my lips as he let me know that Professor Fox was still among us. I asked for a slip of paper and a pen, jotted down a brief message apologizing for my earlier negligence and wondering if Jonathan would be pleased to join me this evening, then handed it back to the porter along with a shilling asking him to deliver it as soon as possible.

I returned to Brasenose and paced about my reception room. *Kormáks Saga* lay splayed out on the desk, lately retrieved from under the chair, expecting me, as I truly had intended that morning, to continue my translation. After an hour and a half of nervous agitation, the knock came. I opened the door, and saw Andrew standing there with a note in his hand.

"Here, sir." He handed it to me while catching his breath. "It seemed very urgent."

"It is, Andrew, thank you. Wait here." I tore open the envelope and read:

> James,
>
> Forgive me, as well, for having forgotten you had forgotten me! March is so terribly rushed. I would be delighted to join you this evening. Shall we meet at the Lamb and Flag around five o'clock?
>
> Jonathan

"A pen."

"Excuse me, sir?"

"A pen," I asked frantically, "do you have one?"

"I..." Andrew fumbled about his pockets, discovered a small stick, removed its cap, and handed it to me. "Here, sir."

I flipped over Jonathan's note, held it against the wall, and scribbled "YES" on the verso face.

"Thank you, Andrew." I handed him the pen. "I apologize if I frightened you."

"All in the job, sir."

I found another shilling and handed it to Andrew along with the message. "Please take this to Jonathan Fox at All Souls as swiftly as possible."

"By Mercury's winged boots, sir!"

I thanked him one last time, then closed the door to resume my pacing. This could not continue for three more hours: my shoes would bore a hole right through the floor, and I would tumble down and land in the lap of the young Austrian economist who lived beneath me, like the chortling lassies he snuck in most Saturdays. I glanced guiltily at *Kormák*, but knew I should not be able to focus. I could head to the Lamb and Flag early; a drink might take my mind off things and calm my nerves. But it could also prevent me from speaking to Jonathan as articulately as I should like.

I hit upon the general idea that, if I walked in any given direction for an hour, and spent an hour wherever I landed, the walk back would bring me to five o'clock. But, as I traced a compass circle about my mental map of Oxford, with the needle point on Brasenose and a radius of four miles, and saw that an hour's walk in any direction would strand me precisely in the middle of nowhere with even fewer possible means of distraction than I currently had at my disposal, I felt suddenly ridiculous and laughed off my nerves. Some tea would do it; and I would have a crack at *Kormák*. And Jonathan had said "around" five o'clock: I could leave at a quarter to the hour, walk slowly, and only be five minutes early.

Or perhaps I could put this odd mood, one of emotional tenderness mixed with driving urgency, to an appropriate use. I had for some time now neglected to send the response to my sister Elizabeth which she really did deserve. This was not from mere laziness; in fact, I doubt laziness had anything to do with it at all. To speak plainly, I was at a complete loss of words. It is always difficult to write of the death of a loved one; it was always difficult to speak to my sister. The simple solution would be to match the business-like tone she had used with me on any occasion for the past pair of decades. But this would feel like a betrayal of an opportunity for a thaw in relations. No: I wanted to send something warm, something open and inviting openness. Unfortunately, I'd had no sense how to begin. Now, though, on sudden impulse, I felt prepared.

Though she was five years my elder, we had been quite close growing up. She was my first playmate, first classmate, even, as I insisted on learning to read quite young, technically my first tutor. We invented fables for each other, tall tales and fairy stories. We plotted pranks on the nannies and governesses. Father was away quite a while serving as a lieutenant in the War. When one or the other or both of us missed him and cried we would hold each other.

We did not have much time to celebrate his return. There were hugs and kisses and little presents and stories for a few days, but all of this vanished in an instant. Though I did not fully understand the circumstances at the time (nor am I certain I do now), I knew from the reaction of the adults around me that the death of Lincoln had been something terrible. My father, though always somewhat reserved, became absolutely silent. He spoke little to me the summer after he came home other than to tell me I would be sent to Exeter in the fall.

After that frigid ride to New Hampshire, where autumn becomes winter so suddenly, I saw my sister only at holidays. While we were always glad at the chance, things were already changed. That quietness had lingered on the house, and we grew so much more when apart than we could recount to each other over one or two weekends.

The rift became final halfway through my second year at Exeter, when I was abruptly called home to attend my father's funeral. Stepping out of the carriage, I saw her look at me for the first time with coldness. Perhaps I reminded her too much of him. Perhaps she believed it was my absence that had made him ill. Perhaps I was just despised along with the rest of the world as she slipped into a very icy religious temperament. Whatever the reason, she had since that day treated me with the polite removal of a bank teller.

I sat at my desk, took a pen and some paper, and began writing:

> Dear Elizabeth,
>
> Thank you for your telegram, for your letter, and for handling mother's affairs. I am sorry to have missed the funeral, as well as for having left you alone. I cannot imagine the difficulty of taking care of all these things without any support. Please know that you have been in my thoughts even more often than usual, and are frequently the subject of my prayers. At this moment, I do not know when I will be able to return to America. However, I would like to invite you to visit me here. Do not consider expenses. Please write back as soon as possible letting me know your thoughts.
>
> Your loving brother,
> James

This was all I could say. It was not what I had hoped, but it did at least invite a response. I folded the letter, slipped it into an envelope, addressed it, sealed it, and left it on my desk. I would mail it tomorrow. The bells played their three-quarters of a tune; all was in time.

I TOOK a long way, through the Bodleian, pausing a moment to admire the statue of the Earl of Pembroke (whose jaunty paunch and *contrapposto* gave him the look of Donatello's David posing a second time after one decade too many of milk, honey, and sack), then leisurely up Parks Road, along the south side of Keble, and down the slender Lamb and Flag passage which parts the two halves of sprawling St. John's and leads to the ancient pub.

I was immensely relieved to see Jonathan already waiting outside in a long, cashmere overcoat that went well past his knees.

"Hello, James." Though I was already mostly calm by now, his gentle voice and warm smile left me entirely placid, even cheerful.

"Hello, Jonathan. Shall we have a drink?"

"Well, I don't know why *you* came here this evening, but if it wasn't for a drink I'm afraid I shall have to remember I made other plans." He winked and opened the door behind us. We walked up to the bar; as I began to weigh the usual options of lager, bitter, ale, or ale number two, Jonathan drew my attention to a set of three further taps on the far side of a wooden support column on my left. They were labeled, in order, by white chalk on small blackboards attached to their pumps with thin twine, "Old Tin Whistle," "Soggy Wolfhound," and "Rosie's Revenge."

"What are they?" I asked, unable to imagine what sort of beverage would advertise itself as tasting of wet dog.

"Cider," Jonathan informed me. "Scrumpy. I can't tell you it's delicious but it's what you want."

The barman, bald, heavy-set, towering nearly to Jonathan's height, with thick, hairy forearms like a pile of leaden pipes lived about by a plumber's cat, approached us.

"What'll it be, sirs?" he almost accosted.

"A pint of the Old Tin Whistle, please," Jonathan piped.

"Aye," the barman placed a pint glass beneath the spout of the leftmost pump and began pulling, then turned his face to me. "And for you, sir?"

"Rosie's Revenge," I chanced.

"Aye," I had earned his respect. "A brave choice."

Not quite understanding the meaning behind this remark but eager to uncover it, I took the full glass of cloudy yellow cider, busy with flecks of apple and skin and what I feared was a bit of a twig floating about the bottom, paid the barman, and followed Jonathan through a low doorway on our right. From there, up two or three steps on our left, we entered a small room and seated ourselves at the righter of two tables therein.

We clinked our glasses, said cheers, and tucked in. I felt as if I were drinking a bushel of apples left drying in the sun for well over a year.

"Careful with that," Jonathan warned playfully, "or you'll be bleeding like Henry after the second. And don't expect me to drag you to Chinon."

We related the events of our past months to each other. He told me of catching up with old friends and tutors over formal dinners and pub lunches, of peeving old enemies by slipping books into their bags from the shelves of the Bodleian, then alerting the librarian that he believed, though he was shocked to say it, that that man over there was attempting to commit a theft. I told him of my trip to Boroughbridge, of the mad, brief stay at York, of Constance (who had now sent me a letter I was ignoring out of courtesy to her better judgment), of the farmers who were all too eager to take my scholarly questions in a certain light. As I told him of the subtle etymological trick by which I proved that it was not only possible, but *quite* possible that *Brunanburh* was a corruption of an ancient name for Boroughbridge, his reserved though mirthful laughter completely overflowed its banks.

"Oh, gosh," he collected himself. "You really will do well at Oxford." He began sipping at the second round he had recently brought back for us from the bar. "Which makes me think: do you intend to stay?"

"I'm glad you've asked that, Jonathan. My inability to answer is, besides your indispensable value as a people's *sommelier*, what drove me to invite you here tonight."

"Drove? I suppose you did seem rather anxious to get hold of me."

"Yes, well," unto the breach, "without going into the details of it, Vigfusson has offered me his position."

A full smile spread across his lips. "That's brilliant, James!" He lifted his glass. "Congratulations!"

"Thank you, Jonathan." I clinked his glass and drank. "But do let's keep this between ourselves for now."

"Of course."

I allowed the smile to fade from my lips. "The only problem is..."

"Yes?"

"Well, he needs an answer by the start of Trinity."

"And?"

"And, as I alluded to briefly before, I am not prepared to give one."

"And why not? You seem to have taken very well to Oxford. She's certainly taken well to you."

"Yes, she has. But," I sipped and began to smile again, "it's the difference between an affair and a marriage."

"All the difference in the world," he winked.

"Joking aside, though, do you see what I mean?"

"Yes, I believe I do. You're fond of England, even awfully fond. But," he gave a one-armed Gallic shrug, "it isn't home."

"Precisely."

"A worthy problem for a mind of your caliber."

"And one with which you must have grappled yourself. You've been living half the world away for, what?, twenty years?"

"Yes, I suppose I have been, haven't I?"

"And India is far more foreign to England than England is to America."

"I suppose it is. Though in a sense that makes it easier. I don't have to pretend to fit in."

"You don't mind living like a stranger?"

"Not particularly. Though, and I don't mention this in mixed company," he sipped to let me stew, "I am one of the Wandering."

"Really?" I asked with something approaching genuine surprise. "Do you practice?"

"Oh no, not in any meaningful sense. In fact, my parents converted, in a political sort of way, long before I was born. I never could have received my education otherwise. We still had religious Tests when I matriculated, you know. Though the oaths were all gone when I took my degree."

"Gosh, how the time passes."

"Yes, astounding, isn't it? Though I wouldn't say we're in the clear yet." His face became serious for a moment, the closest I had seen it come to sadness, then regained its cheer. "It's ridiculous really, but I was sort of proud of Disraeli in a way."

"Your fellow Anglican?"

He laughed. "Yes, I suppose he was, wasn't he? But it's more than a religion, James, and I believe you understand that."

"I do."

"Well." This next pint was passing too quickly. "All that to say, perhaps it is in my blood, but I am content to remain everywhere and nowhere."

"Forever?"

"Forever?" He smiled and nodded to one side. "No, not forever. My wife is sick of it, despite having been born in India. Ever since we sent the boys to Eton, and she started receiving letter after letter about the mother country, it's become a sort of fairyland for her. I couldn't take her eyes off Windsor Castle long enough for her to join me even this one month in Oxford. And the fellows at All Souls have made it quite clear that there is a seat waiting for me whenever I should want to sit in it."

"We may be colleagues then."

"We may." We pictured it in silence. "If you really want my advice, James, it's this: you are younger than you realize. Far younger. And what Gudbrand is offering you is an incredible opportunity for a man of any age. If you accept the role now, you will be able to do anything, anything you should like to do later."

"I see."

"The seasons of life are not so long as they seem. When we shiver, it is always winter. When we dance in the sun, it has always been summer. But we must reap when the harvest is ripe, not just when convenient."

"I believe you're right."

"And Oxford can be a home for anyone, really anyone. It's not like other places."

"I know very well."

"But," he paused, "I think it's also a place you have to come back to. Being here now, it's all the same as I left it. Much more so than London or Paris. And yet, I see London and Paris the same, but Oxford so differently. So perhaps you should try something else for a while. Maybe go to the continent."

I tried to imagine unseen Élysées as we took our last sips.

"I should eat before the next one," Jonathan admitted for both of us. "I'm already getting sentimental."

"As should I."

We had two pies brought out with the following round. As soon as I smelled the fresh pastry, I realized that I had not eaten all day. Jonathan seemed either not to notice or mind the ferocity with which I attacked my plate, for he ate with similar relish. As we helped ourselves, we returned to the sort of small talk which had occupied us at the start of our evening together. Had we heard from Thomas? Very little. And Dominic? Only that he was enjoying himself. Arthur?

"If I remember correctly," Jonathan said, setting words between forkfuls, "I heard you were going to visit him while you were up in Yorkshire."

"Yes, so had I."

"And? How was it?"

"The queerest experience I have ever lived to tell of."

"Oh?" he replied with piqued interest. "What happened?"

An excellent question; I had hardly allowed myself to make sense of the event myself. Now that I had to explain it to a third party, I could not think where to begin.

"Nothing much, really." I dabbed my lips, now making him wait, and took another sip. "Only that Arthur neglected to tell he wouldn't be there."

Jonathan put down his fork and bent over laughing. "If it were any other man, I should never believe you."

"I still don't believe it. When I arrived at Corbenic it seemed like a mausoleum, covered in cobwebs, creaking and drafty. I'm a skeptical man, but if you told me the airy old woman who opened the door had been a ghost I would not doubt you for a second."

"Did you stay?"

"Well, it was too late to go back." Act natural. "And his wife insisted."

"Oh, Emma?" It was the first time I had heard her name since the last time I had spoken it to her. My vision became blurry. My pulse quickened and my chest became tight. I steadied as well as I might the shaking fork in my hand. "A lovely woman."

"Have you met her?"

"A few times."

"What do you make of her?"

"As I said, a lovely woman." He was weighing a thought. He leaned back in his chair and lifted his pint from the table. "Though I will say I've worried about her."

"Oh?" I asked, with what I hoped was a casual air. "Why's that?"

"She..." he leaned closely forward and put his glass back on the table. "If you ever repeat this I will deny having said it."

"Go on."

He took one sip of courage and leaned halfway back. "It's awful to say, though I suppose a sort of compliment, but she's precisely the sort of woman who should never have married for money."

"I see. You believe she was wooed by his title?"

"No." He hit on it. "Not wooed, but won. I'm sure it seems silly to an American, but the rise in station must have meant everything to her father."

"I understand perfectly well. We have our own aristocracy."

"No, your aristocracy is different. Your aristocracy is our middle class. There are no self-made dukes or earls. Perhaps one or two barons. And, whether or not it is true, your titans pride themselves on having paid their own way, as it were. Ours pride themselves on having been born into the privilege."

"Our titans have sons, and they're raised on silver spoons."

"Yes, but one son is one generation. Not a thousand years of portraits and arms hanging up in the manor house of an estate recorded in the Domesday Book."

We had both finished eating, and were coming towards the end of our pints.

"Of course, his title is the first thing Lord Barberry would like to be rid of," he found at the end of his glass. "I half believe he married Emma to prove a point to his mother."

"Is she very much?"

"I shouldn't have said that." Jonathan looked away, visibly embarrassed. "But let's call it a surety that I shall keep your secret too."

"Of course."

"Now," he finished before he said more. "I do have to pack before returning to Eton tomorrow."

"Of course."

"Martha and I will be taking our time through the continent. I can leave you a little itinerary of where to reach me and when, if you like."

"I would very much so."

"Good."

We stood up, put on our coats, and returned outside.

The wind had picked up. "Will we be headed in the same direction?" Jonathan asked, pointing down the Passage.

"No, it's early yet. I think I'll walk about and take the air in a bit more."

"A wise idea. Well," he shook my hand, "thank you for the evening. I have a sense we will meet again soon."

"As do I."

"Good night," he turned half away then turned back. "James, again, you're very young. Don't think too much like an old man. Let the breeze carry you a while yet."

"As far as my wings will take me."

He smiled and turned away fully now. He raised his right arm and said "Goodnight, James," a final time. I returned the word at his back, then watched him disappear behind the winding bend.

3

Though my talk with Jonathan had given me much to think about, and much I still think of today, I cannot say that I felt resolved. If anything, I was more distracted. I had been thinking of Emma since the moment I left Corbenic, but never allowed myself to register this fact consciously. That is not to say that I was actively suppressing my thoughts: to do so would have required a tacit admission that there was something improper in how often she was coming to my mind. Instead, I had let her smile, her laugh, the softness of the skin at her fingertips, ebb and flow about me as if there were nothing more of emotional significance to these memories than to a random reminiscence of a sharp piece of wit I had heard at a dinner, or a particularly fine slice of fruit cake, or a very well-bred border collie that had delighted me once over the course of an afternoon on Boston Common.

Now, the dam was burst. I could no longer deny how she haunted me at every corner. I was dogged, dreary, drowned, and, most of all, embarrassed. I knew this woman even less than I knew the shoeshine who spat on my boots once a week in the Covered Market. And yet, I had dreamt of her thrice in seven days (twice with unwonted clarity) and, in quiet moments where I allowed myself to grow sentimental, felt as if she were nearer to my soul than my very self.

I had met a number of beautiful women, and been familiar with several. Some had made propositions, and some I accepted. Sundry had stirred me; many still do. But Emma was not a suggestion or a lark or a fancy.

At every word I spoke, every grand thought in mind, every overly long, proud, cruelly byzantine sentence I scratched from my pen, she stood by my ear like the slave behind Caesar triumphant asking, "Really, now, James, is that quite what you meant? If so, I don't think it comes across in the way you should like it."

There was no reason I should hear from her. In fact, it would have been perfectly irregular if I did. Married women do not churn out letters to their husband's remote acquaintances like they do to their sisters or cousins or that girl that they met at the convent school. Nor was there any possible way, even if she were being blown about the same gale in which I found myself, that she would ever be aware of my condition. What did I dream I would read on her note card?

"Dear James,

I'm terribly sorry to bother you during what I know to be a very busy time of year for men in your profession but it has suddenly occurred to me that you're the love of my life. Please let me know if you should like to meet for tea in Knightsbridge one afternoon this week, as I am there most days doing the shopping.

Sincerely,
Emma"?

Ridiculous.

"Hello, James, I..."

...shan't even put it to paper.

"James,

Go on then.

Emma"?

Actually somewhat charming, but she could never bring herself to send it.

Knowing this all very well, demonstrating it to myself incessantly with the precise and irrefutable logic of a geometric proof or the *Ethics* of Spinoza, nevertheless, every morning, when I asked Catherine if there was any post, was she sure, had she checked twice, and heard that no, sir, no post, sir, yes she had checked twice, sir, my heart sank deeper and deeper and my mind became once again fixedly convinced that Emma Barberry hated me so well as the Devil hates truth.

This little charade had played out between us with complete regularity for nearly a week, but today, Catherine was giddy. I glared at her from my armchair like a hungover

Hamlet as she repeatedly tried and failed to stifle her laughter while putting down the tray and pouring the tea.

"Catherine, you know very well how fond I am of you, so please understand that it is only for your sake and for that of the husband you will indubitably win for yourself if you can drop off this singular vice of yours that I tell you this, but you simply must be made aware of how silly you seem to be giggling like that over nothing so early in the morning."

"I appreciate your well-intentioned criticism, sir, but it isn't over nothing."

"Oh? Pray tell, what sort of a, of a..." I struggled to find a word that would maintain my air of thoroughly high-brow displeasure, "a *gooseberry* of a joke has got you in such stitches, then? Something lewd, I presume?"

"No sir," she was hunched over now with laughter, "nothing lewd whatsoever. It's only that..."

"Out with it!"

"That, sir, well, that there *is* post today." She nearly fell to the floor, but regained her composure and pulled out a letter from behind her back.

I stood up, silent, and walked slowly towards her to retrieve the message.

"Thank you, Catherine. I'm sorry to have been so rude."

"You couldn't be if you tried, sir."

"Thank you, Catherine. Thank you very, very much."

"Of course, sir." She stood by the table awaiting further orders.

I cleared my throat. "Dismissed."

"Aye aye, sir." She saluted me then turned to leave.

Once she had closed the door, I turned over the envelope. The writing was not Emma's (though I had never seen it I was certain I should know it), but Arthur's. A pit sat deep in my stomach as I returned to the armchair to read:

> Dear James,
>
> I hope you know I feel an absolute dunce [underlining his] to have missed you in Yorkshire. I shall have the chance to explain myself soon: a painter that Emma has decided she's batty about is giving an exhibition at the Ashmolean (what's that line about *tempora* and *mores*?), so I've decided to take her down to Oxford this weekend as I wanted an excuse to see the old place anyway. Would you join us for tea at the Randolph this Saturday at two? When you hear what I've been up to, you'll wish you had been in London with me as well! And if I miss you again, I've let the *maître d'hôtel* know you can stick some caviar on my tab.
>
> As ever,
> Arthur

I was nauseated, first with guilt then with anticipation. I had barely survived waiting to unburden my mind of a much lighter load the previous Wednesday for a grand total of three hours; how was I to make it through three full days? The obvious answer was work; as my students were still on their break, that would mean translating *Kormák*. Unfortunately, as soon as I had managed to enter some sort of flow with the text, I felt it beginning to taunt me. Here I was trying to distract myself with labor while the hero shirks his own to sit at home playing board games with his beloved.

I pressed through my envy and was able to get carried away again as I read of Kormák foiling the harebrained schemes of his rival suitors. I reveled in their well-deserved slaughter, smiling in spite of, perhaps even because of, the wanton grisliness of their end. But my mood soured once more as, after this moment of victory, Kormák fails to attend his own wedding and allows Steingerd to be given to another man.

I felt a personal, almost physical, frustration at this inexplicable twist. The text itself could hardly make sense of the misadventure: though a curse from a witch serves as a sort of formal *diabolus ex machina*, nothing specific actually keeps Kormák away other than his own dissipation. My mind could not maintain the distance required to focus on the technical side of translation; at every attempt it was caught once more in a loop of dumbfounded incredulity. Without much of a choice, I decided I was satisfied with how much I had managed so far and sought out another diversion.

At first I tried losing myself in the fleeting delights of an outdoor season. By luck, the weather had not ceased to be perfect since the days had begun getting longer. A series of walks about the Botanic Garden and the deer park at Magdalen (really the prettiest college) not only put my soul to rest but even made it sing. Still, this song was a short one, resolved before lunch and leaving me in need of something more lasting.

I had nearly resigned myself to the slightly tragic pastime of punting up and down the Cherwell alone when the sight of a boy in a railway uniform reminded me of my train ride to Yorkshire some few weeks ago. I had lost hours in drawing then; perhaps I could catch that same magic again. I had, indeed, been meaning to visit the Union library and devote proper attention to the elaborate decorations; what better way to get to know them than to recreate them with my pen? And so, that same morning, with some inks and a notebook, I crossed over town to the brick, ivied building.

The library was a quiet room, with red leather arm chairs and neat wooden desks upon green carpeting of a simple, white floral pattern. It was my first time in the space. After acclimating to its air of perfect tranquility long enough to feel comfortable spoiling the stillness, I looked up and was immediately stunned by the sight of the ceiling. It was the ribs of a whale, or the hull of an overturned longship; its endless unfolding design of bright branches and leaves made it look, at a distance, as if the stained glass of a cathedral rose window had been stretched out upon it. I took some minutes to recover myself before mounting the staircase to my right and ascending to the murals.

These were the emeralds in the crown, running in a circuit along the entire ring of the library's upper level. Already, though only my age, they were slightly faded. At a whim of old Ruskin's, they had been painted directly onto the walls by sympathetic, romantically-minded young artists, most of whom would go on to become household names. Even sunbleached they shone; the spell was unbroken. I spent that long day in their midst, breaking only for a late lunch of black coffee and soup in the members' bar. Hours evaporated in front of each panel, as I lost countless pages of scrap paper trying to capture these scenes of Rossetti and Morris and Burne-Jones. Before Lancelot's vision of the Grail I felt too great a shiver and continued walking; the rest, the White

Hart, Merlin and Nimue, were traced at great length in their turn.

I was amazed at how readily I recognized the figures and stories. I suppose I had read all the tales as a child, but had never quite fixated on these heroes in the way many boys I knew seemed to. They appeared to me now, though, not as half-remembered youthful fancies, but as perfectly familiar, as almost-near kin I could know at a glance. I felt I was meeting old friends, or old teachers; I felt I was home.

These impressions and studies filled up two notebooks but only one afternoon. Having completed the cycle, I considered moving on to doing sketches about town, depicting finely detailed architectural features or particularly interesting grotesques. But there was no spirit in that; what was needed was something more drastic. Having swallowed my pride (or, my fear of displaying a skill I had not already mastered), I made my first journey to the art supply on Broad Street, passed so many times in the past in a hurry, and purchased some paints and some brushes, some canvas, an easel and palette.

I was right to be nervous; I hadn't the slightest idea of how to begin. The first half-dozen canvasses were wasted on abortive attempts at *natures mortes* of piles of books (all of the covers blended into each other) or tea sets (I could not get the detailed finishing right; they turned out like white and blue lumps). I first inched towards something resembling success when, perhaps out of pity, Catherine agreed to accept a portrait of herself as my humble recompense for having treated her so curtly over the previous week. She came back early that afternoon, after finishing her chores about college, carrying tea trays and washing the linens, and sat beside the window in my simple wooden desk chair. At my insistence, she cupped a crisp green apple with a single-leafed twig in her lap (I believed, correctly, that its color might harmonize well with her hair).

Once she had laughed off her nerves, she really was a splendid model. She sat very still; she knew naturally to turn only her neck and stare into the middle distance. Her smile, with lips just so parted, was subtle and slight but inviting and warm. Her skin, besides the slight blush about her high cheeks which never quite faded, surprised me again and again that there could be so many shades of pure white. Though the result was not Reynolds, I was thoroughly pleased to have produced anything which was recognizably something. Whether she was equally impressed, as she claimed, and felt that the art should belong to the artist or, conversely, at an absolute loss of what to do with the thing but too polite to speak frankly, Catherine only agreed to keep the painting for herself after several minutes of earnest insistence.

In either case, I was gaining in confidence now, and decided to spend the last day blending my craft with my undying urge to remain out of doors. I collected my materials into a sack of rough cloth and carried them across Magdalen Bridge, down Saint Clement's, and up the steady slope of Headington Hill into South Park. From here, high up and east of the center of town, was the perfect view of the city. I began to depict it modestly, with short bursts of spires here and there, then set at filling the skyline with trees and roofs and coloring in the stones.

I worked slowly, at leisure, from morning to noon to starry night. As the sun began to decline in the far west in front of me, and the shades of cloudless, pure blue became heated underneath into orange and pink, I sensed I had found the subject for which I was waiting. Of course, I would never quite capture that sky, those colors, but I did not care fully to do so. To believe I really could, and earnestly strive to, would have been somehow disrespectful. It was beyond my abilities, and perhaps those of any painter, to squeeze the grandeur of the scene before me onto a small square of oil paints. Instead, I felt I was conversing with a friend, picking up little witticisms and turns of phrase and jotting them down in a notebook. Or I was a child, speaking to his grandfather of vigorous old age, who laughed to answer his grandson's questions of the war and of women and of his long-faded days in the sun.

4

By the time I arrived at the Randolph the following afternoon, I was in supremely high spirits and had begun to look forward to the event. I had passed the imposing, five-storied hotel countless times and read several articles about the scandal caused by the architectural plans which gave birth to its compromise façade of "simplified Gothic" (if such a thing exists). But despite my piqued interest, I had never had a reason to enter within. Now at last, I passed underneath its long awning of wrought iron and plate glass which reached all the way to the curb, flanked there by a matching pair of streetlamps, then under a stone archway. An attendant in top hat and tails opened the door for me with "Good day, sir," and informed a young man standing behind the reception desk that I would be joining the Barberry party in the dining room.

I had been to several fashionable eateries about London and therefore came to the Randolph not quite fearing but prepared to accept some intensely awful interior design if the circumstances required. However, I am pleased to report that the dining room of the hotel was, if not stunning or gorgeous, certainly tasteful. It could so easily have been gaudy. Many of the clientele would not have noticed, and most of those who did would have praised it. Indeed, I am certain there must have been as much fighting, if not much more, amongst investors about the interior as there had been amongst the press about the exterior; many of the former group must have maintained that the hotel would never be a success if it did not follow the style of the times and gild the lily with a few more layers.

And yet, as is so rare in our world, the good had won out. That is not to say the room was plain; indeed, it was proud. But it had the simple, innocent pride of a young bride whose shining diamond ring represents the purity of her love, rather than the puffed-up, cruel, menacing pride of a steel baron who twirls a silver-topped cane about his fingers while blowing cigar smoke in the face of a waitress.

The furniture had a purpose-built tact. A theme of red began on the upholstery of high-backed, armless chairs which sat in threes and fours about rounded tables covered in white cloths, developed in curtains about great, shining windows that opened on Magdalen, and resolved into a thin padding of carpet which covered the entire floor. On the walls, in ornate giltwood frames, were a dozen or so large portraits of local nobility and university benefactors (most of which were several centuries old, though others much more recent), as well as a like number of smaller landscape and pastoral scenes. Below the crown molding, on a field of white, marched in file the various arms of the colleges which constitute the University.

Culturally, the place was neither town nor gown: both the teachers and students had no interest in it, while the locals could not afford it. It seemed populated entirely by fashionable ladies in elaborate hats stopping for a bit of luncheon before continuing on to their walking holidays in the Cotswolds and grave, concerned parents down from London to ask their son if he was finally prepared to behave like an adult.

Somewhere in between, by a back window, were Arthur and Emma Barberry. Arthur stood up as I approached the table.

"James," he sounded relieved as he gave me a shake, "a long overdue pleasure."

"Far too long, Arthur," I met.

"I hear you've met my wife," he gestured to where she sat with an overturned hand.

"Mr. Dalthey," she offered her hand as well. She welcomed me with kindness but nothing more, like a mother receiving her son's school-boy chum who had come over in a nervous huff to retrieve a Latin textbook he hoped he had forgotten in her drawing room.

"A pleasure, madam."

"Won't you have a seat, James?" Arthur asked, nodding to the chair in front of me.

"Of course." I pulled it out slightly and sat down.

"I hope you don't mind we've got started already," he alluded to two glasses of Waterford crystal on the table filled, presumably, from the bottle of champagne which rested in a bucket of ice beside him.

"Of course not, though I will insist on joining you immediately."

"Of course," Arthur smiled and hailed down a waiter to help me to a glass. As he poured out my wine, Arthur began ordering food.

"Do you care for oysters, James?"

"Very much!"

"Emma?"

"No, thank you."

"A dozen oysters, then, my good man," he turned to the waiter.

"Very good, sir. Anything else?"

"That will be all for now, but I shall keep you apprised."

"Very good, sir," he bowed slightly over his right arm, angled so stiffly in front of his belly I wondered if it weren't in a cast, then brought our orders to the kitchen.

Arthur raised his freshly filled glass to me. We clinked cheers and sipped.

"To new beginnings, James," he winked.

"To new beginnings," my heart agreed fully.

"Yes, perhaps it's the heat getting to my head or perhaps I am growing sentimental as I careen over into middle age, but I really do feel just splendid."

"I'm delighted to hear that."

"I feel as if I'm entering my, my," a sip found the phrase, "do you understand the term *floruit?*"

"Yes."

"Yes, a scholar! Of course!" He cheated towards Emma to provide a footnote. "You see, dear, in the past, they didn't have records or archives or birth certificates," he snapped back to me, "a bit like the Irish," then back to Emma, "so when we do history we don't always know, say, the exact year a man was born or died or what have you. But we can come up with a general range or a year in and about which a man was working or writing or conquering India. And we call this general range a *floruit*, which is a Latin term that means 'he flourished.' " He looked to me for confirmation. I nodded and he continued. "Well, I feel as if I'm entering my *floruit*. My ideas, my ideals, my aspirations, are finally starting to come into their own."

"That is excellent news!" I had caught his excitement.

"Yes." The waiter returned and placed a silver tray of oysters over chiseled bits of ice in the center of the table. Arthur took the one nearest to him, doused it with a bit of mignonette, shoveled it into his mouth with his tiny fork, and gulped it down. I followed his lead. "We had a demonstration the other week," he resumed, "in Bloomsbury Square."

"Yes, I believe I saw it mentioned in the paper."

"Then don't expect to have heard the truth." He pointed his fork and stared hard at me, ostensibly kidding but seeming perhaps genuinely angry. "You ought to have been there yourself."

"Who's to say that I wasn't? Though if Scotland Yard ask, I couldn't even find the place on a map."

He ignored my attempt at a joke. "And I've been writing constantly," as if I'd said nothing.

"Then I envy you. I've barely been able to put pen to paper for the past several weeks."

"Political things."

"That's right; I heard you've met a man."

Arthur leaned back and snorted. "A man, yes. But the term is an insult to him."

"What is he then?"

"An artist, a poet, a playwright. The only man besides myself who has understood the true, social meaning of Wotan. I call him my 'Perfect Wagnerite.' " Arthur downed his full glass and indicated he should need refilling. "*In fine*, what he is is a genius."

"High praise," I winked and took another oyster. "How has he earned it?"

"Because," Arthur churned the champagne and searched about the corners of the ceiling, "because he understands that his talent is not just a gift but a responsibility."

"You'll have to explain."

"He writes, but he never just writes. Whenever he sits down to compose, he does so first having reminded himself that God or the gods or dame Fate or what have you has entrusted him with the sacred duty of..." he swirled his hand, "of guiding the minds of the people."

"I see. And whither has he guided them so far?"

"So far?" Arthur laughed, only to himself. "So far he is a titan trapped under the thumb of a dwarf." Another oyster, another swig. "You'll look back on this conversation and wish you had found him yourself."

"I don't doubt you." My glass was refilled before I saw I had finished it. "I should be honored to meet him."

"Then come back to London!" he blurted, before leaning in very close and adopting a serious tone. "You know, James. A man of your mind, of your wit, of your ability. I'm sure it, your work here, means very much to you, but," he relaxed now, "aren't you, well, sort of embarrassed not to be doing something more important? We live in a critical age, and we're lacking in generals much more than in foot soldiers.

Are you really going to stay in Oxford forever, reading the *Eddas* and meeting Thomas for dinner?"

"I've been wondering that myself for some time."

"Well, I can tell you one thing. You won't be enjoying this life for much longer. Change is in the air. And our train will quit its station be it with or without you." He smiled as his mind switched tracks. "Do you know what it is about him really?"

"Tell me."

"He...you see, James, many people, even in our movement, have a tendency to romanticize the poor. They read all this Dickens and think every beggar is a plucky little Oliver Twist. But he has no illusions. He sees the poor as they truly are."

"And what are they?"

He finished his glass with an exhalation of relish. "Wretches."

"I see we're identifying spades today."

"I know it may seem cruel, James, but it's simply the fact of the matter. If we really want to help the poor, and we do, we have to be very frank about them. Pretending that the only thing they lack is a handful of shillings will not get anything done whatsoever. All we will have succeeded in doing is shackling them into a new, bizarre sort of slavery by providing them with the means to be fully enthralled by their vices which, for now, are kept in some sort of check by their poverty."

"I think there's some truth to that."

"No," he slammed his glass. "Man must be rebuilt, made new, from top to bottom."

The waiter returned with a fresh bottle of champagne to refill our glasses and remove the dish of empty shells. Would we be needing anything else?

"I'm not terribly hungry. Are you?" Arthur pointed at me.

"No."

"No, well then. Maybe some *pâté*, some *foie gras*. Have you got that?" he asked at the waiter.

"Yes, sir."

"Brilliant. We'll have that, then, with bread and some crackers and such."

"Very good, sir."

As he retreated, Arthur turned back to me. "Forgetting, for now, what you'll do with your life, have you made any plans for the coming afternoon?"

"Well, I had planned to look at some pictures," I said casually.

"Where?"

"Why, at the Ashmolean."

Arthur lost himself briefly in smirking. "Don't tell me you intended to come with us."

"As a matter of fact I had!"

Arthur continued laughing, but more softly now. "I should warn you that this is by no means an intellectual affair. It's one of the little trifles they throw out trying so earnestly as they may to seem relevant."

"I'm aware."

"But are you aware of the state of modern painting?" A plate with heaps of *pâté* and sliced, toasted bread was placed before us.

"Very much so." The liver was sweet. "And I've been consistently impressed by the exhibitions at the Ashmolean. They brought together some pieces of Turner's, which I had read about but never seen, back in Michaelmas, and found myself deeply moved by what I saw."

"Turner." Arthur looked away and laughed again as if someone had just told him that Theocritus was the greatest of all Greek lyricists. "This man..." he looked to Emma searchingly.

"Sargent," she informed him.

"What?"

"Sargent," she repeated, slightly louder.

"Sergeant? Oh, God." He put his hand to his forehead. "Don't tell me it's going to be all *Deaths of Nelson* and *Charges of the Light Brigade*."

"No, Arthur," she said patiently, "that is not his title but his surname. He is John Singer Sargent."

"Well, Sargent. James, you should know this. Emma caught her little obsession two or three years ago." He rolled his eyes at her. "She saw him at the academy when he was presenting in Paris. He caused such a stir that he was run out of town on a rail, but she insists he's a genius."

"You leave me no choice but to judge for myself," I concluded. With that, the *pâté* was finished and the bill cleared up.

"You will follow us to the Ashmolean, then?" Arthur asked as we stood up.

"If you'll have me."

And so, we made the brief walk across the street to the museum. A docent showed us up the stairs to the first of a series of rooms in which Sargent's paintings hung displayed. They were mostly portraits. I laughed to see how their backgrounds were slapped on in broad strokes of color, feeling slightly as if I were being made fun of.

Before the fourth painting, I stopped. I suppose it was a portrait as well, depicting a woman in white. She held an umbrella whose color matched her dress while looking down to make sure her feet were headed in the right direction. Most of the canvas was taken up by the river alongside which she walked. First, I lost myself in the details of her face. Then, I was drawn in by the closeness of color through which the artist had succeeded so silently in depicting the grasses about the water's edge and the flowing mirror image which reflected them, with no clear distinction between truth and its representation. I was dealing with a master. I felt I had been silly, like Aristotle's tutor, whose student demonstrates his superiority as casually as he does chores about the house.

Upon entering this first room, I had walked on my own to the right of the gallery as Emma and Arthur went to the left. Now, behind me, I heard them talking.

"Really now, Emma."

"What could possibly be the matter?"

"You know how I hate all this superficiality."

"And how is this superficial?"

"Look, if I had wanted to gawk at old women with more money than taste, I would have stayed in London and answered mother's calls." He grumbled and scoffed. "That Eagle and Child is right down the road isn't it? I should be writing anyway." I heard his footsteps behind me while I feigned enraptured interest in the ruffles of a sleeve. "James, I won't be joining you for the rest," he smiled. "I trust you can look after my wife."

I smiled back through the mix of terror and elation gushing out from heart to my every extremity. "I can't promise to succeed but can promise to try."

Without a word, he threw back his head, laughed again, and exited the gallery. I neither approached nor avoided Emma. She followed the arc of her orbit about the paintings, as I did in turn. This quiet manner saw us through not only the first but the second room of the exhibition. In the third, we came conjunct before a portrait of a young boy, perhaps eleven, with crossed arms in a sailor's suit.

"He's quite pleased with himself," she said. This was the first full sentence she had spoken to me that day. "I imagine you were very similar at that age."

"No," I corrected her, "I'm afraid I should never have been able to sit still long enough to have something like that painted."

"Are you sure of that? You seem perfectly stupefied most of the time."

Before I could manage a response, she turned and walked to the next painting. It was a lawn, with trees rushing out of the top flank. A woman sat only just to the right of center, faced away from the audience. The color of her hat was that of the farther set of trees; the color of her dress was that of the nearer set of trees. She could be understood as human only by the slight hint of a left hand and the slender skin of a neck, though these colors too were echoes of a patch of dried grass on their left and a square building on the right.

"And this is you," I told her.

"Oh? I'm a bit embarrassed you think I'd wear a hat like that."

"No, Emma, not the hat. Because she harmonizes so effortlessly with her surroundings."

"I'm pleased you think I make such excellent furniture, James."

"You know that's not what I meant."

"And you know I know that you know. Do try not to take things so seriously, James."

Next was a close landscape. Other than a minor corner of clouded evening sky in the top right-hand corner, it was entirely occupied by willows and grasses and a pond full of lily pads.

"I love how easily the leaves become shade and then waters," I opened. "If I stood at the back of the room, it would all seem a disordered clump. But here, being close, the infinite details are perfectly clear."

"Yes, it's quite good, isn't it?"

"It's a masterwork."

"I'll take your word for it."

"Are you artistic at all?"

"Me? No. I'm quite practically minded." She turned away and began walking to the next picture.

"But you play so beautifully."

"What's that?"

"The piano."

She turned back to me. It was the first time our eyes had met all day. Her lips were trembling.

"Yes, well," she coughed slightly and turned back again, "if you really want to know and are not merely making small talk out of respect for my husband, I'll tell you I used to be a singer."

"Used to be?"

"Yes. I very nearly wound up in the conservatory."

"What stopped you?"

"Newer dreams."

"And what did you sing?"

"I was a soprano, doing all the old pieces. Mostly Schubert."

"I didn't know Schubert wrote up so high."

"Not always. But when he does you remember it."

"I shall tell you one thing I remember."

"And what's that?"

"Only that I have some old dreams of my own."

"Of what kind?"

"It may surprise you to hear, but I nearly became a painter myself."

"I see; that's why you feel so entitled to these long-winded opinions."

"I speak only what comes to my heart."

"Then let's speak less and listen."

She paused now in front of a painting as I came to join her. It was dark and light. The darkness was tall grass, foliage, crops of red carnations, a stockinged leg, which occupied most of the canvas. The light came from golden-white lilies, lavender roses, carnations now yellow, the white skin and long-sleeved gowns of two young girls, and the warm, pink-orange hue of paper lanterns (each one a sunset). The girls were in the process of lighting two lanterns more which they held in their hands. Their short-cropped hair was almost tomboyish, but, in conjunction with the look of placid absorption on their faces, its effect was entirely angelic.

Emma and I stood in silence for a while, gazing at it intently.

"It's beautiful," she whispered.

"Yes."

"There's something...pure is not the word, as that would make it sound sterile. But it's so quietly bursting with life. Something so joyful, that takes joy as a matter of course.

Something so tender, something calm, something..." she trailed off.

"Something of the springtime," I suggested.

"Yes."

We continued looking at it for a while, then, moved by twin impulses, turned towards each other. Her lips were parted and shaking. Her eyes had a look almost of disbelief. I imagine mine looked similar. Our hands found their partner. As our fingers folded into each other, waves of electricity ran up my arm and about my entire body. Emma looked down slightly and withdrew her hand to cover her mouth as she began laughing quietly.

"James," she spoke. "I've wanted so badly to write to you, but hadn't the faintest idea of what to say. I made draft after draft in my head, the most daft things..."

"I'm glad to see that you've still got your sense of humor, James," I heard from my left. I turned to see Arthur standing with a wide grin. "They're closing up the gallery, so I figured I'd come collect the lady. There's a carriage outside to take us back to the station."

"Thank you, Arthur," Emma bowed slightly.

"And James," Arthur continued to me, "thank you for joining us. And for keeping an eye on her."

"My pleasure."

WE PROCEEDED outside, where I saw them into their carriage. It had just passed five o'clock. I knew I would be unable to work; I needed to be beneath open sky. As the sun showed no intention of setting, I set off rambling without a destination, down Cornmarket, over Folly Bridge, and onto the towpath along the south bank of the Isis.

Everything was alive. Every bird was singing. Every bee was buzzing. Every flower was dancing. The wind sang in the leaves of the trees. Swans glided silently over the mirror surface of the river. The geese and the playful ducks were woodwinds and brass. The gravel crunched rhythmically beneath my feet like gypsy castanets.

The world had drawn back her curtain and shown me the hidden harmony in everything. She was a flirt, a coquette, she was lifting up her skirt about her ankles. She was looking at me over her shoulder, hoping I would follow her into the meadow.

I walked slowly, with relish, without course. Somewhat past the short bridge over Bulstake Stream, near the sunken plains of Hinksey, just as I felt my pace would never break till I had gone straight off the earth, I picked up the plaintive sound of mewing from behind my back. I turned about and saw a cat standing on the path and looking up at me expectantly. He was no longer a kitten but neither was he fully grown; I judged him to be about six months old. With white about his belly, feet, and nose, the rest of him was light orange, almost blonde. His back and sides, meanwhile, were covered with spots and stripes of slightly darker hair, to the effect that I had to wonder if his great-grandfather had been a leopard. Up and down his tail were short rings of the two shades, his eyes were yellow, and he was (by his anatomy) a boy.

I felt guilty that I had no food to give him. The least I could do, I supposed, was to scratch him behind the ears when he approached and began rubbing himself on my legs. I turned to continue walking, but after several yards, he ran up from behind me and stood before my face. I pet him some more, then resumed walking once again. This little game of kiss-chase repeated itself two or three times, all the way to Osney Lock.

He was too friendly to be feral, but had no collar or tag. He was clearly awfully fond of me, and seemed determined to follow, if not to the ends of the planet, at least to my rooms back at college. Not quite ready for a roommate, but nevertheless feeling obliged by his helplessness, I picked him up, crossed the lock onto Osney Island proper, and brought him into the Punter pub to ask if he belonged to anyone in the area.

The publican, a healthy, ruddy-faced man, was perfectly happy to let him in with me. In fact, he seemed taken with the furball, asked to pet him, and brought a dish of cream to my table along with my pint of cider. Though he had not seen our new friend before, he offered to ask anyone who came in.

I ordered a plate of sausages and cut them into little bits, feeding them to the cat in my lap from the end of a fork. He was extremely hungry; if he did have an owner he certainly had not been spoiled. A fellow from Lincoln, a seamstress, the vicar of St. Thomas the Martyr all came to admire his coat and stroke him along his back, but none was his master. I got a second plate of sausages (this one for myself) and began warming to the idea of taking him home.

As I was finishing my last bit of onion and gravy, I was approached by a young girl, perhaps seven years of age. She had blonde hair cut into bangs over her forehead and wore a woolen dress of white, brown, black, and red tartan with a line of buttons down the front and frills of lace about the neck, the arms, and the bottom of the skirt.

"Excuse me, sir," she stuttered out, "is this your cat?"

"I'm still not quite sure."

A laugh broke her nerves. "How can you not be sure?"

"Well, he started following me along the towpath just an hour or two ago, but before declaring myself his owner, I consider it right to make sure he does not already have one already."

"May I pet him all the same, sir?"

"Of course."

She began doing so. "Does he have a name, sir?"

"Not one I've given him."

He purred softly as she ran her hand about his belly and face.

"Chester," she declared.

"What's that?"

"I think his name is Chester. Doesn't it just suit him?"

"Yes, I think it does."

"How lovely to have him. We don't get cats around the pub often."

"Oh, are you a regular? I didn't take you for much of a drinker."

"Don't be silly, sir. My father is the owner. We live upstairs."

"I find that far easier to believe."

"Sir," she looked up at me, her eyes wet with hopeful expectation, "may I ask you a favor?"

"Of course."

"Well, seeing as Chester is from around this area, and you want to ask people if they own him, perhaps he could stay with us here at the pub and we would show him to customers."

"If that's alright with your father."

She turned to the man where he stood listening from behind the bar. "Can we, father?"

"Oh, so your mother and I can take care of him too?" he shot playfully.

"No!" She held up folded hands and started jumping from excitement. "I promise I'll do everything! I'll feed him and walk him and whatever he needs me to, please!"

"Well, it is about time you started doing something around here..."

"Please, father!"

"Well, since the nice man says it's alright..."

She ran around the bar and hugged his legs tightly. "Thank you ever so much, father."

"Now thank the young gentleman, Bella."

She returned to me and Chester and gave grace profusely. "And of course you can visit whenever you like."

"I shall make a habit of it," I assured her.

It had gotten dark. Though I had a strange sense I should not be able to sleep, I decided it was time to begin heading home. I stayed for one final pint, then put on my coat, entrusted Chester to Bella, and bid everyone goodnight.

The new moon had been three days earlier. Now, as I walked along the river on the path back to mainland, it had returned as a slight crescent in the far corner of the sky. The stars twinkled brightly. I traced all the old constellations, and fancied I could make out more. These ones were Emma's eyes, this was a lock of her hair.

I mounted the Botley Road and turned towards the center of town. As I passed under the railroad bridge and by the station, I thought about how Emma had been there just a few short hours before. The place was charged, blessed by her presence. I continued going east onto Park End Street, over Wareham Stream, over the Isis.

Past Tidmarsh Lane, I began walking up the slight incline which leads by the city's old west gate. The ancient Castle Mound towered there to my right. I paused for a moment, thinking of Matilda in snow-white robes being lowered out of the window of a structure now lost to time and the Parliamentarians, and wondered why I had never climbed to the peak. For a former castle, it was not very well guarded: nothing more than a low wall and thin railing around its base could keep out inquisitive feet. I looked around two or three times, decided the coast was sufficiently clear, and hopped up onto the wall and over the fence.

From the top, I could see everything. I stood before the pair of colossal oak trees slightly off center on the southern slope and scanned the horizon. All of the dreaming spires were in view. Far in the distance lay the flat expanse of Port Meadow. Behind me was St. George's Tower, all that remains of the ancient castle, and, beyond that, the long road flowing to Abingdon.

I turned around slowly in place several times, taking in the entire panorama. Then, I gave rein to my urges, tore off my shoes, and began running wide circles around the top of the mound, giggling to myself like a madman, feeling the kiss of the grass and the dirt on my feet. I stopped, panting, before one of the oak trees, stretched my arms up, jumped, and pulled myself into its branches. I sat there forever, inhaling the earth of the bark, the air of the leaves, the fire of all of the season around me. At this height I believed I could see straight to Blenheim; my heart stared right at the empyrean.

I leapt down from the branch with a bit of a tumble, then lay flat on my back at the mound's very top and gazed up in perfect silence at the stars. No engine of heaven was hidden from me. The movement of the planets, the ebb and flow of the tides, the turning wheel of the year, birth, life, death, and birth again all were perfectly plain to me. I had discovered the key, the common, driving force leading everything on and on and on.

But already, my body was calling me back down to the earth. The lids of my eyes became heavy, heavier than I could keep up. I was half-inclined to sleep right under the banner of heaven. However, I knew someone would be there in the morning to have me arrested as a madman or at least as a trespasser. I arose, said goodbye to the view, to the trees, to the stars, to the feeling that the entire world had opened its arms to me, and walked back down the hill.

Part IV

IN WHICH WE SEE THE SKY

1

We see the true face when it's lit up in joy. Gudbrand was ecstatic. There was more in the man than I ever had guessed. When I came to see him at the end of noughth week and told him I would be accepting the position, he nearly fell out of his chair. Instead, he stood up, walked towards me, pulled me by both arms off the couch, and hugged me tightly. I believe I heard him cry. I also believe he may very well have continued holding me for the rest of his life if I had not informed him that I really must go meet a friend and begged his permission to leave.

He insisted I at least finish my tea, released his grip, and walked towards the window. He was beaming, not with mere self-satisfaction, but with the pride of a father, whose only son I now realized I was. His mouth was pulled taut in a smile; as its right corner twitched I could see the neat, narrow top row of his teeth. He turned again to face me and spoke.

"I am pleased in the extreme, James."

"I can see that, sir," I let the tea steep as I seeped in the smell of old leather.

"Of course, I suppose it is written all over my face." He walked to his desk and leaned back against it, placing his palms down on its top. He seemed so uncharacteristically relaxed that I felt almost uneasy myself. "But do you understand why?"

"Certainly, sir. I know how much you value your legacy."

He looked down and laughed slightly. "Yes, my legacy." His gaze met mine a moment, then returned to the floor. "But it is more than that, James. I am happy for *you.*"

I was not quite sure what to make of this remark. I traced the scarred arm of the sofa I sat on. "I appreciate that, sir."

Gudbrand continued speaking as he walked back to his chair and sat down. "You see, James, I never could bear to watch talent wasted. And, not to suggest that you have a reputation, but," his smile became for a moment a smirk, "I have worried at times that there was something...superfluous about you." His face regained the blank, intimidating look I had come to know it by. "Beyond what is common to youth. And so I am happy, James, truly, to see you have made this decision. That you have come to understand the importance of our profession, of our calling. Of keeping this culture alive, for it would die without us. That you are learning to treat yourself with enough respect to be part of something so precious." There was a warm flicker of smile again. "You have earned that."

I was touched. It had never occurred to me that Gudbrand had taken any sort of interest in my life besides what was strictly professional. Nor was I insulted by his implication of a certain flightiness in my character, as I knew perfectly well that his remark was not only meant in good faith but most assuredly justified. However, my mind turned back to the moment some few days earlier when, in a moment of manic clarity, I had felt absolutely sure of my choice and requested to see Gudbrand as soon as possible. At that time, I was still soaring on the whirlwind of elation whipped up by Emma's fingertips. I entertained no doubts; nothing could be more important and obvious and matter-of-course than the yet-inchoate future my continued presence in England would guarantee between us.

Now, for the first time, I realized I was being duplicitous. This decision, which Gudbrand took with its deserved gravity, had been made more or less out of fancy. But this concern ebbed as suddenly as it had emerged. Emma's face rose again in my mind to eclipse everything else. Her eyes brooked no reason, they were the argument itself. Yes: whatever my motives may be, they had been in earnest. Gudbrand would understand if he could.

He must have sensed that I would not find words to respond, as he did me the favor of continuing. "You have finished your tea?"

I had, without noticing. "Yes, sir."

"Well," he stood up, smiling again, and extended his hand for a shake, "I won't keep you too long on a day such as this."

I walked forward and accepted. "Thank you, sir." He saw me to the door, then I proceeded down the stairs out into fresh air and the full glare of sun.

Dominic was back from Lindisfarne, and had invited me for a walk about the University Parks. He framed our meeting with an intention to receive and discuss the book on the history of the Oxford Movement he had lent at the end of Hilary term. With everything that had happened since, it had never occurred to me to finish it. Instead, life itself had inducted me into its hidden theology, one that was vital, intuitive, speaking through pictures and senses, not cobbled together through syllogy. But, by the same token, it was intensely private, almost incommunicable. A part of me craved Dominic's blessing on these fresh, green ideas, and yet, whenever I attempted to make them concrete or articulate, I felt I was somehow profaning the mysteries.

As I mulled these thoughts over, I stopped for a moment at the post office across from Christ Church to dispatch a letter for Jonathan, now in Zurich, informing him he could let my secret slip, then continued up Cornmarket and right onto Broad Street. I caught Dominic waiting for me outside of the King's Arms, gazing at the nine leaden Muses atop the Clarendon Building. He seemed slightly embarrassed that I called out to greet him before he saw me approaching.

"Excuse me my absence of mind," he said, dusting himself as we walked towards Wadham. "Though I've lived in this city for nearly a decade, I don't believe I'd ever quite noticed those statues before."

"That's quite fine," I assured him. "It's the time of the season. It puts the whole world in new light."

"Yes," he was past his embarrassment. "Though I love a pub lunch, that's why I preferred that we go to the Parks. They've really come into their own this past week."

"I can smell it." The blossoms had been on the breeze for some time. "And, oh..." I slid him the book from my pocket.

"Ah, thank you, James," he smiled down at the cover as if at his child. "I did feel sort of lost without it. I have an attachment to the thing I fear may border on unhealthy, porting it about like Napoleon with his *Ossian*."

"At the very least you've been spared the embarrassment of falling for forgery."

"Yes," he took it in stride, "this is most certainly the genuine article. Tell me, James, didn't it simply transport you?"

"It..." I paused, wondering how I could frame my true thoughts, and whether I ought to at all. "To tell you the truth, I didn't quite finish it."

"Oh?" He masked slight offense. "Why not?"

"I...I suppose I can only stand so much secondary theorizing before I...Well, I find the fresh water flows straight from the spring."

"I see," he accepted. "Yes, it is funny how often we get so bogged down in theology that we forget about Scripture. As I mentioned I have worried about that tendency in myself. In fact, that's largely what inspired me to organize this pilgrimage."

I hummed in general understanding. "And did it succeed?" I was anxious to keep the subject floating. We were sailing too closely too soon.

Before he had time to answer, a scream from the distance sent chills down my spine. We darted our eyes across South Parks Road, where a heaving crowd pulsed before the Museum. Coal-sooted men hurled curses and pickets at policemen who met them with nightsticks. Dominic and I stood there gawking, rapt as the chaos spilled into the street. Against my better judgment, a part of me gave itself there to the tide, waiting for it to roll over me, when an officer shouted and pushed us aside.

I was running now solely on instinct. We abandoned our course and sprinted due east down the Road. We hunched over, our hands on our knees, to catch our breath by the lodge at Parks' southern entrance. Exhaustion had stolen the shock; we laughed at each other like schoolboys escaped from the scene of a prank.

"Oh, goodness," Dominic took off his glasses and wiped sweat from his eyes. "Please do tell Arthur to keep that in London."

"You say that like you think that he'd listen."

Dominic cracked his back and sighed deeply. "Well, it's not up to him. There's an outstanding treaty: Time has agreed to leave Oxford alone."

We entered the Parks, past the hedges and hyssop, and into the shade of the firs. I hadn't been there since the day months before when I'd stumbled about in a fogged haze of grief. My vision was now more than clear but too lucid. The ghosts were all gone, and instead there were sprites. The wind in the branches had ceased to sing dirges, but now belted glory to God. My body was weightless; I needed some grounding before I fell into the sky. I would focus on Dominic: I believe I had asked of his trip to the North?

"Oh, it was just splendid," he smiled at a feather.

"You know," I ran through the dates and rail lines in my head, "I believe we must have passed each other while I was headed back south and you were headed north."

"Oh? Yes, we did, didn't we?"

"Did you find that odd?"

"What, that they go both ways?"

"No, I mean taking a pilgrimage via train. It isn't exactly like walking to Canterbury, is it?"

"Yes, I suppose it is a bit odd. But in a way, it's also reassuring."

"How's that?"

"To see that, despite how much industry has changed, or seems to have changed us, nature still *priketh* our *corages* in the same old fashioned way." He winked and stopped me to point at a robin at play in the hyacinth. "And Chaucer's party went on horseback, you know."

"Of course. I suppose I was so hung up with care for poor John the Carpenter that all other details flew right on past me. But it does show your point. Even the horse was new-fangled once."

"Yes, I suppose men must have looked rather puzzling whenever they decided to start leaping up onto the things. In fact, I've heard a theory that this is the origin of the myth of the centaurs."

"So one tribe living on hither side of the mountain, say, had tamed the wild horses before the others..."

"Yes."

"Then those living on yon side saw them riding about and, having no bloody idea what could possibly be going on, assumed that those two separate beings were in fact one hideous, hybrid mistake of nature."

"Precisely."

"An interesting idea, and rather intuitive. Though I can't say that hearing it makes me feel as if I have lost much by not participating in what apparently passes for an academic approach to the Classics."

"All I can say is: one man's mode of transport is another man's monster."

"Interesting."

"Enough for a walk in the park."

"No, well, of course, what you said is interesting, but it put me in mind of something else."

"And what's that?"

"The word you used, 'monster.' Do you know where it comes from?"

"I haven't the foggiest."

"From *monere* in Latin, 'to warn,' or 'foretell,' like 'admonish.'"

"I can see how the sounds work. Something like 'monstrance.' But I can't say I follow the sense."

"The idea, in the Roman mind, was that the gods send a *monstrum,* a 'monster,' to show humans..." I soaked in the smell of the rose, "to pull back the curtain, if you will, and give us a sign of what is going on in the invisible."

"I see. That's quite an interesting concept. So a 'monster,' some hulking beast with six tails or seven heads, something completely out of the ordinary, completely unnatural, is born unto us as a warning, a demonstration–there's that same root!–of divine displeasure, to shock us out of the daily routine and realize we have to shape up our act, and so on."

"Yes, but that's only one side of the coin. It can mean something positive as well. Just as, well, when we say 'that fellow in the smart hat has taste,' it's implied we mean 'good taste,' even though one may also have 'bad' taste. And if we say 'that haggard old fellow over there in the corner smells,' we mean 'smells bad,' though one can also 'smell good.' In a similar sort of a way, this more general term of 'monster,' that could originally mean either a good or a bad omen, became bogged down in one implication rather than the other."

"I see, and shudder to consider what it means about man's relationship with God that this darker connotation became the default." Dominic smirked, pleased with a sudden insight. "But to think of the lighter, in a sense, Christ too was a monster, embodying the Way itself, teaching it to us all through his own life."

"I suppose you could say that."

"I do think I'm serious here. What we're talking about seems an ancient idea."

"Of course, that's how I described it."

"Forgive me, but I mean not only in the pagan mind, but in the Christian as well, and the Jewish long before it."

"How so?"

"Well, there are countless examples of nature, the seasons, the proper cycles, going completely haywire as a result of God's anger in the Bible. The plagues sent by Moses, the flooding around Noah, and even smaller things like the sun going dark after the death of Christ, are all variations on this theme in one sense or another."

"Yes."

"And of course, there's the 'good' side that you alluded to as well, though we would tend to call those miracles. The parting of the Red Sea, the sun standing still over Gibeon, the changing of water into wine, all show God's ability to suspend the laws of nature to help those in whom His favor rests."

"I see what you mean."

"Now, of course, this isn't quite the same sort of story as a Minotaur or a Pegasus being born, but it does continue the same theme, the same idea, of the ordinary course of nature being interrupted by God." We had reached now the pond, hemmed in its odd oval by many-shaped stones. The coots and the moorhens paddled about the surface of the water, jabbing at flies and at moist bits of moss. "I know from brief mentions in our previous conversations that you are somewhat inclined in this direction, James, but I must tell you that I have always found this one of the primary issues with pantheistic viewpoints."

"Oh?" I drew myself out of the world to the words. "What's that now?"

"Well, if we talk about God and the world as identical, then God becomes beholden to the laws of nature. In a sense, God is less free than we are. We can do whatever we please, good or bad, sin or sanctity, but God must bring the spring and the rain and the winter thereafter. Do you see what I mean?"

"I believe so."

"So in this way, well, God becomes little more than a sentimental label, and miracles become impossible. God can no longer 'do' anything, such as, say," he picked up a stone and dropped it back on the ground, "this stone did not complete any conscious action. It did not make a choice. It simply followed the laws of universal gravitation. In the same way, we're turning God into an absolute object, rather than the subject that He should be."

"I never thought of it that way. And while I should like to say that's not quite what I believe, I can't think of why you're wrong at the moment."

"At the moment, no matter," his mind chanced on something it fancied. "To return to the centaurs, though."

"What about them?"

"Thinking about how those monsters were actually men, it occurs to me that monsters are actually men in the Bible often as well."

"Have you got a pet theory on the Leviathan?"

"No, nothing like that. But God has an interesting sort of relationship with Israel throughout the Old Testament, where whenever they've done something wrong or worshiped other gods or generally departed from His ways, the Lord sends a foreign people to rule over them. And so we have first various native Canaanite tribes, then the Philistines, then the Assyrians and Babylonians, eventually Antiochus and the Romans. But in the way that the narrative of the Bible is structured, these groups are not really human in the way that David or Solomon is. They're really just, to use this term again, forces of nature that God has at his disposal to manifest his anger against the truly conscious protagonists of history."

"That is fascinating, really. I remember, as a much younger man, laughing in scorn with some of my school friends at the description in Exodus of God hardening Pharaoh's heart. We thought that this was just a ridiculous sort of paradox meant to baffle the fools who could let themselves believe it. Of course, we thought we were totally above the whole thing: 'How can God punish Pharaoh for being stubborn when He's the one hardening his heart in the first place?' and so on. But now that I think of it, and hear what you have to say, I realize that this tendency goes much deeper than what we picked up at the time."

"You can tell it's not quite the first time I've thought about it, as well."

"I had guessed."

"Of course, I don't take the Bible quite literally as history, and am comfortable to see it as more of a metaphor."

"A metaphor for what, then?"

"Well." We made way for a family of geese. "Are you really interested in this, James?"

"I am."

"Well, the way I see it, James, is that life is a constant struggle to raise one's own level of consciousness. Our natural tendency, our 'fallenness,' is precisely to fall: to be passive, to follow our urges and impulses. In that state, what some might call a 'natural' state, we are, in a sense, forces of nature just like the tides or the seasons or earthquakes or plagues. Because, just like earthquakes and plagues, we are not really in control of our own actions. We are simply being led by the nose of an infinite, invisible chain of cause and effect. And so the project," he made circles in the air while he stood still to weave his next phrase, "the purpose, the 'Way' of being God's people is, in the same sense, to become 'unnatural,' to rise above base urges, to craft one's own life and decisions. It is only by doing so that one achieves 'individual' consciousness, that one becomes a genuine 'self' and identity, rather than just a bundle of chemicals and electric signals bouncing around a brain."

"That's a compelling way to put it."

"Thank you, I find it so myself. Furthermore, by the same token, the oppression suffered at the hands of the pagans who come and rule over Israel when they reject God's way symbolizes the hell we put ourselves into by giving ourselves over to our passions."

"Interesting." I snuck a smile to myself, remembering the heights passion had borne me to recently. "I can't say I agree with you, but I can say that that is the most fascinating interpretation I've heard so far."

"Thank you, James, I'll take that for the time being." A couple passed under a parasol. "Now, this is also a very interesting difference between the early and latter days of the faith."

"How so?"

"Only that, of course, the early Christians were persecuted by the Romans, but understood this hatred towards them as a sort of honor. They were proud of the opportunity to be martyred for their faith. They embraced it all as part of the tribulations. But afterwards, once the religion was not only permitted but mandated in the Empire, and Apocalypse indefinitely deferred, that view no longer made sense. And so, when the pagans did return, the Goths or the Vandals or Attila the Hun, the Christians of that later time saw them much more like the Israelites had: as a scourge from heaven punishing their own iniquities. Their response, meanwhile, was to get their house in order, as it were, rather than throwing themselves to the lions."

"I see what you mean."

"And that same sort of viewpoint reemerges time and again under similar circumstances. The native Celts of Britain, to cite an example of which you may be aware, parsed the Angles and the Saxons in that sense. And the Angles and Saxons themselves later saw the Vikings that way."

"Yes, I've read my Wulfstan."

"Again, not that I mean to offend you. I know how fond you are of the fellows."

"No offense taken." I touched his arm gently. "I'm not as fond of them as some men seem to think they are."

"Of course," he was well reassured. "All this is a very long way of saying: the trip was splendid."

"Splendid."

"You see, James, it's no secret that I fear the Faith is under attack from a new, more subtle type of barbarian in our own age. And the changes I see, not just in the bodies but in the hearts and minds of men, often plague me with burning concern for the future of our society. But standing there, not just at any holy site but at Lindisfarne in particular, and thinking of how the monastery survived the end of the empire, and the onslaught of the Saxons, then the pillaging of the Vikings, it made me reflect on how the Truth truly is eternal."

"Yes," I said wryly, "it survived all that. But it only took Henry to make it a ruin."

"Yes, a ruin," he lifted a fist in defiance. "But he had the good sense to keep making the mead!" I raised mine in turn and gave cheers to the thought.

"I must say, though, Dominic," I resumed over footsteps, "I find that what you're saying here resonates with much of what I have been contemplating myself recently." I was not yet sure what I intended to say; the sentences were coming from somewhere within me. I knew only the need to set out on fresh waters.

"Interesting. Tell me how."

"Well, you are talking about how to 'live in the way of God' is to be truly conscious. This makes sense to me. Christ calls himself the Way, the Truth, and the Life. And what you're suggesting is, that to be genuinely 'alive' is to be aware of the 'truth' of one's freedom to choose one's actions, rather than simply being the object of impulses. And that cultivating our awareness of this truth through righteous action is the 'way' of the Lord."

"Yes!" he burst out. "A tidy way of rendering it."

"I feel I've been stumbling in the direction of such a view, though perhaps less articulately. And, in conjunction with some other statements from the Bible, I believe I may even be carrying it farther."

"Oh? What other statements?"

"For one such example, the fourth chapter of that first letter of John."

"The disciple Jesus loved."

"Precisely. Then you see what I'm getting at."

"Not quite yet, but continue."

"Well, it is in this chapter that the evangelist speaks at the greatest length about love. Of course, it is also in his Gospel, towards the end of the Last Supper, that Christ gives His 'new' commandment that we love one another as He has loved us. But John develops the thought further here; he states that God *is* love, that everyone who loveth is of God and knoweth God, and so on."

"Lofty sentiments."

"Now my question," we had reached the North Lodge; I paused at the threshold back onto the street, feeling as if I were poised on a cliff, "is to what extent this divine love the evangelist speaks of and the ordinary, human, romantic love we experience are to be differentiated."

Dominic snorted.

"Is it so ridiculous to ask?"

"No, not ridiculous, but I don't even know where to begin answering something like that. The two are so completely different. If anything, I'm inclined to state simply that they must be separated completely."

"Now, that's unfair."

"Of course, I'm being somewhat flippant. But go on, I want to hear your thoughts."

"They're only that, perhaps love, romantic love, is of that good species of monster we mentioned before."

"What do you mean?"

"That perhaps love of that sort is sent to us by God to inspire us, to shove our faces in the beauty of the world, to make it so obvious and clear and evident to us that everything is right and just and ordered by the hand of a benevolent creator."

Dominic shook his head laughing. "It's pretty to think so, James. And I see where you're coming from. But I believe your main error, forgetting all the cardinal ones, is that 'love' in the divine sense, that of God for us and of us for God and of us for each other in God, is not just a feeling. It's much more than a rapture of frantic ecstasy. It's something very quiet. It's deliberate. It's routine, really. Whereas the romance you're talking about, if it even exists, is something very much out of the ordinary. No." The riot outside the Museum had left not a trace. "What I would like to make clear to you is that the love you allude to is but another passion. It's something that we are an object of, as much as of hunger or thirst. As much as lust, though its robes may be nobler. While divine love, properly understood, is about becoming a subject and choosing sacrifice."

I scoffed. "Imagine putting all this effort into becoming a self only to throw yourself away."

"Come now, James."

"Yes, now I'm being flippant. But the idea deserves more than dismissal out of hand, as I'm hardly the first to have had it. Why, throughout the entire age of chivalry, in all the tales of courtly love, it is the beauty and promise of young maidens at home that inspire great knights not only to fight for Christ on the field, but battle against the temptations of Satan within their own hearts."

"I'll grant that, if romantic love can inspire that sort of behavior, perhaps it is the good species of monster. Unfortunately, outside of fairy stories, its results are often more monstrous in the vulgar sense."

"Are they, then? I can cite examples from history if you prefer." I found I was suddenly brimming with choler.

"Please do."

"Well, what inspired your Good King Henry, Supreme Head of your Church, to assert that the scepter of apostolic succession sat by right in his lap other than that fair face of his Lady Greensleeves?"

Dominic was silent. I believe I may have genuinely hurt him.

"What?" I continued, clenching, unclenching a fist. "Unless you believe he was mistaken?"

Dominic adjusted his glasses and tried to keep smiling. "The Lord works in mysterious ways, James. And we all have our thoughts on that Bluff King Hal."

"I won't press it."

"I appreciate that. And, to speak of mistakes," he shrugged, "I do believe this increasingly *blasé* attitude of our society towards divorce, which Henry may have presaged in a way, is something it will live to regret if it should live at all. Do recall, as you alluded to earlier, that this was the beast that brought Lindisfarne low."

We were now outside the King's Arms. We could not quite harmonize this last sour note to a friendly farewell.

"Oh, James?" Dominic tapped me just as I had turned to leave. "You're not musical are you?"

"Only as much as anyone. Why?"

"I've heard great things about the soprano they're bringing into the Sheldonian at the end of third week." He pointed over his shoulder to the theater beside us. "Apparently she hasn't left Bayreuth in a decade and a half, but has decided on a lark to do some touring a bit deeper into *Abendland*."

"I didn't take you to be taken in by that sort of thing."

"Oh not at all. At best I find it silly and at worst a great embarrassment to everyone involved. But her voice, I hear, is transcendent. Would you care for a cigarette?" He extended an open silver case to me, from which I accepted. "Anyway, she won't be singing Wagner."

"What instead, then?" I took a match and lit my cigarette.

"Schubert." Fire. "I suppose that she needed a break."

"Schubert?" Everything flowed back to Emma. I paused for a moment and focused intensely on the cigarette. "I shall have to attend. Thank you for mentioning it."

"Of course. Oh, and James?"

"Yes?"

"I hope you know I leave here thoroughly unoffended and with nothing but respect for your intelligence and integrity." He blew smoke through his nose. "Despite our differences." I realized he had grown a short beard over break which suited him so well that it had so far gone unnoticed.

"I hope you know the same."

"Come see me soon," he put his hand on my arm.

"I shall."

I watched him disappear back down Parks Road towards Keble, then proceeded towards Brasenose across Radcliffe Square.

I had not written to Emma since seeing her off at the Ashmolean, nor received any word from her either. All the same, I was unconcerned. I felt as if I were watching the clockwork gears of the universe from an immense height, and could see everything falling into place in accordance with its immaculate design. I had known that the proper occasion would present itself when ripe, and now, here it was. And so, I sat down at my desk and wrote a short note letting her know, à propos of our conversation the previous week, that a soprano in Oxford would be performing a set of Schubert's *Lieder*. Would she be pleased to join?

2

At least I had something to keep myself busy: the translation of *Kormák* was hitting its stride. I found myself easily absorbed. I scoffed along with the hero when Steingerd's blowhard of a husband beat him in a duel through the absurd technicality of a sliced thumb. I felt almost giddy watching this same braggart get his comeuppance when, shortly after, he is wounded in the groin and left by his wife. And yet, as the story took a detour to narrate the remaining life of this Bersi fellow, I found he was oddly sympathetic. Instead of wallowing in or dying of self-pity, he has a genuine change of heart and becomes a sort of local champion on behalf of the downtrodden. He avenges old farmers, rescues kidnapped maidens, and much more from a sense of duty rather than for personal glory. I recognized in him a sort of selfless nobility, a resoluteness of character lacking in Kormák himself, who, once again inexplicably, now failed to claim his beloved despite finally having the chance.

I was so carried away I had nearly forgotten that the dons expected my speech on the *Brunanburh*-Boroughbridge connection within a fortnight. Some brief days in advance, I drew out the few points that I wanted to evince with as much prolixity as I could muster; Gudbrand, thankfully, was pleased to arrange everything technical. The lecture would happen the Thursday of second week in a dark corner of Queen's College at eight o'clock in the evening. Gudbrand met me at the porter's lodge on the night of the event, once again beaming with pride, and guided me up to the room. When we entered the space, tight with white walls under a low ceiling of warped wooden arms, it was empty but for three rows of chairs and a lectern at the far end. I loitered about this distant part for some fifteen minutes while unfamiliar faces filtered in and took their places, then blended back into the smell of fresh paint. Now and again, Gudbrand would bring one of these over and introduce me contentedly as his successor.

I began speaking as soon as the bells of the hour had faded. Though I must have carried on for three quarters of an hour, I cannot recreate much more than a sentence of what I said. My few, vague conjectures on the subject have been outlined already. I was, for my own part, by no means impressed by them. All the same, I was able to draw from that well of enthusiasm now flowing within me and get carried away with a variety of grand conjectures, not nearly all of which were directly related to the topic at hand. Perhaps this mood was infectious, as I found the final words of the talk greeted with as much of a thunder as could be managed by the applause of some twenty-two men. Perhaps they were simply excited at last to be able to approach the tables stuffed with glasses of red wine at the back of the room. Whatever the case, I proceeded myself in that direction.

I was congratulated by Gudbrand, reassured by most others, questioned, but not deeply, by some students. I believed I had done well enough and felt not embarrassed at a shoddy performance but, indeed, slightly dirty for one falsely good. I longed for a friend I could trust to be plain with me, but Thomas was, I know not how, still on holiday, while Dominic had been already engaged. As I gazed over at one man, alone by the side, I wished that his face could have been more familiar. He nibbled at cheese and sipped from a glass, gray haired and thick bearded, round-bellied but not fat, like a Father Christmas who had only just accepted the position but not fully grown into it. Though removed, he seemed to be not aloof but perfectly self-contained; I felt he was honest.

"James," Gudbrand grabbed me just as I was busily refilling a glass, "I believe you know this here man at a distance."

"Oh?" I turned back. "And who is he?" I was pleased and slightly nervous to see Gudbrand had brought this reserved fellow to meet me.

"William," the newcomer informed me while shaking my hand. "William Collingwood."

"Collingwood," I said, smiling at a private joke. "You know, I owe you a telegram."

"And why's that?"

"I was meant to see *you* give a lecture some two months ago at the Lakes."

William laughed at the thought. "If it helps you feel better, yours was by no means the only empty seat."

"Then poverty is blessed in company."

"What?"

"I mean that I should be delighted to hear your thoughts now that I have the opportunity."

"And I should like to give them, but..."

An attendant now entered letting us know that we were expected to clear the room.

"But," Collingwood peppered his words with chuckling, "I think we've overstayed our welcome."

"Then we shall continue the conversation elsewhere. Gudbrand, will you join?"

"No," he was suddenly once more the stern Icelander. "I fear I will need to sleep. But you shall enjoy yourselves."

"Inevitably."

"Inevitably," Collingwood followed with a wink.

I traced his heels, at a word, out the door, along the Quad, beyond the gate, and free onto High Street, then over Magdalen Bridge and into the Half Moon Pub right on the far side. With a pint each of stout, we sat down at the nearest squat table.

"To threading the needle," William said, raising his pint with an eye up to heaven.

"Between what and what, exactly?"

"Between, well," he nodded aside, "I won't insult your intelligence by saying I believe you believe what you said this evening."

"Was it so obvious?"

"Not quite. And that's what we drink to."

My early impression was right. "I won't insult you either," I said as our glasses met, "but I will ask what in God's name you're doing here tonight."

"I've always been fond of this pub."

"I don't doubt you; but in Oxford in general."

"I came south for some business in London, then capitalized on the excuse to stop here, and wandered into your lecture having seen an advertisement for it outside Queen's."

"But why Oxford at all? For some books in the Bodleian?"

"No," he laughed merry, "for nothing so hardy. Just for the air. You know how it feels to be here in this city."

"We all have a feeling about it or other, but what is that feeling for you?"

"For me? Well," he drank deeply, sat back, and thought, "I took the train from Paddington, then walked a long way into town. I stopped by the Martyrs' Memorial. Do you know much about it? On Magdalene Street?"

I thought of that lonely stone spire, dark-hued, with statues and emblems and dense, detailed fixtures. "Only that it seems to have been there forever."

"And that's it exactly." He wagged a stout finger. "It's only some forty years old."

"I would never have guessed."

"That's precisely my point. It stands there eternal."

"As the city does generally?"

"No; well, not all of it. Affects always come and go, but the substance remains to be built on whenever."

"You know," I savored his thought in the beer, "that is why I had wanted to come to your lecture."

"Oh? Why's that?"

"I am fascinated by this idea too: of returning to the substance."

William laughed, but not at me. "I hear that very often."

"I'm sure, and I don't mean to get us bogged down in clichés, but..." I could not complete the thought satisfactorily.

"But you know the clichés and you know something more than them. Say something of Oxford that hasn't been said."

His lips curled. "You ask me to paint a new color."

"Or an old one in a strange relief." I waited, but saw he had no further answer. "If I remember correctly, though, you did not live here long."

"That's correct."

"So it's not personal recollections you came back for, really just some stones?"

"Stones?" he couldn't believe me. "No, look." He took a big gulp and resolved on the truth. "If you really want to know. I'm skirting about the issue because so many make so much of it, in ways that mean nothing to me. Even John, though I love him to bits. Even Morris, though he's more brilliant than his ego could ever imagine. All that to say, frankly, that this city is the birthplace of the art I cherish so dearly, and still houses so much of it. In particular, and to get to the point, the murals in the Union library."

"It's funny you should mention. Of course I was never a master, but in my younger years I had entertained the idea of becoming a painter and dabbled somewhat in the arts. I've taken it up again recently, just as a hobby, and spent a full day at the Union recreating the murals in ink some few weeks ago."

"One day?" he nearly spilled his drink. "Each one is a lifetime! Forgive me, but I can't imagine you gave them your all."

"Well," I paused as the feeling crept in, "I did feel for some reason that Rossetti's Lancelot was completely beyond me. I revered it like a mystery, scurried on to the next, and left it alone."

"Yes, the Grail eludes us all the first time," he knew it quite well. "But that just means you shall have to try again, when you have learned how to ask of it properly."

"I shall, if I can. And though you shouldn't answer, I do have to ask something of you."

"And what is that?"

"Well, you say Ruskin and Morris make too much of their art, and perhaps they do, but you follow them all the same. Don't you find that a bit odd?"

"I did maybe at first," he shrugged, "but I've found it's irrelevant. You would be wrong to assume the artist understands his art. Try asking a horse where it's going, it would have no bloody idea. It knows how to run and to follow the reins. What makes it good is its readiness to follow the commands of a power it cannot comprehend."

"Very true."

"Besides, I'm not sure how much John really cares about this socialism hubbledybub anyway. It's, well, pathetic isn't the right word at all, but," he finished his pint and gave a long "ah," "but it's a great shame that he cannot let himself simply love something. A painting cannot just be a painting. It has to be good for a reason, and often one that has little to do with enjoyment. They're all like that, really. So much pretense. I mean, 'Pre-Raphaelites'? What a ridiculous name for a movement. And imagine writing so many essays so seriously claiming Sir Gawain has got something to do with Karl Marx or what have you. It's almost embarrassing."

"And yet?"

"And yet," he lilted the words, "and yet they get away with it. For it truly is beautiful art. If the creators should like to spend their weekends or bank holidays writing up little footnotes to accompany a piece we shan't stop them. But I ramble. All that to say: you really must have one more go at the Grail."

"I shall."

"Well," he stood up. "I should like to have another pint, but my wife would like her husband in bed before sunrise. One is one but two never stay two."

"Of course," I stood up as well.

"James, yes?" He extended his hand for a shake.

"Yes." I accepted the gesture.

"Well, James, you seem a good sort. Are you staying in England a while?"

"For the indefinite future."

"Right, Gudbrand mentioned. Well." He picked his coat from his stool, slung it around himself, and removed a pipe from its left pocket. "I've got some men who are interested in Norse culture, as you are. We're looking to put together a society, start publishing translations and journals, maybe a textbook. Let me get you involved."

"I'd be honored to have anything to do with it."

I followed him outside, where he lit his pipe and hailed a cab. As I waved him goodnight, a light rain set in. I turned up the collar of my coat, then went right, without haste, meandering, in the vague direction of home.

3

Arthur did not like the idea of Emma traveling alone. Not, he assured me, from the old superstitions: he trusted her perfectly well. He did not, however, trust the sort of men he knew hung about train stations or outside hotels hoping to take advantage of lost and disorientated women. Furthermore, he had, for some time, been letting his mother's letters go unopened and feigning illness (mild enough that she might stay but serious enough that she would not feel comfortable) whenever she called on him for the better part of a year. That's not to say he harbored any guilt towards her for his negligence. But to fail to do something so simple that would please her so immensely would mean he were absolutely abominable. And of course, he couldn't come to Oxford himself: he would be far too busy and, if he were not, would have to invent obligations due to his severe lack of interest in the subject.

Thus, and in so many words, Arthur prefaced his response to the note I'd sent Emma and informed me that both his wife and his mother would be delighted to meet me on Saturday, May the twelfth, for afternoon tea and an evening of Schubert. He would put them up for the evening in the hotel on High Street, right across from Brasenose, and I would meet them at the Loose Leaf Tea House on Turl Street at half past two. He finished by begging my patience in dealing with Lady Barberry (as she insisted on being called), and swore solemnly to make it up to me on an undecided date in an undefined manner.

This was not the response I had hoped for, nor any of those I had expected. But it was not the one I had feared. At the very least, Arthur himself would not be present. He had not so much as crossed my mind since I saw him last at the Ashmolean, but when I now imagined seeing him in the flesh I realized I should not be able to treat him as both a true friend and as an afterthought to my intentions with Emma at one and the same time. These emotions could be sorted in the due course of time, but for now, in this fragile, infant stage, I must not let things get thrown off track by fear or apprehension. All that to say: I was prepared graciously to accept his offer.

I spent the week after receiving this message much as I had spent the previous two since sending my own. The boiling urge to dance had settled to a simmer. I no longer found myself jumping into trees or befriending wild animals or barely containing myself from embracing every stranger I passed on the street. In an odd sort of a sense, I was extremely relaxed. All my actions came naturally; nothing perplexed me.

And yet, I cannot say that I felt quite regular. For one thing, though I felt perfectly rested, I barely slept. That is not to say I was rolling about the bed all night in nervous agitation. No: I lay on my back quite silently with my hands folded upon my chest. I thought of Emma, of her eyes almost wet, lost in mine at the gallery, of the way her hair, golden, fell about her ivory shoulders like sunlight on a winter morning, or of something so clever she had put just so perfectly. I allowed myself to fantasize: she had come down from London to watch the Summer Eights. We stroll along the south bank of the Isis while the oars crash on our left and the boats rush past us towards the finish line. She wears white lace gloves and holds a white lace parasol in her right hand. In our respective lefts are glasses of Pimm's mixed with lemonade and mint leaves and bits of sliced fruit. She makes a joke about one of the rowers. I, in mock-outraged jealousy, quicken my pace and leave her behind a bend in the path. She stands still in disbelief, then sees me emerge from around the corner bearing her a bowl of fresh strawberries and cream. What sleep I did have, meanwhile, was full of odd visions, lives of a parallel past, in places totally foreign and yet somewhere intimately familiar.

Nor, for that matter, was I eating much. When I did, it was not from hunger but from a vague, half-remembered sense at the back of my mind that the routine was necessary. Without this foggy recollection of the generally accepted rules of life on Earth, I would have been perfectly content to float through my days without ever touching food. Or perhaps I would become like the mad sages of lost ancient China, and have no sustenance but the wild honey drops of dew.

Everything was perfect. Everything was clear. Everything was warm and colorful and fresh and intriguing. A walk in the park was grand. A chat with a friend was brilliant. Tutorials with students were an absolute blessing. I walked in beauty. I walked on air.

As I walked that Saturday, May the twelfth, down Turl Street, it occurred to me for the first time that the Loose Leaf Tea House was exactly the sort of place I would not have expected Lady Barberry to choose to spend her afternoon. I had passed it countless times, and could see through its broad open windows that it was perfectly lovely, with plain white walls and ceiling and exposed beams of thinly lacquered wood. Numerous friends, meanwhile, had regaled me with tales of its impossibly impeccable strawberry jam. But Arthur had given me the impression that his mother was the type to feel naked in anything cheaper than silk. All the same, here she waited, nestled between antique shops and stationery stores, in a most unassuming location.

As soon as I entered, I saw Emma seated in the far right corner with her face towards the door. We locked eyes before I had time to remove my hat. She smiled, and I began walking in the direction of a large crop of feathers sticking from a wide-brimmed, powder-blue hat upon the head of who must have been Lady Barberry. She turned around towards me when I was some few steps away.

"Mr. Dalthey." She smiled gently and offered me her gloved hand. I was immediately struck by the impression that she looked how I imagined Emma herself would look in middle age. Her hair was blonde as well, though slightly faded now, and curled into ringlets where Emma's was mostly straight. Her eyes were lighter, closer to properly blue, but they had the same easy look of quiet wisdom. A very few, thin lines flowed away from them, like the first drops of rain on a sand dune, and likewise from the corners of her mouth. I found myself thinking that she must have had Arthur quite young.

"A pleasure, Lady Barberry," I bowed slightly.

"Please, call me Alice. And please have a seat."

"Thank you, Alice," I said somewhat nervously before turning to Emma. She offered me her hand as well. I wondered if my heart could be seen bursting out of my chest as I held it. "Emma."

"James."

I took my seat. Before me on the table was a triple-tiered stand of porcelain plates. Each was ornamented in gold leaf with blooming azaleas pink in the center. Upon them were small sandwiches, cakes, biscuits, scones. Next to the stand was a matching teapot, from which Alice poured me a small cup.

"So you're the poor Percival they sent up to Corbenic," she began.

I laughed. "Well, I did go up there, but I wouldn't call myself poorer for the experience." I accepted her offer of cream. "I was made to feel perfectly welcome, and I know how busy Arthur has been."

"Yes, his writing." Alice took a scone from the stand and cut it in half upon a small plate in front of her. "Of course I do love him just dearly, but he does carry on as if he were the *Weltgeist* in short pants."

Emma nearly spat out her tea.

"Excuse me," Alice continued in my direction, "but Emma and I were just talking about how Hegel has absolutely ruined men." She looked intensely at her scone while slathering it in strawberry jam. "They were bad enough when they just wanted to be Caesar. Now they consider it an intellectual duty to be God as well!" She took a heaping spoonful of clotted cream and laid it on top of the jam, then locked eyes with me once again. "Yourself excluded, of course, Mr. Dalthey."

"I've never been so honored to be told I'm not a man."

"Well, now, and that is my point. You've clearly got a sense of humor. These young men, though, and I suppose it's been going on for a while, but..." she took a small bite, "it just gets worse and worse!"

"Perhaps it skips a generation, madam. I can't say any of the problems I've had with my students is that they're too serious."

"Yes, perhaps. The late Lord Barberry was, after all..." How could she put it? "Well, we shall say that he was a good dancer."

"And from what I have the pleasure of remembering," Emma chimed in, "always in excellent spirits."

"Yes, bless you, dear," with a hand on her arm. "He was so fond of you, too. But, James," she turned back to me. "You mentioned your students, and here I realize I've been going on for minutes on end about my nonsense without even taking the time to ask you anything about yourself, your life, what you do." She sipped and restarted before I could speak. "You can see why Arthur leaves all the letters I send him unopened on the drawing room table every time I come to visit."

Emma and I locked eyes again and again, speaking worlds through silence. "Perhaps, ma'am," I suggested, my hand on my heart, "he has resealed them for especial safekeeping."

"Gosh," Alice looked sideways, "you truly are lucky to be just handsome enough to pass off such rank flattery as charming. But come then, do let's have a word about you. I take it you're American."

"Is my accent so pronounced?"

"Oh, no, don't worry about that dear. You've almost nearly cured it. But look what you've done to your scone." She pointed her knife in the direction of my plate where, perfectly absent of mind, I had cut a scone in half and covered the inner faces in clotted cream and jam. "You've gone and put the cream on before the jam."

"Excuse me, madam, but, at the risk of offending your most reverent culture, I put the cream on first because it receives the jam on top of itself much more readily than the jam receives the cream."

"That's precisely my point:" she began pouring herself a second cup of tea, "you're a very practical people."

"If I am practical, it must only be manifest in the way I dress my pastries. It is certainly not a quality I have been known to demonstrate in any other facet of my life."

"Somehow I doubt that."

"Alas, it's true," Emma said with a sigh. "James is an incurable romantic."

"A priest, then?" Alice asked.

"A professor," I answered.

"Yes, right, your students," she sighed now too. "And you were just starting to restore my faith in your sex. At least tell me you're in something perfectly useless."

"Old English, ma'am," I offered her with hope.

"That, well," she wiped her fingers on her napkin. "That can go any sort of way, I suppose. How did your father take the news?"

"He, well," I gazed at my face in my spoon, "fortunately, madam, he did not live to have to live through the shock."

"Gosh." She looked down and furrowed her brow. Her tone changed immediately. "I'm truly sorry, James."

"It's really no matter," I assured her.

"No, no. You see, the truth is, I'm quite nervous with new people, and I suppose I use humor as a sort of defense."

"A common quirk," Emma told her.

"Common, yes, but a vice, not a quirk. I really feel awful, James, to have brought that old cloud back to rain on you."

"Please don't." I begged softly. "It was long, long ago."

"Well," Alice picked up the thread of the frayed conversation, "and which college are you associated with, James?"

"It is an odd situation. I am living in Brasenose, for now. And I'll have offices over at Christ Church next year. You see, I've recently accepted an offer to be chair of Scandinavian Studies."

Emma's cup clanged its dish. "You've accepted?"

She gazed at me searching. To look in her eyes was to look in a mirror. Our lips curved in smiles in tandem. I felt our hearts beating as one.

"Yes," I looked away and back at Alice. "Just recently."

"Very interesting," she was piqued if not puzzled. "I suppose they'll have you doing plenty of research, then."

"Yes," I told her. "In fact, that's what brought me up to Yorkshire in March."

"I see. And what were you looking for there?"

"The location of the battle of Brunanburh."

"I'm afraid you'll have to enlighten my ignorance a little further."

"That is, well, there is an ancient document, the *Anglo-Saxon Chronicle,* we call it. It's generally rather routine: incomplete sentences of rote prose recording deaths of earls and ascensions of bishops and so forth. The sort of thing that would only be interesting to an antiquarian. But, for some reason, in the entry for the year 937, it breaks into poetry for some seventy five lines. I won't call it masterful verse, but the shock of the rupture enshrouds it in mystery: why do we have this bright burst of beauty, a lone, lofty mountain rising from a sea of the mundane?"

"Remarkable. Poetry comes upon all of us suddenly, I suppose, but to see it in such sharp relief, I can see why it captured your interest."

"It has captured the interest of many."

"And what does this have to do with Yorkshire?"

"Well, the poem describes a fierce battle, a turning point in the struggle between English civilization and the barbarism represented by the Vikings. But despite this apparently grave historical import, no one has any idea where it took place. Indeed, many claim it did not take place at all. I humbly suggested the town of Boroughbridge, near Corbenic, as the location, and went up on a scouting mission to see if it fit the description."

"Is that so? Very clever. Did you find what you were looking for?"

"I can't say I found the battle, but I do believe I found the cause of the poetry." I met Emma's glance for the blink of an eye.

"Hmm..." Alice seemed very intent on her tea. "And that is what you write about?"

"At the moment I don't write much at all."

"That's a shame. You know, you have a beautiful way of speaking, James. I imagine you would make a good novelist. You've really never tried that sort of thing?"

"No, though..." I paused as the thought of a weird dream-vision, stolen upon me recently during one of my fleeting moments of sleep some few nights before, came suddenly back into mind. I was unsure of whether to speak it. "It's true I've been mulling over a story of late."

"Something you'd like to write?" Emma asked, eager.

"Something that's toyed with me."

"Well," Alice interceded, "I can say for myself that I should love to hear your idea, if you don't mind sharing."

"If you'll suffer me."

"Please."

"Well," I dove in headfirst, "I picture some place in indefinite past. Perhaps Britain, before the Romans, somewhere far out in the wilderness. There's a small cabin, almost a hut, built up out of the ground, with stone walls and sod and grass growing out of the roof. A young boy lives there. One day, his father comes from his own father's funeral, and without a word places a curious, large metal disk over the hearth. Over the years it is darkened with ash and soot, and becomes even more obscure than it had been in the first place. The boy grows up, leaves his home, and wanders for many years. One day, his father dies in turn, and the boy returns home for the burial. Afterwards, he is back in his childhood home, clearing things up, consoling his weeping mother, and he takes down that old metal disk from the mantel.

"He brushes off a section of it with his sleeve. He sees an engraved picture. Curious, he grabs a cloth and cleans off some more, then more, and with more and more rapture, as he sees battles and weddings and births and souls passing and singing and dancing and weeping and winter, the turn of the seasons, the gods, constellations, everything under the sun and above it that ever has been and that shall be forever. And seeing all this, finally seeing it, he is overcome with joy and grief all at once. For the entire world, everything joyous and moving and beautiful, had been waiting for him, right there in front of him, and he had never even bothered to dust it off and look."

I peeked to see Emma fixed intently on me over folded hands.

"That's a lovely story, James," she said, "and it resonates with me so much, with so much of how I've been feeling these days."

"Yes," Alice blew her nose in a handkerchief, "an intriguing story. Why don't you try writing it?"

"Well, that's just the problem." I stated. "I'm afraid even to touch it. It could never become on the page what it is in my mind."

"Yes, something is always lost in translation when we whittle our thoughts and our cares and our loves down into bare words. But that makes them all the more magical when they really do make us feel something. Would you like more tea?"

"No, thank you."

"Emma?"

"No, thank you."

"I see. I suppose I shall finish this battle alone." She poured herself a large, final cup. "For what it's worth, that's why I have always preferred music. It can speak directly to the heart."

"Then you shall love our program this evening," I told her.

"I don't doubt it. I didn't just come to let my son feel he had done something nice for me, you know."

"You love Schubert well, then?"

"Oh, dreadfully. I always have. Even before I heard Emma breathing such life into him."

"Do you make any music yourself?"

"No, and for everything but lack of trying. I must have taken piano lessons for fifteen years, practicing hours a day, but never get beyond Anna Magdalena's notebook."

"At least you got farther than I did."

"Well, so far as I could. As difficult as I found it, though, I cherished every minute. I only gave it up because it became so much more convenient to listen to others."

"Yes, we are lucky to have them."

"Schubert, though, he really is something quite special. You know, I heard it said once that Mozart is a genius, while Schubert is a miracle. Does that make any sense to you?"

"Intuitively."

"I believe it's because, well, Schubert is right between Mozart and Beethoven, if you see what I mean, not by birthdate, of course."

"Go on."

"On the one hand, he is a master craftsman. A purist. He has that perfect, geometrical, ordered sense of point and harmony that Mozart and the older masters, Telemann, Bach, Boccherini have (perhaps not to the same extent, but for the sake of argument). At the same time, though, he's starting to leave these premade forms behind to play more with, well, the specifically human instead of the absolute: with emotion and sentimentality, with feelings and not just triangles and parallelograms. And it's not quite to the point of being soppy like Berlioz or showy like Liszt or completely inchoate like Brahms (about whom I simply refuse to let you get me started), but right in the middle, the momentary blossoming of spring after deep frost of winter and before the unending, oppressive, maddening heat of summer, a harmony between harmony itself and, well...not, *disharmony*, but..."

"*Harmony and Invention?*"

"Yes!" she exclaimed.

"Then it seems our Red Priest had outflanked the Romantics some hundred years *avant la lettre*."

"Oh, but it's always the same old thing. Schumann and Wagner were just having a latter-day *Querelle des bouffons.*"

"What's that?"

"You mean you weren't there yourself? And here I was starting to fear you immortal. Well, *en bref*, long before his grandson had all that nasty trouble, Louis XV found his court quite nearly in shreds over the issue of how lively an opera should be."

"I'm amazed that they fought over something so vital for once."

"For once, yes." We shared a laugh. "But have I made that all clear? It does seem an eternal dynamic, this back and forth, form here and function. Alas," she landed her cup with a flourish, "I've finished my tea. And you understand me as well as you shall."

"I do," through a smile.

"I do as well," Emma agreed. "In fact, what you're saying is so much of what made me fall in love with Schubert myself."

"Of course, Emma. I knew you would understand," Alice told her gently. "And really, dear, I know I make quite a nuisance of myself telling you this, but you should take up singing again."

"I do mean to, in fact," she looked down and blushed. "It's funny that you should mention it, as I've been practicing recently for the first time in years."

"Is that so?" I asked.

"Yes."

The world fell away from her face. We must have been staring at each other even longer than the centuries it seemed, for Alice scraped back her chair and said, "Well, would you look at the time!"

"And what time is that?" I brought back my self.

"A quarter to five. We really must be going."

"Of course."

She put some coins on the table and thanked the server as we all stood about and collected our things.

"Gosh," Alice leaned suddenly forward, her hands on the table.

"Are you alright?" Emma asked with concern.

"Yes, dear, thank you, but would you believe it? I suddenly feel..."

Emma put her hand on Alice's back and scrutinized every inch of her face.

Alice looked back at me. "I'm really showing my age here, James, but..." she took her hands from the table and straightened her back. "If you will excuse me, I'm afraid I shall have to go back to the hotel."

"No..." Emma started.

"I'm truly sorry, dear, I don't know *what's* come over me, but I feel I shall be terribly ill if I don't lie down immediately."

"Then I shall come with you," Emma said plainly.

"Yes," I agree. "And let me fetch a carriage."

"No, no, no." She waved her hand at me dismissively. "My man Geoffrey is right outside. He shall be all that I need." She waved towards the door and called, "Geoffrey!"

"Please, Alice," Emma implored her, "you can't expect me to leave you."

Alice turned and put her hand on Emma's. "I insist, dear. I want you to enjoy yourselves."

A man with a black jacket and gray tweed pants, quite bald but dark-moustached, had appeared next to Alice and taken her by the arm.

"Thank you, Geoffrey," Alice nodded, "and James," turning to me, "do send me a draft of that story."

I HAD agreed to meet Dominic with the two Ladies Barberry outside of the Sheldonian Theatre shortly before the performance was billed to begin at five o'clock. If one pictures the theater as a series of horseshoes stacked neatly on top of each other, nestled behind the Bodleian with their mouths open towards the Divinity Schools, we found Dominic waiting outside of an open door at the end of the shoes' left arm through which a large crowd was already beginning to push. He spied and greeted us as we came around the curve of the building from the fenced gate on Broad Street, where the theater is guarded by some thirteen grotesque-bearded herms in mock-Roman dress and laurel crowns.

"Hello, Emma," he said, accepting the offer of her hand, "always a pleasure."

"Thank you, Dominic, it is a pleasure to see you as well."

"And you too, James," he nodded towards me, "a pleasure perhaps less rare, but no less exquisite!"

"The feeling, as ever, is mutual."

"Now, Emma," he resumed back to her, "I had heard that your mother-in-law was to be joining us as well."

"She was, bless her, but unfortunately she found herself feeling suddenly ill at the end of tea."

Dominic gasped and put a hand to his lips. "No..."

"Yes, unfortunately," I confirmed. "Emma begged permission to accompany her to the hotel and take care of her, but Lady Barberry insisted on having no assistance whatsoever other than that of her valet Geoffrey."

"I see," he tutted.

"We come here now," Emma came in, "only under her strictest, most precise instructions that we enjoy ourselves."

"Well, you shan't struggle to do so," Dominic replied. "I haven't seen her myself, but the legend precedes that the singer is simply magnificent. It's a shame Lady Barberry shall miss her. And frankly," he shrugged, "that I shall have to miss *her!*"

"For her legend precedes her as well?" I asked playfully.

"By miles, by leagues! I've heard everything about her. And I do not mean to say that I have heard everything that there is to know about her, her height, her weight, how she dresses her scones, what have you. I mean that every possible judgment of character that could apply to any person in any direction or sense, good or bad, saintly or evil, I have heard applied to Lady Barberry on repeated occasions and from manifold trustworthy sources."

Emma and I laughed. "And they were all true!" she rejoined.

"A woman after God's own heart," Dominic winked. "Well, shall we enter?"

We walked through the door and into the heart of the horseshoes. Entering the main space of the theater, we saw that the broad, open floor of polished oak had upon it a black concert-grand piano (how they managed it in there remains a mystery). A single music stand, now bare, stood to its right. All about the room were rows of light-wooded benches in two stories, already mostly filled with audience members. Above, covering the entirety of the ceiling, was a painting of Truth, in the form of a miracle cherub, shining like Apollo in a fiery cloudburst, descending upon the arts and sciences to dispel envy and ignorance and greed.

We went up a short series of steps and squeezed into the front row of benches. From this vantage point I could see, on my left, a cream-pink organ with powder-blue pipes flanked by windows perched upon the wall of the upper level along the mouth of the horseshoes.

As is almost always the case, the performance did not begin until a quarter of an hour after its billed starting time. All while we waited, the theater beat on with chatter and echoed in anticipation. Silence fell sharp on the heels of our Master of Ceremonies as he walked out onto the bare floor. He thanked us ladies and gentlemen for attending this most special evening, and asked us please warmly to welcome our coming performers. He bowed slightly, and walked to the benches accompanied by a light rumble of applause.

First, a man in a black suit and spectacles with a long white beard about a slightly sagging face entered with an arm full of sheet music. He emptied this onto the stand of the piano, then turned and waved towards the wings. A young boy with a stool ran out and seated himself beside the piano, prepared to turn pages as this fellow played. At long last, the lady herself, draped in a mink stole, with done-up brown hair, a rectangular face, long opera gloves of white silk and a flowing scarlet gown, greeted by applause much firmer now, glided to the music stand and placed her own notes there upon it. She welcomed us to her with arms open wide, then put us to hush with her raised palms, turned to the pianist, and nodded.

He began those high-reaching, those soft-bubbled notes of the *Frühlingsglaube.* She eased herself into the tune, as light as the breezes she sung of:

Die linden Lüfte sind erwacht
Sie säuseln und weben Tag und Nacht

These lines were simple enough, but how to translate the third?

Sie schaffen an allen Enden

Of course, "they shape at all ends" is rather a literal rendering, word for word in a way. But there is no English for *schaffen*'s full sense here: "to be endowed with and employ a creative capacity"? And it must be understood that the *Enden* are both the ends of the earth and our own ends: our purposes, goals, and our deaths.

Here I was overthinking what should be enjoyed in pure silence. I leaned back, closed my eyes, and let the *frischer Duft* and *neuer Klang* roll over me. *"Nun, armes Herze, sei nicht bang,"* they whispered in my ear. Yes. I understood. *Nun muss sich Alles, Alles wenden.*

I spent most of the concert thus seated, through *An die Entfernte,* through *Iphigenia,* through countless pieces I had never heard before and may never hear again. The voice, though so high, was a deep, rolling river, not roaring, but slowly, deliberately carving its way to the sea. After what must have been approximately an hour, the singer returned to the subject of spring with *Im Frühling*. Once the piano trailed off after the third and final *Sommer lang,* the applause grew even more thunderous than what it had been at the end of the other songs. I opened my eyes, and saw the soprano bowing repeatedly towards the cheering of the crowd with her music pressed onto her breast. Realizing that this was the end, I began clapping as well.

"I see you have rejoined us on Earth," I heard Emma whisper.

As touching as I had found the final piece, and how moving its thematic reappraisal of the first *Lied,* I did feel as if something more were needed as the musicians went back into the wings. It appears I was not alone in this opinion, as the shouts of *"Brava!"* began to be mingled with others of *"Encore!"* until the entire crowd was on its feet demanding one more song.

The musicians returned and bowed again; the audience regained its quiet if not its calm. The pianist, now playing from memory, began an arpeggiated D minor (plus the second) which rolled up and down and up again incessantly. The singer, also no pages before her, began Goethe's lyrics to *Gretchen am Spinnrade*. I sat rapt on the edge of my seat as I listened to the lost, lovesick maiden pouring her heart out in fear and confusion. As she pined after Faust, I could feel she foresaw his betrayal, her death. I turned some way through, and saw Emma facing down and slightly shaking.

When this *Lied* was ended, I, Dominic, most every soul in the theater shot onto his feet and burst into applause. The thunder continued for several minutes after the musicians had once again left, now not to return. As the cheering died down and people began collecting their coats and hats and shuffling out into the early night air, I saw Emma was still sitting down and looking extremely pale. I put my hand on her shoulder.

"Are you alright?" I asked.

"Yes," she replied. "It's a beautiful song."

She gathered her spirits and personal effects and flowed with the river of people outside. Once there, Dominic asked if we should like to join him for supper. As Emma, I saw, was still not quite herself, and we'd have to eat something at some point, I agreed on our mutual behalf.

We walked through the open gateway of the Clarendon Building, across Broad Street, and ducked under the low roof of the White Horse pub, nestled between the twain sprawling arms of old Blackwell's. We found a long table towards the end of the narrow place, then ordered some ale and some lamb and some chicken. Dominic offered a toast to Saint Schubert, to which we all heartily clinked.

I was anxious to be alone with Emma, and had very little to contribute to a conversation I longed to see ended as quickly as possible. Thankfully, Dominic was prepared to do enough speaking for all of us. He was simply beside himself to have heard that University College was planning to build a memorial to Percy Shelley.

"They sent him down, you know," he informed us, slicing his chicken too slowly, "and only in his first year!" Each bit took a minute to chew. "He wrote a tract on the *Necessity of Atheism* and sent a copy to every don and cleric in the university. Can you imagine?"

"Incredible."

"And the *most* incredible thing," he said, beginning a second pint I now wished I had discouraged more forcefully, "is that they offered to give him a hearing! But of course he had nothing to say for himself and refused to answer any questions. What did he imagine would happen?"

"I can't say."

"And now, they're going to commission a marble statue of the fellow, more tragically heroic than he ever could have dreamed of himself, and put it right in the heart of the place that had such better sense about him less than a century ago! Isn't that odd?"

"In extremis."

I was pleased to see Emma recover her humor. Indeed, as Dominic assured us a third time, unprompted, that he really was not upset he just found it quite queer, I saw her laugh under her hand. At last, we returned outside. Dominic begged our forgiveness, but he really must rush back to chapel for Compline. He took a deep breath to switch into the sacred, folded his hands, then blessed us the sign of the cross before walking away.

We were almost two months past the equinox and, though it was now approaching eight o'clock, the sun had not nearly begun to set. Emma and I decided to take a long, slow walk back to her hotel down Queens Lane. Once we had turned the corner beyond slender Saint Helen's which leads to the Turf Tavern, we knew that we were quite alone. We took each other close by the arm, and went gently along the pavement laughing with endearment for Dominic.

"Of course, he's right," I said. "What *did* Shelley expect? But, by the same token, what did *Dominic* expect? I mean, can you imagine if Shelley *had* gone to his hearing? I can just picture him, standing before the Sanhedrin in his academic robes, the dean asking, 'Did you write this?' 'You say I did.' "

Emma laughed, "Gosh, now that you say that, I'm even *more* surprised he didn't bother showing up. You'd think he'd have leapt at the chance to play Christ. But we can't help our natures." We carried on walking, now quietly. "What do you make of him, anyway?" Emma restarted.

"Shelley or Dominic?"

"Shelley."

"I know little of the man, but it's excellent poetry."

"Yes."

"And yourself?"

"Well," she paused here to lift up her skirt for a puddle. "I suppose I'm sort of horrified by him in a way. I think he may be slightly evil."

"A wonder to be only slightly evil."

"Yes, but I am being quite serious, really. There's something so grand in scale with the treachery of Macbeth or of Brutus that one has to respect it against one's better judgment. While Shelley's is so petty it becomes inexcusable."

"I'm afraid I don't know what you mean."

"Well, he did drive his first wife to suicide."

A vision stole on me: the Barberry household in winter, quiet and empty. "I see."

"And it's not just the profligacy alone. A man's eye may wander, but he ought to have the decency to feel embarrassed about it. Whereas Shelley will pour out the rest of his life desperate to paint his vice as the loftiest of virtues. It would be pathetic if it didn't ruin so many lives. Even end them, in this case."

I wasn't prepared to respond.

"He's a bit like Rousseau, really," she continued. "There's something perfectly twisted, *sinister* about these men who constantly bandy on about liberty, but to whom liberty means nothing more than freedom from having to raise their families."

"You're making me think now," I finally landed on something to say, "about the old truism that philosophy begins with wonder."

"From Aristotle."

"Yes, precisely: his idea that one looks about the world in stupefied awe and begins to philosophize out to explain it."

"Not the worst theory."

"Not the worst, surely, but one I am less confident in than most."

"And why is that?"

"Because, well," I cleared my throat, "because in *my* greatest moments of awe, I find I am silent, accepting of and open to mysteries, not frantically pawing about to reduce everything to logic."

She smiled at me. "Yes, it is an odd impulse. I suppose, James, it is because an experience like that, that moment of awe, requires something of us in turn. If we are going to believe, to take these feelings seriously, that requires action and courage and sacrifice from us. We can wave it away, pretend it was nothing, get back to folding the laundry, what have you, but that's a sort of sacrilege, and wasting a chance most will never have and which we ourselves will most likely never have again. So suddenly, we little wretches must become heroes. And that's something most are not prepared to do."

"And so we choose the coward's path, and explain it all away."

"Only sometimes."

"Only sometimes. But putting Aristotle aside, I began this as I also believe there may be a different root to philosophy altogether."

"Oh?"

"Yes. You see, when I search out the origins of this little science, for lack of any method more objective, I try to take an historian's approach: to look at how and why it arose in the first place and in the most rude, material terms."

"And how and why is that?"

"So far as we are concerned, with the sophists of classical Athens."

"I see."

"We think of Socrates and Plato as the start of all this, but really, they only found themselves and their students through arguing with the sophists. And the sophists, first and foremost, were lawyers. They didn't care so much about 'truth' in itself or in absolute sense. In fact, they considered the notion as sort of absurd. Their concern was in playing with words, to make little verbal games to prove that wrong was right and good was bad and remove the burden of guilt from their clients."

"That's true."

"So, to return to your point about Shelley and Rousseau, I believe there is something for us to learn from this historical reality. For, it really is rather strange that a man should have a 'philosophy': so many odd terms and obscure intimations, stitched together with such grand leaps in logic, without hardly referring to anything concrete in the world. Why bother? What is it all for? What does it accomplish? Well, all that to say: I believe it accomplishes precisely what it was designed for those thousands of years ago, that one arrives at philosophy, as an individual and as a group of individuals over time, in response to some charge of guilt, though of an internal kind, out of the law court but deep in the heart, as a sort of nervous compulsion to allay a restless conscience."

"That's quite grim, isn't it, James?"

"I suppose."

"That isn't to say you aren't onto something. It simply isn't quite how I think about philosophy myself."

"And how do you, then?"

"Well, despite what you may have assumed from my earlier comments on liberty, I do take freedom quite seriously. In fact, I see *that* as the cardinal axiom of everything else, where you would seem to place guilt. For here one is, in the world, in a moment. And one can choose to do quite literally anything in it."

"Anything?"

"Yes, James, anything. And I think philosophy is only honest, fit for purpose, when it begins with such a frank admission of absolute freedom. From there flow all the real questions. What should one do? What does one want to do? Why does one want to do it? Why doesn't one do what one wants to? And so on."

"Well, why doesn't one do what one wants, then?"

"I have a sneaking suspicion one inevitably does what one wants."

"Then why all the hemming and hawing?"

"Fear, mostly." She stopped and turned to me briefly, attempting a smile, then we kept on walking with no sound but footsteps. "But to give you your credit, I do believe there's a neat parallel there."

"Where?"

"Well, we were discussing these contrasted possible origins of philosophy: guilt and wonder. While I still put freedom at the heart of the matter, I do think those others echo the twin impulses one can follow when making decisions and living a life."

"And what are those impulses?"

"Fear, as I mentioned, and joy. For our actions are either negative, rooted in fear, trying to avoid an undesired outcome, or positive, rooted in joy, asserting some goodness and living in it, following through on it."

"I see. And I can guess which of them you prefer."

"It's more than mere preference. If you allow, I'll get quite metaphysical."

"Please do."

"Well," she set sail, "all fear, I suppose, is ultimately fear of death. And death, in the most abstract sense, is the cessation of being. So for us, we the living, fear itself, in a way, is always inherently baseless. For either we truly die and indeed cease to be, in which case death is no experience at all, void of content, something neutral and unworthy of dread. Or, death is an illusion, we are eternal, and the suggestion that we could ever not *be* is absurd. So we are like children, startling ourselves over imaginary monsters under the bed.

"Why this matters, why I bring this up, is that these two modes of living, joy and fear, are therefore not equal or equally true. Joy is the true way, the answer, the 'why' of why one exists and the world is still here in the first place."

"I believe you've uncovered something."

"Yes. To..." Our pace slowed somewhat as she stammered and struggled to sort out her thoughts. "To get to it, to get to what I really should like to say to you tonight, James..." She looked at me, hoping to get it across without words, then tried all the same. "I suppose, as I alluded to earlier, it is only because I take freedom so seriously that I find men like Shelley abominable. What they long for is the wrong sort of freedom, a perverse sort. For example, well," she tilted her head, "you've been in England long enough, I'm sure you've heard of Oscar Wilde by now."

"Certainly. Walter Pater still makes it down to High Table every now and again, and seems to have few other names he can drop."

"Yes, well," she laughed and continued, "Mr. Wilde moves in some of our circles as well. He lent a manuscript to Arthur once, who thought it was so brilliant that he insisted I read it for my edification. An essay with a working title, something like "The Spirit and Socialism." It doesn't matter. Of course, like everything he writes, it's all a big joke. But also it's fully in earnest. In essence, his argument is that it's all such a bloody bother that one has to take care of others. One would like to be left alone to write and think and paint, but instead one has to worry about putting bread in the mouths of the poor. So wouldn't it be grand if the state would just handle all of this for us? We could finally forget about the hungering masses and do what we should really like."

"And?"

"And, well..." She stopped, put her hands to her shaking head, and laughed once in spite of herself. "Well, I think it's the most awful opinion I have ever heard! So far as I have always seen, what makes life so beautiful and charged and purposive is that we can and do care for each other. That we are beholden to one another, that our actions have weight, that these ties which bind us also have meaning beyond any trivial fancy. And so, to want to be 'free' from caring, as if caring were a burden, is a hatred of everything that is pure and good and innocent and true. It's a rejection of human existence itself." She put her hands down and glanced at me, smiling through terrified eyes. "I'm sorry, James, I'm so lost, I don't know how to say it."

I smiled back, I hoped, reassuringly. "I understand."

We were stood now outside of the church of St. Peter-in-the-East. Emma turned towards me. We stared into each other's eyes. I put my hand on her cheek, then wrapped her strongly in my arms and kissed her, first softly, then deeply and passionately. For those moments we soared above everything. There was nothing but touch, the smell of her hair, the warmth of our bodies that floated in space. And then, just as suddenly, we came back to earth. She took her face away, placed it on my shoulder, and began weeping profusely.

"I'm in love with you, James," she looked at me again. "I've never said that to anyone before. Do you know what it means?"

"I do, Emma, yes, I'm in love with you too."

"I feel like I'm alive with you, James, finally alive, like I'm a schoolgirl, like I'm walking on air. But," she shook her head, "James, I don't know what to do."

"You could..." I paused. "Are you going to stay with Arthur?"

"I, well, to be honest...Thank you." She took my offered handkerchief and blew her nose, laughing in sputters at how her hands trembled. "To be honest, I had been speaking with a lawyer before you and I ever met. But," she laughed gently now, "well, I suppose every girl wants to be Effie Gray until she's faced with the real opportunity."

"I see," but not quite. "Is it the money?"

"No, no, the money isn't an issue, but..."

"And I suppose you will need cause..."

"There is cause, James, but..." She smiled at me and placed her hand on my chest. We slipped back into a kiss. I pressed her against the stone wall of the church as the lines were cut loose and we became totally unmoored.

Bells from above, all at once, tolling ten brought us back to ourselves. The sky had already been dark, but now sank to pitch black. Emma took back her face and gazed at me, straightening her skirt, smiling bravely but still seeming frightened and lost. "Please take me to the hotel, James."

We walked out onto High Street, close but no longer touching, crossed over the road, and walked west in silence. When we reached the entrance, she turned, took my hand, and squeezed it tightly.

"I will write to you soon, James," she promised.

"I know."

She squeezed my hand once again, then disappeared behind the door.

4

I am ashamed to admit how quickly I began to fear. Even as soon as I undressed that evening, a sinking feeling had begun to weigh on my stomach and knees. The spell was broken. That is not to say I had stopped loving her, or loved her any less. But for a brief while before, I had been looking at the world through the eyes of God. In this beatific vision, the suggestion that anything could be wrong or amiss was a contradiction in terms. Now, I was man again. I was dice in the hands of chance. I was strapped to the wheel of fate. I had been torn from omniscient ignorance and handed back over to care.

I felt dirty. I felt guilty, more over the fear itself than over anything we had done; harboring any anxiety about our love seemed a sort of blasphemy. I passed a little syllogism back and forth in my mind: if it were not to be, then it was not what I'd hoped; if it were, then surely it was. But these mechanical thoughts did not make me feel any better. Indeed, a rebuke always followed at their heels. Why should I need reassuring? The fact that I was in any way conscious of the possibility our love could not be true proved that it wasn't. If one wonders "is the sun shining?" one must be in the dark; if one wonders "is it raining?" one is dry.

Or so I feared: and yet, but quietly. This was not a return to the raving madness I had suffered in mid-April to almost hysterical effect. It was silent as a cancer, and only noted in very still moments: if I had lain awake till dawn or taken the face of a stranger on the street for hers, only to see it dissipate into a cloud of reality.

Quiet, that is what I became, as one day became two became weeks. It went unnoticed by all except Catherine who, on the day she brought the second of the only two pieces of mail I received that term, asked very politely if someone had passed. I thanked her, told her no, and opened the letter up once she had left. It read:

> Dear James,
>
> Helen and I have run into Jonathan in Zurich, who (immediately but only after receiving your permission to do so) informed me of your splendid new position. I apologize for not having been able to get this bit of news from you firsthand, but we had been enjoying ourselves so thoroughly on the continent that I called in all of my favours in Oxford to have our absence extended as long as possible. As I should be returned shortly after the time you receive this, I hope you don't mind that I've taken the liberty of organizing a small get-together on

Saturday the 9th and inviting everyone I could think to.

Sincerely,
Thomas

PS - Please find included here a drawing from my son Spencer. I knew you would appreciate.

I removed a piece of thick paper from the envelope and unfolded it. The drawing, in charcoal, was of a woman with long, flowing locks of dark hair in a billowing white dress. Her arms were extended as she lifted her leg into an *arabesque*. Every finger was stretched out and curved up like feathers. Her head, slightly turned towards the viewer, faced down, while her smoky eyes fixed on a slight slope of rocks and grass and flowers below her and to her left. The title, scratched in black ink in the bottom right-hand corner, read "Vivien in the *Val Sans Retour.*"

The image taunted me. Like those unfaithful lovers, cursed to wander endless forest, I had hemmed myself in with my angst over Emma when I ought to be lost in a rapture of joy. My impatience, long smoldering, was now vexed beyond any containment. My body was a steam engine that could no longer remain passive or still. The gears must move; I needed something to pour myself into or risk bursting and taking the whole city of Oxford with me. I had no tutorials or essays or grammar exercises to focus on; my students had finished all that for the year and were busy revising for exams. All that remained was the translation of *Kormák*, which I had left unattended for well over a month.

I had chosen to translate this saga out of a fondness for the hero. When I had first read it, he seemed picaresque, his verses light but charming. Now, as I tossed aside Thomas' note and sat back down at my desk, pouring over the final few pages, I found I had soured on the man entirely. Kormák was infuriating. Here, in a moment almost absurdly gallant, he rescues Steingerd, the love of his life, from the clutches of ravenous pirates while her new husband, an ineffectual merchant she'd married only for comfort, cries on the sidelines for help. Even he is so impressed by Kormák's valiant deed that he forfeits his wife as rightfully belonging to the poet.

Though Steingerd rebuffs him, it was clear she did so hoping finally to see Kormák assert himself fully. But instead of taking that act of will, staking his claim on reality, reaching out and grasping what he claimed so intensely to desire, Kormák shrugs his shoulders and wanders off singing his woes. This was intolerable. He had everything I wanted, craved, needed now so desperately from Emma, and let it slip through his fingers simply because he preferred to romanticize misery over having his living beloved. I wanted to leap at him, grab him by the throat, knock the fool silly then some sense right back in him. Why? How? How, at this critical moment, could he be so careless and diffident?

I squeezed the pen so tightly in my hand I had to throw it down lest I break it. I hurled the book across the room before I could tear it to shreds. I let out a scream, losing a temper I had not known for decades. With my head in my hands, after several deep breaths, I collected myself long enough to make sense of the outburst. Of course, Kormák was myself. Not only with Emma, but for my entire life, I had let the world carry me wherever it wanted. Accepting Gudbrand's offer, coming to England, even entering academia in the first place, every major decision in my life had been made simply for lack of something else to do. What did I want? What truly mattered to me? Where was the passion and meaning and bother?

Of late, I supposed it was Emma, that our love had bestowed some nobility on my decision to remain in Oxford. And yet now the entire matter bared itself to me as patently absurd. What did I truly expect to happen over the next year, even under the best of circumstances? She would leave Arthur and come live with me in some little closet at Christ Church? Or in a shack somewhere at the outskirts, poor as church mice, her making me dinner and editing my papers? What would Thomas think? What would anyone think? I would be a pariah, and rightly. Through this delusional sense of some romantic grandeur, I had betrayed a friend, destroyed a family, and abandoned my home.

It was time to make a choice, to act. I could no longer be at the receiving end of life. I glanced back at the drawing that Thomas had sent and for a fleeting moment everything became clear. I saw Emma with a parasol crossing the dunes at Montauk as I stood by an easel and reflected her grace. I saw us standing together on top of a mountain, gazing out at the infinite westward expanse of America, the landscape raising its hands up in glory to God. I saw a cabin in the Berkshires and children roasting chestnuts at the fire, a treat from my sister who was finally family. I saw pride in a son who had learned from his father. I saw warmth and contentment, commitment and care. I saw hope for a future, cut loose from a decadent past.

I arose from my seat, glided in long strides to the bedroom, and began packing all of my possessions with the silent intensity of emergency surgery. But this could be done later; there were more pressing issues at hand. I took a coat and hat, went downstairs, out of college, and hailed the first cab to take me to the station. There was an office there for the Cunard Line, and one for Western Union. At the former, I laid out nearly every coin and banknote I had for the final two tickets aboard the next crossing; at the latter, I spent what little remained sending Emma notice to meet me. Though my entire body was buzzing with electricity, I was bathed in odd calm, collected and sure.

Two days would be all she would need. I would go to the little party Thomas had organized for me tomorrow, wear the mask one last time, shake hands and make jokes and pretend that it mattered. Then on Sunday, Emma and I would arise and enter a New World.

5

The summer nights are long in England. Even here, in the southern part of the country, the sun of new June would tarry in a far corner of heaven until only two hours before what should have been the middle of night. As I stepped out of Brasenose at nine in the evening, dressed in white bowtie and waistcoat, the sky was still perfectly light.

I did not have far to walk; Thomas had arranged to have the party at All Souls directly across Radcliffe Square. He must have had at least a few favors left over, as the event tonight was the only I have ever seen held for a single individual on such short notice and for so little cause on the otherwise dearly guarded and neatly manicured North Quad. A porter had been assigned for the occasion to welcome us through the high, wrought-iron gate that pours directly onto the Square. Once I had given him my name, he bowed slightly, opened the portal, and ushered me in.

In light yellow stone, some ten feet above ground, were the windows of the library; across were those of the chapel.

Dominating the scene, directly before me, were the tapering lengths of twin towers. Upon the quadrangle (actually something of an oval) were tables dressed in white linen. The one teemed with bottles of champagne; the other was covered in crystal flutes, most already full, but many still waiting. Behind both were servers distributing glasses and setting out fresh ones. As I stepped through the grass and spied out the bustling figures, excitement crept up on me steadily. Partly because I felt in on a secret, but more so because it occurred to me now how badly I wished to see Thomas. He would understand tacitly, shore up my courage, and give me his blessing. I reached the two tables, took a glass, thanked the server, then turned to see whom I might recognize.

"James!"

It was Gudbrand. He put his left hand on my arm and offered his right for a shake.

"Gudbrand, thank you so much for being here tonight."

"Of course, James, I never would miss it. I'm sure you imagine these months have been trying. It's not really something that one comes to terms with. But seeing how you have matured, and trusting that you will be bearing the torch, it's meant so much to me in my most quiet moments." I wondered who would break the news; I saw him crying in his hands. He continued before I had time for regret. "And that wonderful talk that you gave us in second week!"

"Thank you, sir." I shook myself, flushed. "Though the true joy was mine in the giving."

"It was...ingenious, really. Tell me, if you don't mind, how did you fall upon this little theory of yours about Boroughbridge?"

"If I knew the source of inspiration, I'd drink from it more often." There is always a way to be honest.

"Of course, as would we all. Let us say, then, there was something in the air when you visited."

"Something in the air."

"Good evening, James!" I heard now behind me. I turned to see Dominic sipping a flute. "Cheers!"

"To his great success!" Gudbrand offered and joined in the clinking.

"Now, James," Dominic continued as we three formed a circle, "could you possibly tell me where you've been for the past month? I don't terribly mind you not coming to see me, but it seems that no one has heard anything from you at all."

"Yes, I'm afraid I've been terribly busy."

"Busy?" he asked quizzically. "But you've not been teaching since fourth week."

"Yes, well, as I believe I've mentioned I've also been working on a translation."

"The last I heard, though," a grand inquisitor, "and this came not as a rumor but from your own mouth, you'd barely touched the thing in months."

"Yes, well, by that very token," the questions were starting to tax me, "I had to start taking my work much more seriously."

"Really?" Dominic seemed almost surprised, but then smiled. "I always saw you as smarter than to take your work seriously."

"I'm smarter than to do it for anyone else. But I suppose it was time to feel proud of myself."

"Well, you know how pride goeth, though I do agree you may have been lingering a tad on the far side of a golden mean. I'm glad to hear that."

"As am I," the storm was past. "In fact, I'd be particularly curious to hear your thoughts on the thing." I pictured myself tossing a parcel of notes and translation to the porter at Keble, with Dominic's name and a promise to send my new address as soon as I had one. "I know it's not what you would normally read, but something in this one is special. I can send you what I have so far, if you let me know your thoughts."

"I would be honored, James, thank you."

"John!" I heard a shout over my shoulder, then whispering, "That's him over there."

I looked towards the voice, and saw the Brows and the Monocle walking closely together towards me. It was the first time they had appeared either before my eyes or in my mind since that hazy night in London so many months earlier. They joined our circle.

"Hello, John!" said the Brows.

"Congratulations on the award!" followed the Monocle.

"James," I corrected.

"Yes, yes, of course," they both grumbled, then lifted their glasses to drink to my health.

A pit sank in my stomach, as the presence of these made it clear that Thomas had indeed invited everybody. It was only a matter of time.

"James!" Thomas sauntered towards me with a thousand-yard grin.

"Thomas!" A spontaneous smile smothered the fear. I extended my hand, but he brushed it aside and embraced me, then pulled away and lifted his glass.

"To yourself!"

"And how in the world have you been?"

"Just exquisite. But why do I ever leave Italy? I always regret it the moment I'm over the Alps. Though I must say I had much grander a time in Zurich than I ever expected at the hands of the Swiss."

"And how is Jonathan?"

"Brilliant: thoroughly pleased with his sons' schoolboy progress, and his wife just displeased enough to have something to keep herself worried."

"Perfect."

"Oh, just. I half suspect he'll be joining us back in Oxford soon."

"Did he tell you so much?"

"Not in so many words. But if a man such as you can come to his senses, I'm certain that Jonathan must. Wait..." He began fumbling about his inside jacket pocket then retrieved a thin, square box of red leather with a frame of yellow trimming. "Here." I opened to see a line of cigarettes wrapped in black paper with a strip of gold around each tip. "Courtesy of the Russian Imperial court."

"Oh? Has the *tzar* pushed his borders so far west already?" I placed the box in my pocket. "I really should be paying more attention at Privy Council."

"Oh no, not quite yet. But everyone passes through Florence. Now, I've also heard that you're to be published."

"Then you've heard correctly."

"And what's this translation?"

"A saga, the life of the Icelandic poet Kormák."

"Splendid. Is it perfectly grisly?"

"Not quite: believe it or not, it's really a romance."

"A romance?" Thomas balked. "I didn't know Northmen had those types of tender feelings."

"Not normally, no, but in certain seasons..."

"James!" There it was. Arthur was coming to join us, smoking a large cigar. His collar was open, and a white scarf hung about his shoulders, as if they were still last night's clothes. "Good on you, you've made the right choice. England needs minds like yours. In America, you'd, well..." he scowled at the ash falling from his cigar, "I don't have to tell you. How are you feeling, our man of the hour?"

I managed to continue smiling. "Just grand, and yourself?"

"As grand as one may, under the circumstances."

"And what are those?"

"You can imagine. You know how busy I've been with my work. And now, with all this on top of it."

"Oh? Was it much of a bother to come here tonight?"

"Here?" He took a deep drag from his cigar and billowed gray smoke. "Of course not, James," he squinted. "I wouldn't miss it for the world. If anything, it's a break from the trouble back home."

"What trouble?" My heart was in my throat.

"Emma didn't tell you? I thought you were quite chummy these days."

"No, I haven't heard anything."

"She's," he blew a loose ring, "well, she's 'expecting.' "

Ice ran down my spine. Ringing filled my ears, as if I'd been hit by a cannonball. My vision lost focus. My eyes clouded over with vague clumps of color.

I couldn't fit all of these pieces together. Where had I gone wrong? What should have been different? I flew from the Quad through the past several months. If I'd kissed her right then by the fire in the library? Then taken her with me to Rome or Vienna? No: the guilt would have poisoned the pureness between us. If I'd sent her a letter, built trust, correspondence? But that would take up too much time. And what if that day he caught us in the gallery, smirking sadistic as if he knew we couldn't say what he'd seen, I'd clocked the smug bastard then square on the jaw? Emma would struggle to love me through prison. Then after the concert, when we were alone, when we held each other so close in our arms: what if I'd held her a little bit longer? No: by then it was already midnight.

But what if I just had been properly patient? What if I'd really done nothing at all? I leapt from the past to another reality. I had moved quietly back to America, not seeing Emma since leaving the North. And then, five years later, somewhere in the ashcans, I have my first gallery show in New York. There among critics, the overdressed ladies, the students who scoff or who praise far too much, I see Emma floating, a queen in her kingdom, pointing and smiling and nodding her head. "Are you Mr. Dalthey?" she says as she spies me. "I do think I met you once, long, long ago."

That could have been, maybe, with everything different; but then we would have to have been not ourselves. The more that I searched, and the more I found nothing, the more I knew this was the end all along. I closed my eyes, leaned back, fell into my body, accepting the place where I stood now in time.

Awake, I heard Arthur still talking. "Of course, she's just giddy to have an excuse not to get off the couch. She never does anything. Well, except for the singing. Bloody Schubert.

I blame that on you." He pointed the cigar in my face. I was not prepared to answer.

"Well, a child is always a blessing," Thomas spoke for me.

"So they tell me," Arthur hissed.

"Especially your first!" Thomas jabbed his shoulder. "I look forward to thrashing him for so constantly misusing the ablative supine." He turned to me and must have seen I'd gone pale. "Are you alright, James?"

"Yes," I drew a deep breath. "Thomas, would you join me out on the Square for a cigarette? I need a moment of peace to settle into my celebrity."

"Of course. Arthur, do you mind?"

"Of course not. Enjoy yourselves, gentlemen."

Thomas and I walked briskly across the quad. The porter let us through the gate, and we stood shoulder to shoulder some yards to the left. I removed the leather case from my pocket, my hand shaking intensely, retrieved two cigarettes, and handed one to Thomas. He took a match from his own, lit it, and touched the fire to the tip of his cigarette.

"So," he broke the silence, "a barbarian romance? How does that play out?"

"Much like the others." I accepted the match and held it before my face.

"A tragedy, then?"

"A farce." I let out the smoke from my lips. "But it's pretty."

"What more do we want?"

So much; and so much I wanted to say. But now with the first shock subsided, my thoughts and emotions were racing too wildly for me to begin taming them into sentences. I tried to distract myself, focusing on a tune that Thomas started humming beside me. As I struggled to determine which *Deh vieni* he was fumbling through, I realized that it was a seamless, flowing blend of the two. In that moment, in a flash, somewhere between the seducer at the window and the helpmeet in the garden, I beheld fully nude my absurd situation.

I poured it all into a laugh. It started in spurts, but grew solid and loud. Thomas had the courtesy not to prod and carried on with his improvisation. This outburst deflated me, like a long, slow note from the collapsing bellows of an organ, emptying me, calming me but leaving nothing behind. It took everything out of me; all that remained was sardonic fatigue somewhere under the numbness. Though not quite convinced they rang true, I formed at the least from this hollow some words.

"Thomas?" I began. "Do you ever get the feeling that we cling to these stories, these romances, simply because we couldn't keep living without them? We paint life in bright colors to make it seem grand and gay, like a ball and a carnival. When really, it's overall boring. It's dull. It's routine. And often, quite painful. We wake up, we sweat, then we sleep and we die. But these yarns that we spin let us think it's all worth it, that there's beauty in life, that there's meaning and harmony, just long enough to push over the hill."

"Yes," he stared into the end of his cigarette. "Yes, I have thought so myself, especially back then when I was your age. But do you know what else?"

He gave me his half-smile, then took a long drag. He looked west as he tapped the near end and sent ash drifting carelessly downward. The sun had now set, so far as we saw beyond the sudden wall of Brasenose across the quiet square, but the clouds held a rich violet hue that became gradually warmer and, at last, burning gold as they circled the spot where the disk had slipped past the horizon. I can't say whether Thomas embarked on his speech with something resembling a sense of direction, whether he took this pause of no more than a minute but, in tinted memory, stretching on beyond Judgment, either out of a need to put now into words what were yet merely vague inclinations or simply *ad lib*, for dramatic effect. He spoke, to be sure, from the soul.

"I won't hold you back if you really believe that. That we're ghosts, phantoms floating towards a desire we never quite reach nor remember the birth of, yet so dogged by its trace we refuse to give up, close our eyes, say goodnight. You've reached to that point, and I trust your decision. So blow out the candle! But I think we both know you'll be home with the sunrise." He turned his face back to the edge of the sky. "I suppose life is long, and suppose it is tiring, and at times we seem stubborn still running right back to it. But what keeps us alive is much more than the spell of a fairytale, much less. In a sense, it is nothing at all. See, it seems you would claim that our life is a burden, that we need something special to make our strife worth it. But where is this strife? Can you point to it for me?" He looked at me square in the eye.

I couldn't quite meet him, and looked away, searching, then saw, by the churchyard, a boy far past bedtime. With his mother behind him, a bowl, and a pipe, he blew out soap bubbles that popped meeting air. He fixed his technique, took a low, deep, long breath, let out smooth and slowly, and curved a great globe that flew off through the square. Of course, he set after it, losing himself, and dropping the bowl that he'd held in his hand. Shards of clay, mess of foam, spread about all around him. He left off his chase, gasped, and melted in tears. His mother laughed gently, "Oh gosh, someone's sleepy!" She lifted him, kissed him, and bore him away.

I heard Thomas speaking beside me. "We could have been anywhere tonight. And yet, here we are."

"And yet, here we are."

THE REST of the evening passed easily. Thomas and I finished our cigarettes and returned to our circle. We drank, we made jokes, we told stories. I laughed along, sipped routinely, even offered a few anecdotes. But all the while I was somewhere else. Once it was quite dark, or as dark as it would be, around eleven o'clock, I excused myself and bid farewell to those about me. I was one of the first to leave my own party.

I was not, in truth, tired. After undressing, I stood by my desk and stared at the light of a candle dancing with shadows on the wall behind it. My friend from the Press, who had given me my commission, had been at the party this evening. When I told him that I had been drawing and painting, he suggested I do a short series of scenes from the saga to go with the translation. I really ought to be in bed, but while midnight is a time for rest, it is also the first moment of a new day. I pulled out my chair, sat down, and began.

Something for the frontispiece; perhaps a portrait of Steingerd, the true love of our ill-starred hero. Her back was towards me. Her head turned to the right to look over her shoulder. The face, not quite a circle, was blushed somewhat on the strong cheekbones. Half a smile could be seen on her lips, slightly parted. Her eyes, lightly shaded, were open wide with longing and expectation. As I finished her hair, flowing down to her shoulders with a double-stranded braid in the center, I realized she was Emma.

I could not send it to her; I could not send her anything. Nor did I think I should keep it myself, gazing at it at odd hours, harboring it like a grudge, worshiping a hidden, silent god. But for the book it was perfect. I would send the image back to the realm of pure form it had come from. It was not mine to hold. The spirit had graced me and gone; the ghost had breathed in me and left with the tide. I was honored to have known it, and, in an instance, reflected it onto the page. All that remained was to set it adrift, to let others find it. If they had eyes to see, in it they might discover the world.

Special thanks are due to Kelton Madden, for the Call to Adventure, to Jonathan Keeperman, for transforming my Google Doc into a novel, and to Anne Clarke, without whom it would not have been born in the first place.

Special thanks are also due to everyone along the way who read drafts and gave feedback: my parents, Megan Bunce, Michaela Niamh Brady, David Leon, Adam Husain, Michael Palmieri, Kairee, William Rice, Osemudiamen Edionwele, Bob of Bob's Corner, James Maye, Maxwell Foley, Paul McNiel, T Chevéz-Mathews, Keturah Hickman, my brother Daniel, and Mike Elias.

The most special gratitude belongs to the enchanting Aisha, whose brilliance has been so illuminating that words lose their strength in attempting to capture it. Her magical presence is felt on every page.